Roses and Rot

KAT HOWARD

ROSES

AND

ROT

SAGA PRESS

LONDON SYDNEY **NEW YORK** TORONTO NEW DELHI

SAGA PRESS
AN IMPRINT OF SIMON & SCHUSTER, INC.

1230 AVENUE OF THE AMERICAS, NEW YORK, NEW YORK 10020

Saga Press and logo are trademarks of Simon & Schuster, Inc.
For information about special discounts for bulk purchases, please contact Simon & Schuster Special Sales at 1-866-506-1949 or business@simonandschuster.com.
The Simon & Schuster Speakers Bureau can bring authors to your live event. For more information or to book an event, contact the Simon & Schuster Speakers Bureau at 1-866-248-3049 or visit our website at www.simonspeakers.com.
The text for this book was set in Adobe Caslon Pro.
Manufactured in the United States of America
First Edition
2 4 6 8 10 9 7 5 3 1
CIP data for this book is available from the Library of Congress.
ISBN 978-1-4814-5116-1
ISBN 978-1-4814-5118-5 (eBook)

FOR MY SISTER

ACKNOWLEDGMENTS

Unlike Imogen and Marin, I have a family who loves me and supports my work. Thank you, so much, to my parents, my sister, and my brothers. I could not have done this without you. I love you guys.

When I think of what it means to have a good mentor, I think of my grad school adviser, Rebecca Krug. She has supported my writing since the day I told her that I was going to take two months off from writing my dissertation to go to San Diego and learn to write fantasy and science fiction, and has encouraged me in every leap since.

I cannot say thank you enough to Maria Dahvana Headley and Megan Kurashige, who read a draft of this book when it was the hottest of hot messes, and helped me find the story I was trying to tell. Their encouragement at that point kept me going. Thank you also to Megan, who gave me great insight into the life and career of a professional dancer. Marin's gift is due to her. All remaining errors and dramatic license are mine only.

Thank you also to Neil Gaiman, who read a somewhat less-messy draft and told me I needed to write the hard parts. And that I really needed a new title. I did.

Thank you to my glorious agent, Brianne Johnson, who read so many versions of this book and pushed me to make it better, who has been an unwavering support and advocate of me and my writing, and who I am so, so lucky to have in my corner. And thank you, thank you to Sarah McCarry for being there in a period of professional crisis, and introducing us.

Thank you to my excellent editor, Joe Monti, who helped me make this the best book I could, and to all the excellent people at Saga Press who have made it shiny and gorgeous. I couldn't have asked for a better home for my story.

Thank you to all of the women who made art, and inspired me to make my own.

More strange than true. I never may believe
These antique fables, nor these fairy toys.

—WILLIAM SHAKESPEARE,
A Midsummer Night's Dream

1

Marin sat on my bed, next to my half-packed suitcase. "I wish you weren't leaving, Imogen."

I couldn't say the same, not and answer honestly. "I'd be leaving for college in two years anyway."

"Yes, but that's two years from now." She picked through my T-shirts, separated one with a rose embroidered in tattered ribbon on its front from the pile. "This is mine, by the way."

"Sorry, forgot," I said. I took her hand, rubbed my thumb over her fading scars. Mine hadn't healed as well, which had been the point. "You know I can't stay here, Marin."

"I know," she said, looking down at our joined hands. "I can't believe she's letting you go."

"Blackstone's fancy. It gives her bragging rights." I had planned my escape carefully. I knew I had to feed my mother's ego enough to outweigh the pleasure that thwarting me would give her. It had been an agonizing two weeks after I'd been accepted, before she decided to let me enroll. She didn't say yes until she'd found a press release about some ambassador's son attending attached to an invitation to a parents' social.

I had made sure she found it.

"True. And she can delicately cry about how much she misses you, but she doesn't want to get in the way of your dreams, mothers sacrifice so much for their children." Marin gave a sniff, and pretended to wipe tears from her eyes.

"That was almost scary, how much you just sounded like her."

"Thank you." She bowed. "I've been working on character interpretation. It helps my dance." She paused. "You'll come home for Christmas?"

I squeezed her hand, let it go. It was the previous Christmas when we'd gotten our sets of scars. It wasn't exactly my favorite holiday.

"For you? Of course. And there is email there. Cell phones, even. I'm going to boarding school, not Mars." Christmas break would only be a couple of weeks. For Marin, I could endure it.

"Marin, if you're not down here in three minutes, you're walking to class." Our mother, her voice creeping up from downstairs.

Marin rolled her eyes and picked up the bag full of pointe shoes and tights and all the other assorted dance paraphernalia she had dropped inside my door. "She'd make me, too. Driving along behind me all the way."

"Marin, now. If you don't take your training seriously, you'll never be the best. There are hundreds of girls out there, thousands, with talent. I'm trying to give you an advantage, but you need to take it seriously." Our mother, again, more impatient this time.

"Is this the week you start the new classes?" I asked.

"Extra training for an extra advantage." That same sarcastic mocking of our mother's voice.

"You're already better than anyone at your studio."

"I'm good for here." She shrugged. "I need to be better if I want to dance for real. Extra classes will help."

She stopped in the doorway, looked back. "I just don't understand why I can't come, too. To Blackstone. If you had told me about it, I could have applied. Didn't you want me to be there with you?"

"I've been saving money to pay tuition for the last year and half,

Marin. And I still couldn't have gone until next year if I hadn't gotten a scholarship. There was no way I could afford to pay for both of us." I'd hidden the account from our mother, then paid all the tuition up front so I wouldn't have to worry about it accidentally disappearing.

She shrugged her bag onto her shoulder. "Fine. Whatever. See you at Christmas."

When I unpacked my suitcase in my new dorm room, Marin's rose T-shirt was inside. I traced my hand over the ribbon, telling myself that she would be fine, that I had done what I'd had to do.

I didn't go home for Christmas, or any other holiday. I didn't even speak to my sister again for four years. We didn't live under the same roof for almost seven years after that.

2

A decade after I'd stopped living with my sister, I was packing to do so again. This time, I wasn't just packing a suitcase, but my entire apartment, and Marin wasn't sitting on my bed, she was on speakerphone.

"I get in four hours after you do," she said. "So I'll just meet you at the house at Melete. Unless you want to wait?"

"At the airport? For four hours?" I asked, taping shut the box of dishes. Most of my things were going into storage. I wouldn't need them at Melete. All incidentals—including dishes, sheets, towels, and the like—were provided as part of our residence at the artists' colony.

"You're right. That would be silly. I'll meet you there."

"Are you okay?" I asked. "You sound nervous."

"It's not nerves. It's the echoes from your speakerphone. Love you!"

"Love you!"

Marin did sound weird, though, and I was pretty sure it wasn't from being on speakerphone in my almost-empty apartment. It was a weirdness I thought I understood—I was nervous too, about living in the same house, and the memories that might bring back. I loved my sister, and I missed her, but it was hard to put the past behind you when the past was living down the hall.

I taped up the last box, smoothed my hands over it to check the seal. Living together would be fine. We would both be fine.

The shuttle I had gotten into at the tiny Manchester airport sped down the pock-marked highway. We crossed a river, gleaming like silver ribbon wound through the green of the hills. I felt like I was being driven through a Robert Frost poem, and I shook my head as we passed the freeway sign marking the exit for his house. Because of course the Frost house would be Melete's neighbor. One more perfect thing about it.

"This place—it's too amazing to be real, Marin." I had called her after she sent me the link to Melete's website. An artists' colony. Full funding for nine months, including housing and meals. A personal mentor to work with—an artist who was working at the top of her or his field who would also live at Melete in order to guide your work for that time.

"I'm applying. You should, too, Imogen. It would be so great if we were there together."

"It would take a miracle to get in. I bet they get thousands of applications."

"Probably. But it might as well be us," she'd said.

"You have a point."

So I had put together a portfolio, written my artist's statement—an activity that always made me feel like I was writing some strange manifesto that had nothing to do with why I actually wrote—and sent in my application. I'd been astounded when I'd gotten the email telling me I'd made it through the first round.

"I knew you would!" Marin had said. She had, too. "I've got such a good feeling about this."

Her good feeling turned out to be right. We were both among the forty fellows awarded residencies at Melete.

Before she lent her name to an artists' colony, Melete had been one of the three original Greek Muses—the sisters Aoide (song),

Mneme (memory), and Melete (practice). The colony's founders wanted it to be a place for up-and-coming artists to be able to practice their art without interference from the outside world.

It had been around for just over seventy-five years, long enough to generate a distinguished list of alumni, a terrific reputation as a cauldron in which artists could refine their talent, and even a few scandals, one so dramatic as to almost close Melete's doors. That last bit wasn't listed in the application materials.

Everything had been too good. I didn't trust the polished website, the shiny testimonials. No place could be so perfect. So I had looked, and looked hard for the tarnish on the shine.

There was curiously little written about the scandal anywhere, but even with the dearth of mentions, the tiny blip stuck out because it was the only discordant note in the near-identical chorus of glowing praise.

Something—and the details were obscured, spoken on the slant—happened about fifty years ago. A fellow involved with one of the mentors, an extramarital pregnancy, a disappearance that might have been a suicide. Allegedly. Everything was qualified by that word, "allegedly," and—very carefully—everything was phrased to suggest that it could have happened anywhere, that nothing that Melete did or didn't do could have changed things. At least officially. But there were changes in the program after that, mentors no longer in the same housing with fellows, and allowed to bring their families to live on the grounds, so at least some of the rumors must have been true.

But everything that had been said publicly since then was near-Stepfordian in its similarity. Everyone who had attended had the experience of their lives, and even the most successful alums continued to mention Melete in acceptance speeches for ever-flashier awards. The excess of glory made me nervous. Nervous enough that I had left the application—completed but unsigned—sitting on my desk.

"The deadline is tomorrow, Imogen."

"I know, Marin, I know. I just . . . there's something weird about it."

"You are seriously the only person I know who decides not to trust someplace because it's too perfect."

"I want to sleep on it."

"Fine. Maybe you'll get some sort of sign in a dream. Will that be good enough for you?"

I laughed and hung up.

I didn't dream of Melete, or of winning a literary prize, or anything else that might be taken as an omen about going. I did, however, sit bolt upright at around three in the morning, realizing that I was about to lose the chance to possibly study with my favorite living writer because of a bad feeling. I picked up my pen, rolled it through my fingers, stretching the stiffness from my scars, signed it in the red-black ink I used for luck, dated the application, and sent it off.

Even though she applied before I did, the fellowships were all announced on the same day. Celebrating our acceptances with Marin on the phone was one of the happiest moments in my life—I was so proud of us.

Melete's campus was tucked away in New Hampshire, about an hour out of Boston. Close enough to New York that artists could come up and give guest seminars and performances, or that the fellows could go down to the city and see shows, but still isolated enough that we could be alone with our art. Our practice. It was possible to feel utterly apart from the world while you were there, if that was what you wanted.

As we drove through slanted sunlight and green-leafed trees that scraped the sky, the outside world fell farther and farther away. Here were graveyards old enough to have footstones as well as headstones marking their bounds, inside of stone walls that had stood for hundreds of winters. I cracked open the window and let the late August breeze tug and tangle my hair.

"Here you are," the driver said. "Enjoy your time at Melete."

I gathered my bags, then looked at the house where I would be living for the next nine months, and burst out laughing. In front of me was a beautiful and slightly mad-looking Queen Anne, painted in autumnal shades of red and cream and gold. It had gabled windows and spindle work, and a porch that wrapped around the front and left side. Best of all, it had a tower. Had I been asked to design my ideal writer's house, this was what I would have come up with.

I barely registered the house's other details as I rushed up the steps to the front door, and then continued up the spiraling staircase to the tower. The room at the top was indeed a bedroom, and unoccupied, the key still in the door. I turned the key in the lock and walked into the center of the room. Stood, eyes closed, breathing in.

For that breath of time, my doubts and worries fell away, and I was utterly happy. It seemed just possible that all of the praise for Melete was nothing more than true, that I was in an extraordinary place that was exactly as perfect as it seemed. Best of all, it was my writing that had brought me here. For a moment, everything felt golden.

I slid the zipper of my suitcase open and started unpacking. Then stopped. Unpacking could wait. I went to the window and looked out.

Ivy twined around the window frame, a dull green that I hoped would turn scarlet in the fall. Through the glass, I could see some of the other buildings, houses and studios, of the place that would be home for the next nine months.

Home.

A strange word to think about. The house I grew up in was never home, and I had left it as soon as I could. After that, I had moved through a series of temporary places. Dorm rooms, cheap apartments, two months on a friend's couch when things were tight. Most of them had been no more than addresses. None of those places felt like mine. Maybe, at least for a little while, Melete could.

"Didn't it occur to you that maybe it would be better to wait until we were all here before you claimed a room?"

The woman in the doorway was whippet-thin and had a messily chopped shock of fuchsia hair. She looked angry at everything, and specifically at me.

"Considering we could move in any time from two days ago until tomorrow, not really," I said.

She stood in the doorway, as if perhaps the weight of her presence might make me change my mind. I started putting my lingerie away, hoping that unpacking something that personal would send the signal that I had no intention of trading. "I'm Imogen, by the way. I'm a writer." I smiled.

"Helena. I'm a poet. I have two collections out already. Both with independent presses. This is supposed to be my room."

Okay then.

"I'm sorry, but I don't see how that's possible. There was nothing in here when I arrived, and the key was in the lock." The welcome packet I had received had specified that while residences were assigned, individual rooms were not. They were available on a first-come, first-served basis during the move-in period, and keys would be left in the doors until the rooms were claimed.

"Whatever," she said. "It was supposed to be mine."

"If someone promised you that, they were lying. Or at the very least, mistaken. Check your welcome packet."

Silence. She was gone. I shook my head and continued unpacking.

The tower was the highest part of the house, its own small third floor. Mostly unpacked, I walked back through the rest. The second floor was made up of the other three bedrooms, all generously sized. Each bedroom had its own full-size bathroom. Whoever had designed the house had clearly been thinking of harmony between the people living there as much as aesthetics—there would be no need to fight for showers in the morning. One door, at the far end of the hall, away from the stairs, was closed. I assumed it was Helena's, and didn't knock, glad, at that moment, for closed doors and distance.

The front door opened.

"Hello? Anyone here?" a voice called—a voice I knew.

My heart flung itself into the back of my throat as I clattered down the stairs to see my sister. Marin smiled, arms open, and I stepped into them.

As we hugged our hellos, I marveled, as I always did, at the strength of her. Dancer's muscles, and skin and bones made fearless by a life dedicated to throwing itself against the constraints of gravity.

She squeezed me one more time. "I'm so happy you're here, Imogen. So happy. Keep me company while I unpack?"

"Sure." I grabbed one of her bags and followed my sister up the stairs.

"This one," Marin said, after walking back and forth between the two unoccupied rooms, gazing from the windows. "I like the view of the river."

I stood next to her, looking out as the sun sparked mirror flashes off the water. "I can't believe how different it looks from here— I look out at the opposite side of the house, and you can't even see the river. It's like living in two different places."

"Well," she said, opening up her suitcase, "for the first time in far too long we're not, and I'm glad."

"Me, too."

Watching Marin unpack was like watching a very precise whirlwind. She seemed like chaos, but everything wound up folded and hung, neat and exactly where she wanted it.

"Have you looked around the campus yet?" she asked.

"My plane was delayed getting in, so I didn't get here that much before you did. Long enough to mostly unpack, and to steal an unoccupied room from one of our housemates."

Marin rolled her eyes over the story. "Maybe she didn't understand the whole 'open move-in period.' Or she has unbelievably bad people skills." She zipped her suitcase closed and tucked it in the back of her closet. Just like that, her room looked as if she had always lived here.

"Maybe. Maybe it was just a bad day. I hope she gets over it. I don't relish the idea of living for nine months with someone who hates me from the start. Speaking of bad people skills, have you heard anything from our mother?"

Marin's mouth twisted. "The usual passive-aggressive bullshit. The idea of Melete seemed very nice, but was I sure I was doing the right thing by attending, and yes, I would have a great teacher, but if no one else saw me dance for a year, would they remember me, blah blah blah. I told her we weren't allowed to communicate in any way with the outside world while we were here."

I gaped. "You didn't."

"I did." A dimple winked in and out as she grinned. "Doesn't mean she won't fill our inboxes with nasty email, but it does get us out of dealing with her."

"You are a genius. An evil genius, and I love you." What she had said wasn't quite true. No one who wasn't a resident was allowed on the campus, but we were certainly allowed to communicate—to email or FaceTime or call. Not that I wanted to, when it came to our mother, so I was delighted that Marin had put up that extra barrier.

"It was the best way I could think of to keep our sanity. Mom's always going to be Mom, which means she's never going to be happy, and will do her best to make sure we aren't, either. Literally the only thing she asked when I told her about being awarded the residency was when I'd be performing, so she could come 'visit.' Which I knew was code for 'stage some sort of scene.' Remember opening night of *Swan Lake*?"

"How could I forget? That was maybe her worst." Our mother had always made a point of attending Marin's performances, and an even greater point of making sure everyone knew she was there. That night, she had fainted—from excitement, she said later—in the middle of Marin dancing the Black Swan variation. She had done so noisily enough to bring the entire production to a halt, and she got more words in the next day's review than Marin did.

"Right? Or at least her most dramatic. So yes, it was an utter delight telling her that no one who wasn't a mentor or resident was allowed on the grounds." Marin stretched, rolling her shoulders and shaking the last vestiges of travel away. "Want to take a walk, get to know the place?"

"That'd be good."

We wandered through the other residences, marveling at the ridiculous and amazing all around us. It was the opposite of cinder

- 1 2 -

block and sameness—nothing on campus looked like a normal house.

"That place looks like Cinderella's castle," Marin said.

It did, formed in miniature, down to the front door fashioned like a drawbridge. It was even painted the same shade of semi-sparkling blue that her ball gown had been in the Disney movie.

"The one next to it is like something out of a Russian novel, all onion domes and red," I said. "Who designed this place?" Gravel crunched beneath our feet, and the air smelled honey-green, like warm grass.

"The people who came here as architects. Or maybe the sculptors. I forget exactly. But it's a thank-you tradition. They do bridges over the river, too. Kind of amazing, right?" She grinned, her whole face lighting up.

It was impossible not to smile back. "So far, everything about this place is."

We returned to our house as the sun was setting, dappling everything in golden light. We heard the voice before we saw her, pure and clear, singing, *"O mio babbino caro."*

The woman singing was standing in front of our house, eyes closed. She looked like a darker-skinned Louise Brooks in leather leggings and a slouchy T-shirt—effortlessly cool.

Everything narrowed to a point—the small magic of her voice, the setting, that song. Hearing her was an ache in my heart.

"Brava, brava!" Marin called out.

"Thanks. Seemed like the time and place for it. I mean, how do you stand in the middle of this and not sing?" She spread her arms open wide, taking in everything. "I'm Ariel, by the way. You two live here, too?"

"We do." Marin smiled. "A fact that is still sinking in. I'm Marin, and this is my sister, Imogen."

"You have a great voice," I said. "Are you an opera singer?"

"Singer singer. My voice doesn't really do the opera thing, but I love that aria. It just gets me, right here." She thumped her fist over her heart. "I still kind of can't believe this place is real. I mean, look at this house. Are they all like this?"

"The house next door has a moat," I said.

"Seriously, a moat?" Ariel asked.

"I know. I'm trying to convince Imogen that we should stage an invasion. Or go skinny-dipping in it. I haven't decided," Marin said.

"Invasion," Ariel said. "You just know people skinny-dip in the moat all the time, and we're not here to be conventional."

"I like how you think," Marin said, and bumped her shoulder against Ariel's. She had always been so much easier with new people than I was.

"What are you planning on working on while you're here?" I asked. One of the quirks of Melete was that we weren't required to work on anything. No one had to give recitals or have portfolios reviewed before they left. It was, in fact, completely possible to be accepted, then come to Melete for nine months to just hang out— or, in the language of the official paperwork, to take the time in residence to think deeply about the nature of your art. But there was an unwritten tradition of working on a large, ambitious project, and many of those projects had proven to be breakout ones, an ever-growing list of the origins of the next big things.

"I'm writing a rock opera about Joan of Arc. When it's staged, I'll be Joan."

I turned the idea over in my brain. "That really works. She is one of the few people I can think of where the idea of a rock opera sounds fitting, not weird."

"Working on it seems just scary enough," Ariel said. "Which is the way I like to pick what I'm going to do next. You know, how much does this idea make my stomach hurt? Oh, all the way to nausea? Why yes, that's exactly what I'll do."

"Just being here for me is a kind of terror," Marin said.

I blinked in shock. This was the first time I'd heard Marin say anything about Melete that wasn't a rave. She had never hesitated when we discussed applying, never given any hint that this wasn't the thing she wanted more than anything else.

"Seriously?" Ariel said.

"Leaving my company for a year, it's insane. Just not done. There's no guarantee I'll have a place to go back to." Her foot described a half-circle on the ground as she spoke, a piece of a dance step, Marin's version of fidgeting.

"Why come then?" Ariel asked. I was glad she did, so I didn't have to. It was fine for someone we'd just met not to know this huge, important thing. Not so much for a sister.

"To study with Gavin Delacourt. Hopefully, working with him will be enough of a career boost that I won't need to go back to my old company. To make myself be extraordinary." She shrugged. "Same reason as anyone—to be so good that nothing else matters."

"That's the truth," Ariel said. "How about you, Imogen?"

I hedged, not stepping close to the specifics. Talking about my work made me feel like the weight of my words might break the thing in my head. "Something big, and, like you said, something that scares me enough that I know I'm supposed to be writing it. I feel like this is the best time to try something huge and ambitious, the kind of thing I wouldn't even consider somewhere else."

Ariel nodded. "I couldn't even think about a project this big without a place like this to work on it. In my real life, there would have been no way to buy myself the time to take it seriously."

"Exactly." I smiled.

Still, I watched Marin, who hadn't bought herself time by coming here, but maybe had given part of it up. I wondered what had happened, to make a risk this big seem safe, or whether safety had stopped mattering to her.

"Happy as I'd be to talk art with you ladies all night, I haven't even started to unpack," Ariel said, "and I really should."

"I still need to finish, too," I said. "Which is sad, since I've been here longer than you both."

"We should have that all-night art talk soon, though," Marin said. "That's part of why we're here, right?"

Plans made, we went back to our new rooms. I glanced down the hallway as I walked up. Helena's door was still closed tight, a bar against the rest of the house.

Once I got upstairs, I opened the windows to let the night in. The dark blanket of the night was my favorite time to write. It was easier to think about impossible things then, when there was no one else around to see or judge. It was the time of day most conducive to naked honesty, the time that made me feel like it was safe to tell secrets, to reveal desires.

At my desk, alone in the falling evening, I opened my notebook. Even though I hadn't said so, I knew exactly the thing I had come to Melete to write—a novel told in stories, told in interweaving fairy tales, about the girls who get lost in the woods, and how it is that they come to be lost there, and whether or not they can save themselves. About the stories that lead them into the dark places of the forest, of their lives, and then become the maps by which they find their way out. I had known for a while that this was something I wanted to do, a story I needed to tell.

I picked up my pen, then set it back down. Put my hands on the desk to steady myself, and breathed deep, pulling the late-summer air into my lungs.

The truth, the night-dark truth of it, was that I was afraid of what it meant to write this book, of how close to the bone I would have to cut myself to do it. I was afraid if I thought about it too deeply, talked about it too much, I would talk myself out of writing it. I had done that before.

It was so much easier to hide, to stay safe and write the kind of thing I knew I was good at, the kind of thing I had sent in as a sample of my creative work when I applied. Quiet stories about girls with tragic pasts who faded away and became less. Lots of metaphor, lots of melancholy. I could write them beautifully, make you cry, before you realized you didn't know anything about the character you were crying for.

Easier to write, but less real.

Not now. Not anymore. I was here to see what I could do if I pushed everything else aside except the story. To see if I could, like Marin said, make myself extraordinary.

I stretched my hand, rubbed the ache out of the scar tissue, and picked up my pen.

You always tell yourself that there's someone who has it worse, and if you lived through the abuse, there almost certainly was. There's a horrible sort of comfort in reassuring yourself in that fashion— maybe you were hungry some nights, but you had food. Maybe you got slapped, but at least you didn't get beaten. Maybe you got beaten, but at least you never had broken bones. You think of the worst thing that happened to you, and then you think of something even worse than that. If you survived, you always can, and so by pained, contorted logic, what happened to you wasn't really that bad.

Maybe your mother tried to break you, to tell you that you were nothing, that you'd never matter, that you were a waste of her time, but she never succeeded. Maybe you still have scars, but those marks on your skin mean you've lived long enough to heal.

Maybe you lived, once, a life full of secrets. Ones you could never tell, not because you didn't know the words, but because you had learned, time and time again, that the words didn't matter. People would rather believe a pretty lie than an ugly truth, and you were always the one who wasn't believed. So you learned the power in silence, and in secrets. Maybe you still look over your shoulder, but at least you got away.

And after all, if you'd had a childhood that was different, one that didn't always feel like walking on knives, maybe you would never have found your voice. If you hadn't been forced to swallow your words, you would have never learned the power in speaking them.

This is what you tell yourself. This is how you keep breathing. This is what happily ever after means.

I woke soon after going to sleep, as the fingers of dawn were beginning to pluck at the edges of the sky, to find my room full of butterflies. An entire kaleidoscope of them, orange and red and black and electric, Nabokov blue. Their wings were opening and closing slowly, and it seemed as if my walls moved in time with the beat of some unknown heart.

I lay in bed, not moving, barely even breathing, just watching. Minutes passed, or maybe hours. It felt like I was in a cathedral, some holy place outside of time.

The next time I woke up, the butterflies were gone, no sign that any of them had ever been there. I had nearly convinced myself that it was a particularly vivid dream when I saw, on the open page of my notebook, a smear of iridescent dust.

I don't like the idea of signs and portents. People like to say fate is inescapable, but I believe there's always an escape. We make our own luck, and we do that by bending our will and energy toward what we want. I think that if you look for an omen, you'll find one, and it will tell you exactly what you desire it to, for good or ill. It would have been easy, had I wanted, to think of that tiny, shimmering smudge as some sort of sign, but I didn't need it to be. I didn't need signs. I had myself.

3

Marin had hung amber-colored curtains over the windows so that the light turned her room warm and honey-gold. We strung red fairy lights around the top of the ceiling, just beneath the molding, then stepped back to take in the effect.

"I like it—elegant and welcoming," I said.

"Did you bring your stars?" she asked.

"Of course I did." Marin had given me a set of glow-in-the-dark stars to stick on my ceiling when she moved into her first apartment, sending them completely out of the blue. What she had called a "reverse housewarming present" had broken through four years of silence, and helped us start talking again. I had put them up in every one of my bedrooms since. "They're arranged in constellations and everything."

"Your favorite mythologies, all set out on the ceiling." Marin folded herself onto the bed, then began sewing the ribbons on a new pair of pointe shoes. "Just like you always said you would have."

"Rearranging the stories so the ones that should be next to each other are," I said.

"You used to tell me stories about the stars when we were kids," she said, not looking up from her sewing. "When I couldn't sleep. About the two princesses who lived in the star palaces. Remember?"

"They had a constellation carousel, to move the sky into place for their adventures." I pressed the heel of my hand against my chest, soothing the ache of the memory.

"I loved those stories. Did you ever think about writing them down? I mean, not to sell or anything. I know that's not the kind of thing you write now, but, like, just to have?" She snipped the thread, and picked up the other shoe.

"They were more just things for you, not for writing down," I said. I had, though. My first semester away at Blackstone. When I still thought she wanted me to come home for Christmas. I had been planning on giving them to her then. Instead, nothing but silence from her, and the beginning of our years of separation.

They were packed away, with everything else I had put in storage—I didn't want them, but couldn't bring myself to destroy my own work. "They weren't ever meant to be for publication. And no, I didn't apply here with Star Princess stories."

She laughed. "I didn't think you had. Still, I sort of miss them."

"Fine. Next time you can't sleep, you can knock on my door, and I'll tell you a story."

She looked up, and smiled, and I almost, almost told her the truth about the stories. It wasn't that I couldn't say it. I could. But there are times that you don't speak, because silence hurts less. There was no need to reopen old wounds when we both wanted them healed. Instead: "Do you want to have dinner tonight?"

"I would, but I'm meeting Gavin."

Gavin Delacourt was a principal dancer with the National Ballet Theater. Onstage, he moved as if gravity were an option for him, as if the air itself were his partner. Even outside of the dance world, he was a star, regularly appearing in tabloid lists of eligible bachelors and beautiful people and gossiped about as the possible inspiration for one character or another in Hollywood dance fantasy films.

She tucked the finished shoes in her bag. "We're figuring out the plan for the year."

"Will you go down and take class with NBT?"

"That's one of the things we're going to talk about. How to balance the time here with the need to be in training with a company. Plus, I want an audition with them by the time this year is over. I don't want to push too hard, but I don't want to just let it go, either." She stuffed the finished shoes into the side of her messenger bag, then twisted her long hair into a tidy bun at the nape of her neck.

"Marin? Did you mean it when you said you were terrified to be here?"

She sat back down. It was how I had known the conversation was going to be serious when we were growing up, when my kinetic sister would voluntarily stop moving. "It's a big risk. Time is never a dancer's friend, and a year off is a lot. But I needed to get out of where I was, and to do it with enough drama to be talked about, so people don't forget about me when I'm not onstage. The world's full of next big things, so it's not enough to just be good, I have to be good and be the dancer they're looking for.

"But working with Gavin is a great opportunity, and he chose me, specifically, to work with, which has to mean he thinks I'm worth the time."

"And that you have the talent," I said.

"I hope so. He's such a technically gifted dancer—every movement, every angle is utterly precise. That's what I'm missing in my work, and if I can get that"—her face set—"if I can get that, I won't just be good, I'll be great.

"If I'm lucky, the benefits balance the risks. I'm not thinking about what happens if I'm not lucky. It's too terrifying. Anyway, I need to go check into my studio."

I checked my phone. "I'm not sure if I'll be here when you get back—I have my first appointment with Beth later. But, Marin, if you need anything—"

She cut me off. "I know. That's why we're here, too, right?"

Ariel and I were trying to wrestle her trunk up the stairs to her room. It was an actual steamer trunk, leather-strapped and brass-hinged, an heirloom that had belonged to her great-grandmother, and so even though it was less practical than cardboard boxes, she had used it to ship her things to Melete. It was beautiful, but even unpacked it was heavy, and it was currently stuck on the second turn of the stairs.

"Are you going to be done anytime soon? I need to get my lunch out of the kitchen," Helena said from the landing above us.

"You could help. We'd be done faster," Ariel said.

"All of my stuff is in my room. Neither of you helped get it there," Helena said.

"True, but we would have, if you'd asked," I said.

"Would you really?" The thing was, she sounded genuinely curious, like the idea of asking for help would never have crossed her mind.

Ariel stood up, wiped the sweat from her forehead. "Go get something. Anything. And I swear, I will carry it up and down the stairs as many times as you want later, if you help us move this damn thing now."

Helena cocked her head. "Okay."

Ariel looked at me. "What have I just done?"

I shoved my hair out of my eyes and laughed.

Helena snaked herself between the wall and the trunk to help us lift it. "If you have everything out of this, why does it need to be in your room? Just put it in storage or leave it in the front room or something."

"Count of three?" I said, and we all heaved on cue.

"Because it's like home," Ariel said, yanking up and backward as we finally got the trunk unjammed. "And because my great-grandmother was a nightclub singer, until she got married. She traveled with this. It reminds me of what I come from, of who I want to be."

"That's a good reason," Helena said.

"Glad you approve," said Ariel.

We wrangled the trunk the rest of the way up the stairs and down the hall to Ariel's room.

"You can go bring me my lunch," Helena told Ariel, "but you don't have to walk anything else up and down the stairs."

"Thanks for helping," Ariel said.

Helena nodded, a sharp jerk of her head, then walked off.

"It's like she spent part of her life being raised by wolves," Ariel said, watching her go. "She only almost knows how to be a human. Do you want me to bring you anything while I'm carrying my penance, er, Helena's lunch?"

"No." I grinned. "I'm good."

I rechecked the directions my mentor, Beth Edwards, had sent me, then slid my phone into the back pocket of my jeans in case I needed them again as I walked. The mentors lived on the Melete grounds as well, but their houses were grouped on the opposite side of the studios. "Close, but not so close I can read over your shoulder while you're working," Beth had emailed.

As I walked, I could see fellows moving into their studios, carrying instrument cases and paint-splattered bags. Somewhere in the midst of them a piano crashed through a phrase, paused, and then repeated. I felt like I was walking through the opening montage of a movie—everything was just a shade brighter than real.

At some point, I knew, being at Melete would feel settled, normal. I would be used to seeing houses with moats, or constructed with the same impossible geometry as a Dr. Seuss drawing. It would be no big deal for an Oscar-winning actor to smile at me as we passed each other walking, and I wouldn't blush as I smiled back. Until then, I would revel in the novelty.

Farther out, on the edge of the Commons, was a rose garden. Drowsy with bees and full of late-summer blooms. A riot of color, the surrounding air drunk on the scent.

Just past the roses, I veered left off the path, toward a faded Cape Cod–style cottage so weathered it could have been plucked from some coastal peninsula and then set down in the New Hampshire forest.

It was a weird thing to be standing outside Beth Edwards's house. She had won the Orange Prize for the book she had begun while at Melete, a novel in stories about the young women at the center of the Salem witch trials, and that had only been the beginning of her success. She was seven books into her career now, all of which had appeared on bestseller and awards lists. She'd been profiled in *The New Yorker* and *Vogue*. And still, she was a writer's writer, her technique both brilliant and seemingly effortless. I loved the sparse precision of her language and the way that she was unflinching about writing emotion in her work, even when it wasn't comfortable to read. She was one of my most lasting influences, the reason I had chosen the structure I had for the book I would work on while I was here.

When she visited my college on a signing tour, I had been too nervous to go, afraid that I wouldn't be able to do anything other than babble at her. I wasn't confident I was going to do any better today—my heart was racing, and anxiety surged like electricity through my joints. I rubbed at my hand, stretching the scar tissue, and sucked in a breath. Even if I babbled, working with her was why I was here. Forcing my spine straight, I walked past the rows of tiny purple flowers and knocked.

It's a clichéd observation to make about a hero, but she was shorter than I expected, the top of her head only coming up to my shoulder. The scents of cinnamon and vanilla floated past her out the door. "You must be Imogen. Come in. I made cinnamon rolls.

"So, are you completely overwhelmed yet? I know I was when I was first here as a fellow. It took me a full two weeks to stop expecting someone to knock on the door and tell me mistakes had been made and I needed to leave. Mugs are in the cupboard to your right, if you want coffee, or I have tea." She slathered icing across the tops of the cinnamon rolls.

"I prefer coffee, thanks." I helped myself to a mug. "And I'm too excited to be overwhelmed."

"Well, that's good. Here you go." She slid a plate over to me, and then poured tea into a daisy-patterned cup with gilded edges.

"Let's go into the other room. I enjoy everything about this house except for the kitchen chairs, which could double as torture devices."

I followed her down the hall and into a room filled with books. Once we were settled, she said, "Tell me what you're writing."

"Actually, I'd rather not." The words came out of my mouth before I could stop and reframe them into something more polite, before I could consider whether maybe she knew best, and what I wanted didn't matter. I clutched the fork in my hand so hard I worried it might bend.

Beth set her cup carefully in its saucer and looked at me. The silence stretched and held. That was it, then. Not even fifteen minutes into my first meeting with my literary idol, and I'd fucked it up already. My stomach attempted to turn itself inside out. Then: "Good for you. Good for you. Protect your art. Too many people don't do that, and nothing—nothing—you do matters as much."

She sipped her tea again. "Take a breath, Imogen. I won't hate you for speaking your mind."

I did, and I ate another bite of a cinnamon roll. Then another. "These are great, by the way."

Beth smiled and nodded. "I like to eat, so I learned to cook, and I learned to do it well, because I can't stand half-assing things. Now, you do know what you're working on while you're here, yes?"

"Yes. I started writing it my first night in residence. I know what it will be, I just don't want to talk it to death before I have it written."

"Good. You don't have to explain your artistic choices to me, so long as they aren't sitting around and not writing. I'm picky about my fellows, and I have no tolerance for people who use the opportunity of being here to do nothing. It's nice to see that I'm not wrong about you. Now, what do you want out of the time you and I will spend together while you're here? Be honest."

I sipped my coffee. "I want to know where I'm failing, so I can get better. I want to be able to talk to you and get advice about setbacks, and frustrations, and how to work through those."

"Not my agent's number, or a blurb for your book?" She raised a brow.

"No, because if I'm good enough, you'll give me those without my having to ask for them."

Another pause, and then she laughed, huge and bawdy. "You're right. If you're that good, I absolutely will. That way, I can brag about discovering you. I think we'll do well together, Imogen. Let's talk about the practicalities. How often do you want to meet?" She got up and walked into the hallway.

I scanned the bookcases while I waited for her to come back, looking for some clue to her interests, influences. Something I could file away and use as a tool to make my own writing better. Magic words.

She returned with a yarn-filled bag. "Not being busy makes me itch. About a year ago, I learned to knit. Now I feel lazy if I'm sitting down to do anything other than write and I don't have yarn in my hands."

"I'd like to meet about every two weeks, I think. But I don't want to show you my writing until it's done. I hate getting feedback on an unfinished project, and I don't want to waste your time on problems I can figure out myself."

"I'm here to have my time wasted in precisely that fashion, but if it won't help you to discuss your work directly, we'll talk about other things." Beth's knitting needles clicked against each other. The yarn was thick and lavender-colored, but I couldn't see enough to tell what she was making.

"But if you change your mind, and you need to talk about writing, or show me pages, or change any of our meetings, don't be afraid to speak up, whether that means getting together less frequently or more. Every day, if that's what you want. You're here for your art, so put it first."

"I will, thanks." I set down my cup, thinking that the meeting was over, glad I had made it through without embarrassing myself.

"Now, I'm going to indulge my curiosity for a moment. Your sister is here also, yes?"

I leaned back into the couch, feeling the seams of the cushions press against me. "She is, and we're living in the same house, which is great. It was Marin's idea to apply. I wouldn't be here if not for her."

The sound of knitting needles reminded me of the clatter of typewriter keys. "I don't think there has ever been a sibling pair here at the same time before. It's such a fascinating dynamic. Having two artists in the family doesn't cause friction? No professional jealousy or sibling rivalry?"

"Our dad died when we were young, so it's pretty much always been just the two of us. It's never even occurred to me to think of Marin as a rival, someone who I ought to be competing against."

Though our mother hadn't seen things that way. Having a daughter who was a dancer was a reflected spotlight for the mother backstage, and our mother hoarded that reflection, clutching it to her heart. She basked in Marin's applause, and told herself that she had earned it, too. Having a daughter who was a writer was a flashlight shone into corners that ought to be kept dark so that no one saw the monsters tucked away in them. She wanted that light turned off.

I tucked my hand under my thigh, out of sight. "We work in different fields, so it's not like we'll ever be in direct competition. I actually think it's made us more secure as artists, having someone else close who knows what it means to work this hard. I mean, we're sisters, so we haven't always gotten along, but even when things have been difficult between us, we've always supported each other's art."

"That's good." Beth nodded. "To have that sort of support, and to have someone close who knows what it's like to have a life that doesn't look like everyone else's. So many people don't understand that. It's one of the things I love about coming back here—working with people who do.

"Well, unless there's anything else, I should let you get back to settling in, and to your work. I'm happy to be working with you, Imogen."

"I'm happy to be working with you, too."

I scrubbed the heel of my hand over my heart as I walked back home, almost light-headed with relief at how well the meeting had gone.

Late summer's lazy wind blew through the rose garden I had passed before, bending blossom-heavy heads like dancers' arms. The long afternoon shadows followed them, twisting and turning. A ballet of thorns and velvet petals and cold, perfumed darkness. I stepped off the path and into the thick of the flowers.

The wind blew sharper then, tearing the petals from their stems, sending them spinning in a red-black whirlwind. Melete's noise fell away, and I felt seasick, sideways, as if I had been shoved partially out of my own skin.

A woman stood in the center of the whirlwind, sharp-boned and long-haired, her dress like petals sewn with silk, and for an instant, it looked like her eyes were entirely black.

Then the light shifted, and they weren't. The tornado of rose petals was gone, and all the bustle of Melete filled the air. She smiled at me, long red dress rippling in the breeze. I waved and turned back to the path.

Stress, I told myself. Stress from the anxiety around meeting Beth, and maybe I was more light-headed with relief than I had thought. Over my shoulder, the rose garden was no more or less than it was, fragrant beauty in the late afternoon sun, tended by a woman in a sundress. That was all.

The third night we were officially in residence, I wandered into the kitchen to pick up my dinner and found Marin and Ariel already there. "You should join us," Ariel said, setting out another glass.

"Thanks." I set the bento-style box my dinner was packed in on the table with the two others. Two. Shit. "I'm going to go upstairs and see if Helena wants to eat with us."

"She's kind of horrible," Ariel said.

"Aggressively rude. Like she's feral, and doesn't know how to be a person," Marin added.

"Then she'll probably say no. But I still feel like I should ask. Unless she's really that bad?" Maybe I was luckier than I knew, living on a different floor than they did.

Ariel sighed. "The Catholic guilt has kicked in. Ask."

I knocked on Helena's door, waited, then knocked again. Feeling relieved that I wouldn't have to deal with the consequences of being polite, I turned to go.

"What?" Helena stood in the mostly closed doorway.

"The three of us were going to eat dinner together. Want to join us?"

She narrowed her eyes, gnawed on her bottom lip.

"If you're busy or something"—feral, I substituted internally—"you don't have to."

"Fine." She burst through the door, pulling it immediately shut behind her. "We're supposed to take opportunities to bond as artists while we're here, right?"

Right.

Marin and Ariel both looked surprised to see Helena join us, but recovered and set her a place. Ariel poured wine, then raised her glass. "To us, and to art." Her exaggerated pose erased any hint of pretension from the words, making them a welcome, a celebration. Marin and I toasted, and, after a second, Helena did, too.

It's the little things that break the ice. Helena and Marin both hated roasted red peppers, and pulled them out of their salads. Ariel stole them off their plates—they were her favorite. She and I had both worked as baristas, and shared the same contempt for people who ordered nonfat no-foam decaf like it was a sacrament. "Like, what is the actual point? Everything that is delicious in the drink is gone." Ariel shook her head. Helena didn't want to talk about her childhood, either. The air in the room relaxed as the meal progressed, our voices became less cautiously polite.

Then, rolling the red liquid around the bottom of her glass, Helena asked, "What would you trade for guaranteed success?"

"Like, 'I have one hit record and can retire comfortably on my royalties' success, or like 'I am become Beyoncé, destroyer of worlds' success?" Ariel asked.

"The latter. Everything you've ever wanted. All your dreams come true, even the ones you won't admit to having."

"I wouldn't sell my soul. I might sell my younger brother." Ariel grinned, making it clear she wouldn't.

"If we can trade other people, I'd trade in our mother in a heartbeat," Marin said. "Though I suppose that doesn't count as a sacrifice, considering how horrid Mommy Dearest is."

"Is she really that bad?" Ariel asked.

"Worse," Marin said, tucking her burned hand out of sight beneath the table. Her scars were barely visible, even if you knew to look, but old habits linger.

"Like growing up in hell," I said, my own hand aching in sympathy.

"I doubt that," Helena said, her face hard. "But even if it was, what would you trade to show her you'd made it? That would be worth something big, right?"

The quick answer would be to say that I would have stayed. Lived the extra two years at home, in the hell that my mother made it. But I couldn't say that in front of Marin, wouldn't make her feel like she was part of the hell that life had been, not when she was the thing that made it bearable.

"I'm starting to feel like you're asking me to sign my name in blood at a crossroads, Helena. What about you, what would you give up?" I asked.

"Everything. Anything. Whatever it takes."

It's a thing that's easy to say when you're sure no one will ever offer you that trade, because it's an impossible deal to make. But looking at Helena's face, I believed her.

"If only it were that easy," Marin said. "No bleeding feet and aching muscles. No auditions where you get passed over for a worse dancer because you don't look right for the part, whatever that means that day. No endless hours of rehearsal sabotaged by injury. Selling your soul sounds like the easy way out to me."

"I'm just glad my only option is to kick ass the usual way, so I'll never have to find out what I'd really give up," Ariel said. "Seems like a good way to learn some really uncomfortable things about yourself."

"I don't understand any of you," Helena said. "If it matters enough, you say yes. You take the deal. You don't look back. If you aren't prepared to do that, what are you doing here, anyway?" She put her dishes on the sideboard, and went back upstairs. Her door slammed shut.

"Oddly enough, dinner went better than I thought it would," Ariel said, pouring the rest of the wine into the three remaining glasses.

"You never did answer her, Imogen," Marin said as we cleared the table.

"I know." I had been afraid. Afraid that I would answer like Helena: Anything.

4

It had rained the night before, a torrential late-summer storm. The air was soup-thick with humidity as I drank my coffee on the porch. Marin came out and sat next to me.

"Did you sleep okay?" I asked. Our mother hated thunderstorms, and so she would put on noise-canceling headphones and drink herself into oblivion. Those nights, I knew I would be safe, and so I craved them. Marin, however, hated the howl of the wind, the roar of the thunder, and more often than not would crawl into bed with me during storms.

"No, but it wasn't the thunder that kept me awake. I had the weirdest dreams." She hunched over her own mug of coffee, breathing in the steam.

"Weird how?"

"Like, women's voices. Singing. Not with words or anything, just like they were singing along with the storm. Then I'd wake up, and think that I could see them outside my window, or in the river."

I leaned back against the smooth wood of the railings. "Wow. You're not rehearsing *Giselle*, are you?" It was one of the creepiest ballets I knew, complete with a graveyard full of vengeful Wilis, heartbroken women who returned from the dead to dance unfaithful men to death. I loved it, but if any ballet would make you think you were being haunted in a storm, it was that one.

"No, but maybe we should. Myrtha would make a good showcase

role for me." Marin sipped her coffee. "Seriously, though, you didn't hear anything?"

"I did, Marin. I heard the storm. Which sounded like women's voices because of the wind in the trees. We're not being haunted."

"But you heard them." She was insistent.

I set my mug down. "Are you okay? Did something else happen?"

She drank, shuddered. "It's gone bitter. No, I'm sure you're right. Just the storm, and not being used to how things sound in a strange place. I'm fine."

She stood up, shook herself loose. "I'll see you later?"

"Did we settle on four or four thirty?" I asked. We were meeting Gavin for a drink.

"Four, if that still works."

"It does. I'll see you then."

One of the buildings ringing the Commons was a bar. The kind of place that sold burgers and salads made of things that mostly weren't greens, where you could get out of the house and get your french fry fix all at once. It was made of old, smoke-tinged wood and thick plastered walls, one of which was painted with a surrealist fantasy of liquid clocks and a mechanized forest and a battalion of flaming horses—a gift from an earlier year's visual arts contingent. The bar had also been gifted with the astoundingly creative name of "There." As in, "Are we going There for drinks again?" Because the personalized meal service that was part of the residency was so good, There was the only other option at Melete, so indeed, we were: Marin, me, and Gavin.

Rumor was that while the food was decent, the service was indifferent at best, which may have explained why it was nearly empty during happy hour in the first week at an artists' colony. Marin was in the back corner, across a table from Gavin, waiting for me. Getting together here had been their idea, and Marin had been oddly shy when she brought it up.

"We're apparently the first set of siblings ever to be here at the same time, so he's curious. Plus, well, I'd like to introduce you." She was bent over her dance bag, face obscured by a curtain of hair.

"So I can see if he passes inspection?" I joked.

"It's just a drink. You don't have to come if you don't want to."

"It's fine, Marin. Of course I will."

After only a five-minute wait, the bartender slid me the bottle of blackcurrant cider I'd ordered. Unopened, no glass. I reached over and borrowed the bottle opener, then took my drink to the table. Marin made introductions.

"A pleasure, Imogen. How are you finding Melete so far?" Gavin asked. He made the polite question feel genuine, as if my answer mattered.

"It's lovely, thanks."

"Marin tells me you're a writer."

"Yes." We were all doing very well at this particular round of small talk.

She stood up. "I think that's our food getting cold. I'll be right back."

Gavin leaned across the table and lowered his voice. "Are you happy to be here? I didn't want to ask in front of your sister."

"I beg your pardon?" Apparently, the small talk was over.

"Marin mentioned that you had some reluctance about applying. She was worried that you only came here because she asked."

She hadn't told me that. "I really am. She did push me to apply, but I wouldn't have done it if I hadn't wanted to, and I'm glad I did.

"How do you like working with my sister?"

"Marin's a brilliant dancer." For a second, as he watched her walk back with our plates, his poise slipped away, and he looked real, like he was breath and blood, instead of a magazine page. Then the second passed, and that unreal perfection fell on him like a shadow again.

Silence slid over the table and stretched, cat-like, as we ate. Marin fidgeted, picking at her fries with nothing like her usual appetite. Gavin raised his eyes to her face every time he drank, using the motion as a cover.

It struck me that I was chaperoning the world's most awkward date. Or a date that might have been less awkward if I wasn't there to witness it. "Marin, do you know where the ladies' room is?" I grabbed her arm and pulled her with me without waiting for her answer.

The door swung shut behind us. "I feel like an enormous third wheel. Be honest—would you rather be alone with him?"

"Maybe?" Marin said. "I mean, not when I asked you. It was supposed to be drinks, so you could meet him, then things started to sort of happen."

I grinned. "That's adorable. Okay. Go back out there. I'm going to get a really important phone call."

She hugged me. "Thanks, Imogen."

I waited a couple of minutes, then walked back to the table. "Marin, Gavin, I'm so sorry. My mentor just called and asked to move up our next meeting. I promised her I'd have pages, and I don't have anything written. Will you excuse me?"

"I'd be a terrible example if I didn't," Gavin said.

"We're fine." Marin smiled. "Go."

"Lovely to meet you, Gavin."

"And you." He stood as I left, perfectly polite, perfectly correct.

On the way out of the door, I looked back. They were deep in conversation, leaning close across the table. Impossible at this distance to say what they were talking about, but at least they were talking, instead of sitting in silence and not quite looking at each other. Then Gavin reached out, tucked Marin's hair behind an ear, and she smiled. So did I.

Strange, but somehow also comforting, to think that even one of the dance world's most beautiful people was still human enough to get flummoxed about a crush.

Since I had used needing to write as an excuse to leave, it only seemed fair that I actually go home and do that. I picked up my pen and used the scratch of the nib across the page as white noise, shutting out everything but the story.

Once upon a time.

Once upon a time, all the clocks chime midnight.

Cinderella flees from the ball as her illusion unweaves. Beauty races toward her Beast before the last echo of the clock falls silent.

Illusions fall. Magic ends. The clock chimes.

Nothing lasts forever, and midnight is a purposeful stop. A pause to remind you that there is always a clock ticking. There will never be enough time, and for every Beauty who saves her Beast, there will be a voiceless mermaid who dissolves into sea foam.

But there is another thing about midnight. It is when illusions break. When you can see the truth beneath them, if you are looking. There is always a crack in the illusion, a gap in the perfection, even if it is only visible with the ticking of a clock.

Midnight is when you look, if there is a truth you need to see. If you are brave enough to bear what you witness.

For just a moment, the smoke dissipates, the mirrors shatter, and the glamour is gone. All that's left is the truth of the story, the truth in your heart, your darkest secret.

A glass shoe, abandoned on the stairs.

Once upon a time.

Tick.

Tock.

Pen down, and I rolled the tension from my shoulders, shook the stiffness from my hand.

It's easier to see the places where things end. Endings are clear, endings are dramatic, endings are obvious events. A pair of panties, not yours, found, the slap of a hand across a face, a ring returned. Something that was, and isn't, now.

Beginnings are hidden in the shadows of time, are gradual, are two half-glances in a dark bar. Tiny things that no one even notices, but that hold everything.

After a week, I had been at Melete long enough for it to start feeling like it was mine. Part of that familiarity was from running over and through the place until my feet knew the ground beneath. I felt connected, like I had learned Melete's borders and boundaries, like it had shown me its secrets.

I ran through the falling light of evening, arms loose, the muscles in my thighs warm. Grass bent and sprang beneath my feet, and I heard the rush of the river under the rush of my breath.

I had started running my freshman year of high school as a way to not be in the house, to escape. Even that small escape hadn't been easy, but it had been possible. According to my mother, "letting herself go" was the cardinal sin a woman could commit, and being overweight or out of shape were both major signs of a woman letting herself go. She checked the sizes on our clothing, and if they were what she considered to be too large, the clothes would disappear from our closets, leaving us the choice of whittling ourselves back into the size she felt was appropriate, or using our own money to buy replacements that would disappear at the next inspection. So if I wanted to run, all I had to do was tell her that I thought I was gaining weight. She would narrow her eyes, pinch the flesh under my arm or on top of my thigh, and tell me that I certainly could stand to tone up. The freedom was worth the humiliation.

I learned to love the motion of running, the action itself. The fact that I could trust the muscles in my legs to carry me, if I needed to go. Running made me feel strong and capable. Like, if I ran far enough, I could outrun everything—that my thoughts would just go white, and there would be nothing in the world but movement.

Once I had been able to move out of my mother's house, I had stopped trying to outrun my life and ran for the pleasure I felt in movement. Legs and arms the tick of a metronome, distance disappearing beneath my feet. Now, I ran to clear my thoughts, to untangle plot threads, to ground myself in my own skin, something that was necessary to counterbalance all of the hours I spent living solely in my head.

I kept to the path, weaving through the fellows' houses, then the studios, then the other buildings that ringed the Commons— including what looked like a completely empty There—then farther out, into the woods. The air smelled rich, green as the trees, and a breeze cooled the sweat against my skin. Birds called their evening greetings, and something else, smaller than I was, chipmunk or squirrel, ran through the forest as well.

The sun slid farther toward the horizon, and I turned around, looping my steps back on themselves.

I emerged from the forest and ran back through the populated areas of campus. The mentors' houses, the fragrant air of the rose garden, the artists' studios. Some of the dancers' studios had walls of enormous glass windows. They could be curtained over for privacy, but tonight, Marin had left hers uncovered. As I ran past, I saw them, Marin and Gavin, dancing. I stopped.

I don't forget how talented she is. I've seen Marin dance almost my entire life, and I've seen her talent since I was aware enough to know what that meant, to know how much better she was than the other girls onstage in pink tights and tutus. I've gone to her performances and watched recordings. But sometimes the reality of her ability slips from my mind until I have a reason to be reminded of it, and here, like this, she was breathtaking.

Marin exploded through the air, in and out of Gavin's arms. Every arch of her wrist, every movement described by her leg, was like watching a story in a language I hadn't known I understood. When they danced together, it was clear that Gavin was the best partner Marin had ever worked with. I could hear the music, just seeing them move. They were the song.

My abused muscles quivered in the cold, and I stood, transfixed.

It was a catch and lift they were working on. Marin flung herself into the air toward Gavin, and his hands pushed her higher still, until she was poised just on the edge of his grasp.

Then a toss and she flew again, spun, and dropped back into his hold, but only after almost, almost falling. Beautiful in its peril, trust enfleshed.

Again and again they ran through the motions, making slight adjustments that I couldn't see. But I could see that she flew higher, fell faster. My heart raced to watch it.

Then he said something, and stepped closer, and it was not with the grace of a dancer, but something very mortal, hesitant and nervous. And even though it was a not a wild flight through the air, there was peril in Marin's answering movement, as she stepped into the circle of his arms. Peril, but grace there, too.

And then his hands moved on her body, and her mouth touched his, and I turned away, and I did not watch.

5

The Mourning River, which Marin could see from her window, cut through the grounds at Melete, dividing the place almost exactly in half. Clear and swift-flowing, it was arched with bridges, installed with the same sense of artistic chaos that suffused the rest of the design here. I stood in the center of a miniature version of the Thames's Tower Bridge, and I could see the Rialto Bridge just downriver. The experience was like standing on a fold in a map, impossible geography made solid.

I still hadn't gotten over the slight feeling of unreality that Melete gave me. The night before, I had felt the sensation that someone was watching me work so strongly that I had to close my windows and curtains before it went away. I had slept fitfully, and woken up before dawn feeling like the shadows were staring at me.

But the late morning was bright and clear. Light dappled through the leaves of the trees, and I closed my eyes and tilted my face toward the warmth.

"Those trees are my favorite."

I looked toward the voice.

"The ones you were looking at. They're called elf maples."

He might have been an elf, the modern film version, all red-gold hair and cheekbones so sharp you could cut yourself on them, worn jeans, and a T-shirt as green as the leaves. He smiled, and I felt heat rise just under my skin.

"It sounds like a name from a fairy tale," I said, and it did, so much that I filed it away in my brain for later use, imagining people who made their houses in trees, and stepped, dryad-like, out of them. An entire forest of trees that were also people, the rustling of their leaves a slow, ongoing song with seasonal movements.

"Someone else told me that, once." His eyes went very far away. "She didn't like fairy tales, though. She said they made things sound too easy."

"Not all of them do," I said. "Not the true ones."

"True fairy tales?" He turned back to me, all the way back from wherever he had been lost. "Do you think they exist?"

"I don't think that someone named Sleeping Beauty literally slept for one hundred years," I said. "But there are fairy tales where there is a cost, where the veins of the story run deeper than ball gowns and handsome princes. I don't think they're real, but I think they're true."

"Interesting," he said. "Is that what you're here to write?" He nodded at the notebook on the bridge in front of me.

"Something like that. Are you a writer?"

"No, I leave the words to people who are better with them." He walked closer, and leaned on the edge of the bridge, watching the river flowing beneath. The light through the trees, through the leaves of the elf maples—which I would have called by the much less romantic name of box elders—slanted across him, covering him in alternating patches of bright and shadow, obscuring his expression. "I'd forgotten how beautiful it is here."

"Forgotten? So you've been here before." He must be a mentor, in that case. Fellows weren't allowed more than one residency.

"I have. And only recently returned. I'm Evan." He held out his hand.

"Imogen. I just started my residency." His hand was rough, callused. I wanted to ask if he was a sculptor, but that would mean admitting I had noticed.

"Do you like it here so far?" he asked.

"Very much." I smiled. "It's more than I expected. Better, somehow. Which is weird, because I'd thought that it sounded perfect. Are you happy to be back?"

"Melete, this part of the woods in particular—they're among my favorite places. They feel right. So I always like coming back to them. Even when there isn't such excellent company." He smiled, and my blood fizzed.

The wind rustled through the trees, shaking loose the seedpods from the maples to spiral in helicopters down the air and into the river. Goosebumps rose on my arms, and I shivered.

Evan looked up at the darkening sky. "Storms can come in fast here. If you're not the sort of person who likes to get caught in them, you might want to go in."

The wind grabbed at my hair, turning it to snakes, and the leaves were silver fish against the slate-grey sky. Thunder rumbled in distant echo. "Maybe next time, when I'm dressed for it."

"How will I find you, the next time there's a storm?" Evan smiled. The rain fell, heavy drops that splotched his shirt.

"Do you have a phone?" I asked. I very much wanted to be found.

"Not with me."

"The old-fashioned way, then." I fished in my bag for a pen, then scrawled my number across a notebook page. The wind nearly tore it from my hand as I passed it to him.

"Until next time," he half-shouted over the rising wind.

The skies opened, bucketing rain. I ran for home.

Soaked to the skin, mud-splattered, and dreaming of hot chocolate and a hotter shower, the sheer delight of dry clothes, I clumped up the porch stairs and through the front door. I toed out of Converse that squelched when I walked, and fought the urge to wring the water from my sopping hair. "Marin?" I called. "Are you here?" I didn't want to drip my way up three flights of stairs.

Face flushed, she stormed out of the kitchen. "What?"

"I was hoping for a towel and dry clothes, but if this is a bad time . . ."

"No. It's fine." She bit her words as if they were apples. "I'll get them. And maybe while you're waiting, you could explain to Helena that I'm not a whore."

"I—what?" Marin was already halfway up the stairs, so I stood where I was.

"Your sister is fucking her mentor." Helena slouched down the hallway. "Also, you're disgusting, and I can see through your shirt."

"Good. Yes. Glad to know my secret plan to call down a rainstorm so I could flash my bra to the entire campus worked. Also, how is Marin's sex life any of my business? Or yours?"

"It's not." Marin held out a towel, leggings, and a T-shirt. "Which is what I've been trying to explain."

I peeled out of my soaked clothes and toweled off.

"How do you not care?" Helena asked me, eyes ostentatiously averted from my nakedness.

I did care, but I was pretty sure not for the reasons Helena did. I let the towel fall and pulled on the dry clothing. *So much better.*

"I don't care because Marin is an adult who is capable of making her own choices. So long as it's consensual and she's happy, it's none of my business who she has sex with."

"It is, and I am," Marin said, the color still high on her face.

"Well, there you go. And even if it were my business, he seemed perfectly nice when I met him. So there really is no reason for me to step in here, and even less of one for you to."

"You've met him? Of course you have. Ugh." Helena looked like she might spit right on the floor. She cut her eyes back to Marin. "He's using you, and you're too fucking stupid to see it."

"Still not sure how that makes me a whore," Marin snapped.

"Right. Because he didn't promise you anything to get you to drop your tights. Whatever. Some of us have to actually work to get what we want while we're here." Helena stalked upstairs.

"So, that was pleasant," I said. "Want some hot chocolate?" I wanted it even more now, and it had been Marin's favorite comfort food when we were growing up.

"Yes. I'll drop your gross clothes in the wash."

"I can—"

"I'll do it."

I raised my hands in surrender and went into the kitchen. I had forgotten that was what Marin did when she was stressed. She cleaned, straightened. Did something to impose order on the chaos.

The milk was warming on the stove when Marin came in. "So, what brought all that on?" I asked.

"Thin walls," she said.

It took me a moment to register what she meant, and then I snickered. "Well, if you're whoring yourself out, at least the sex is good."

There was silence, and I worried that I had overstepped and said the utterly wrong thing. Then Marin burst into laughter.

"Yes, yes it is," she said.

I carried the mugs over to the table and set them down next to her. "Feel better?"

"Much, thanks. I know there are going to be people who think the worst about me because of this, but she really freaked out."

"There are always going to be people who think things. Obviously, you and Gavin are both hideous, unpleasant people with no redeeming personal qualities, so why would anyone want to have sex with either of you, unless they were getting something in trade?"

Marin grinned, then looked down into her cocoa. "It's still pretty new. This thing. The two of us. I thought maybe it was just going to be casual, but I really like him."

"Are you worried about that?" I asked. "The liking him, I mean."

"I wasn't until Helena freaked out."

"Do you think she's right, that he's using you?"

She shook her head. "He's a brilliant dancer with a great career. There is literally nothing I could give him that he doesn't already have. But people will think I'm using him."

"They probably will," I said. "And some people will think he's abusing the power he has over you. Scandal is more fun to talk about, and there will always be people who would rather believe the gross stuff.

"But if you know it's not true, and Gavin does too, then it really doesn't matter. Just be happy, and tell the gossips to go fuck themselves."

Marin leaned her head on my shoulder. "Thanks. It means a lot that you'd stand up for me. So, what were you doing out in the rain?"

"Flirting with a cute boy."

Marin raised an eyebrow, and then shook her head sadly. "Whore."

"Runs in the family, I guess," I said. We tapped our mugs together in a toast.

6

"Hey, Imogen." Ariel knocked on the half-open door to my room. "You have a letter. It looks fancy."

"Really?" I pushed back from my desk.

"Here it is." She leaned against the door frame.

No stamp, so it had come through Melete's in-house mail system. The envelope was decorated—a sketch of a bridge, surrounded by trees. Hand drawn, the pencil smudged in places from handling. "Elf maples," I murmured, and smiled.

"Do you know who it's from?" Ariel asked.

"I think so. This guy I met the other day."

"A cute guy?" She waggled her eyebrows and mock-leered.

I felt myself blush and ducked my head, embarrassed by the reaction, and so of course turned even redder.

"Never mind." Ariel laughed. "You just told me. I'll let you read your love letter in peace."

I slid my finger beneath the flap and opened it. The stationery was gorgeous, a thick cream, and the ink deep green. He had drawn leaves here, too, borders of them all around the words.

Dear Imogen—

Forgive me for not calling. The storm stole your number. But I took the liberty of sending you this letter so that I might convince you to go to Melete's Night Market with me.

It will be held this Friday, in the common area at the center of the campus. I hope to attend, and hope even more to see you there.

Yours, waiting,
Evan

I smiled as I refolded the letter and tucked it into the top drawer of my desk. I had no idea what the Night Market was, but I was definitely going.

Friday night the trees around the Commons were strung with fairy lights, and they sparkled like fireflies in the darkening September sky. The air smelled like the burnt sugar of caramel corn and the fading sweetness of the grass that crackled underfoot. Evan was waiting by the entrance.

"Imogen! I'm so glad you came." He hugged me hello, both of us holding on a moment longer than mere friendliness.

"I loved the letter. Do you draw, then?" I was still curious about what kind of art he made.

"Only well enough. I'm a sculptor—right now, I work mainly with metal. I was worried you'd think getting a letter was too weird."

"I like getting mail. It happens so rarely anymore, it's almost like getting a present along with the words. I should give you my number, through, to make things easier."

"I didn't bring my phone—I didn't want to be disturbed."

Hard to argue with that. "Next time, then. So, what is the Night Market?"

"Let me show you," he said.

Walking through it was like walking through an enormous cabinet of curiosities. Wax-stoppered apothecary bottles of perfume sat on velvet the color of a faded rose. A man with a map tattooed on the globe of his head sold thick silver jewelry designed like miniature barquentines and sextants.

A poet busked, calling out verse that was both spontaneous and awful: "Haiku, limerick, or sonnet, spoken here in praise of your lord or lady, and then disappearing like smoke." Evan dropped a bill in the open pencil case at the poet's feet, but held up his hand to forestall the poetry. "My lady cannot be improved, even by praise in verse."

"Beware perfection unremarked," the poet said. "Peril lies within."

"I certainly hope that wasn't his idea of romance," I said.

"I'll make a note," Evan said, smiling. "As wooing techniques go, cryptic, creepy poetry is right out."

As we walked past, a shadow rose, clawed and horned, from the poet's back. The light shifted and it was normal, his only shadow a copy of himself. Still, I looked twice more over my shoulder as we continued on.

"How often does this happen?" I asked. The sky had grown darker, the fairy lights in the trees now like closer stars. Fire pits had been set up just off the path, and we stopped at one for s'mores. They tasted like pieces of campfires, like memories of childhood summers that never were. I wanted to take the moment and press it between glass, safe forever.

"Part of the appeal of the Market is its mystery, so there's no regular schedule, though there are traditional times. The one around Halloween is a spectacle, and there's always one just before Christmas. But really, it appears when it wants, or when it's needed.

I know that sounds ridiculous, but it really does seem to be the best way to explain the randomness."

"I love that idea," I said. "Like there's some guiding force here that says, 'Oh, the artists are sad. Everyone is spilled paint and paper cuts. Let's have a party.'"

Evan laughed. "It's a lot like that. Though, it's also an organized randomness. There are rumors just before, to give people time to get ready, and the artists who exhibit or perform always know in advance."

"There are performances?" I asked.

"There are always artists who exhibit, usually the ones who need a stage. Being invited to show your work here is considered a bit of a coup. There's a singer tonight. If you want to stay."

I smiled. "I'd like that."

"Imogen!"

I turned to see Marin, holding hands with Gavin. The effect of his presence was stronger here than it had been in a darkened bar. There was a wildness about him in the shadowed trees and fire-light, a quality that made me understand why glamour used to be thought of as magic, as dangerous.

Gavin smiled, kissed both of my cheeks, and the spell was broken. "A pleasure to see you again."

"And this is—" I began.

"We've met," Evan said.

"I'm surprised you're here," Gavin said. Except that when he said "surprised," it sounded like he meant "pissed off." I glanced at Marin, and she shrugged, as puzzled as I was.

"I had some free time. Gavin's commissioned some work from me," Evan said by way of explanation. "Though surely you don't expect me to spend every moment I'm here working on it."

"We've discussed my expectations. I'd thought you understood the arrangement." As if Evan was a child who needed scolding.

"Believe me," Evan said, "it would be impossible to forget."

"Well, since you are here, perhaps I should leave you. I'd hate for your time to go to waste.

"Imogen." Gavin nodded at me, his arm around Marin, guiding her away.

"What was that?" I asked.

"A very long and uninteresting story," Evan said, his eyes on Gavin's back.

It hadn't seemed that way, but then the music began, and asking Evan for more details became much less important.

Stage presence. Star quality. Phrases you think you understand, until you encounter someone who embodies them. Ariel did. She was a force, electric, and from the first note, we were hers. It wasn't that we couldn't look away, it was that no one would want to turn from the bright flame of her to the ordinary pieces of the world. It seemed like everyone at the Market gathered in the center of the Commons to hear her.

We screamed and clapped and cheered. Ariel shouted her song into the sky, and we threw ourselves after it. The song was one I didn't know, but it was impossible to hear it and not want to move, to celebrate the music. I danced with Evan, and gloried in the feel of his hands on my waist, and the ache in my thighs that was from more than just dancing.

Another hand grabbed mine, and carried on the force of the music, I let myself be pulled away. Another hand, and then another, until I was dizzy and lost, trapped in a knot of bodies.

Somewhere in that panicked lostness, the music changed. It wasn't Ariel singing anymore, but something that raced my heart and prickled my skin. Dissonant. I struggled through the crowd, but shoving my way through was like trying to navigate a living maze.

My breath came faster, and I tore away from hands that grabbed at me, turned my eyes from faces gone feral and cruel in the starlight. They were no one I recognized. They were almost inhuman. Bones gone to sharp edges, fingernails to talons, hair to wings and fur and rose petals.

Then a hand—callused and work-roughened—found mine, and Evan's voice was in my ear. "Imogen. Imogen, I've got you."

I clung to his hand, the realness of it, and closed my eyes against the impossible surrounding me. I could feel myself fall, as if from a great height, back into my skin.

"You're fine, Imogen. It's safe."

Safe. I was quite sure I hadn't been. "You didn't see them. Didn't hear it."

He couldn't have. If he'd seen what I had, had heard that unreal song, he wouldn't be walking so calmly. Every step, I waited for footfalls, for the wild music to restart, for the strangeness to pounce on me. My head throbbed, and I couldn't quite focus my vision.

Finally, as we got to the edge of the Commons, I could breathe again. The pressure in my head faded from being squeezed by a vise to hangover-level. No more music that hadn't been Ariel's voice, only the practical clatter of booths being packed away—by real people, not furred and clawed nightmares. Everything I could see in the Commons looked normal, expected. Still, I stretched my eyes toward the shadows, trying to see what they hid.

"Can I walk you home?" Evan asked.

"I'd like that," I said, relieved that he had offered, that I hadn't had to ask. I kept my fingers entangled with his as we walked. The silence wrapped around us like a blanket, and it was enough that I could pretend things had been normal.

When we got to my house, Evan wished me good night. "I'd like to see you again, Imogen."

I raised my hand to his face, traced my thumb over the sharpness of his cheekbone, then stepped in and kissed him. His mouth was sweet and dark, the chocolate from the s'mores. I fisted my hand in his hair and pressed my body against his as if I might lose myself again without him to hold on to.

Then I stepped back, savoring the taste of him on my lips. "I'd like that, too. Send me a letter."

The next day, my head was too full of thoughts from the night before to let me clear out my mind and work. Unfortunately, the almost-dream of losing myself in a crowd of dancers overwhelmed the remembered heat of Evan's mouth. Every time I relaxed, I could feel myself being pulled into a dance that became a trap.

I had showered twice when I got home the night before, once not being enough to wash the echoes of grabbing hands from my skin. I'd slept with earbuds in, Bach cello suites on repeat, in an attempt to purge the strange song from my brain. I refused to let it stay in my thoughts, but the notes were still clinging to me, and the sound of them curdled my blood.

I wandered down to the kitchen and poured myself an enormous mug of coffee. Helena scuffed in, bare feet pale under black silk men's pajamas. "Morning," I said.

"Yes, unfortunately, it is." She grabbed my mug from the counter and stumbled back out.

I shook my head and poured myself a second mug, then took it to the library before someone made off with that one, too.

Our house's library was on the first floor, in the back. Three walls were lined with bookshelves. There were two well-worn reading chairs and a long table where people could work. The fourth wall had an old brick fireplace and a mantel inexplicably carved with Tudor roses.

The library's collection was eclectic. There were worn paperback romances mixed in with Dickens, a shelf of serious-looking physics books next to one full of J.K. Rowling and Stephen King. Poetry was mixed in with graphic novels, and *Gormenghast* snuggled up to *Good Omens*.

I was looking for one of the big fairy tale collections—Grimm or Andersen—for reference. To see the way the stories were structured, how the technical elements fit together. And to help keep my mind on work, and not wandering off to think about music that sounded like it was chasing me.

"Enough," I said out loud, just to hear something that was normal. I pulled Maria Tatar's *The Annotated Brothers Grimm* from the shelf. I would read them out loud to myself if that's what it would take to clear my head.

A packet of letters fell out after it.

They were tied together by a green ribbon, and the ribbon sealed with wax. The mark sealed into the wax was some sort of branch hung with berries. It was hard to tell exactly what they were—at some point, the seal had been broken, and the letters read.

Rather than putting them back where I'd found them, I sat down and untied the ribbon, folding it and setting it to the side. The packet of letters smelled faintly like rosemary.

They weren't dated. The handwriting was neat and elegant, much lovelier than my own haphazard scrawl, but not what I thought of as old-fashioned—which was somewhat surprising, considering the way they were written. They were all addressed to *My Thomas, True,* and signed *Your own, J*—language that felt purposely stylized, almost archaic.

My Thomas, True,

One year today since you were gone from me, and I walked the river and the bridge, thinking of you. Wishing that the distance between us might grow thin, that I might be where you are.

If I close my eyes, my skin remembers the feel of your hands.

I write poetry, as I have done constantly since you left. I sit before the glass you made for me as I do, and I wait for your return. I know the time of it, to the second, and I will be there, waiting. You are in my thoughts and in my words and in my heart. I trust that I am in yours as well.

Your own, J

Glancing through the rest of them, I wondered if they had ever been sent. They weren't stamped or postmarked. J made references to Thomas being in an unreachable place, that she would hold the letters and keep them safe against his return, that he could read them then, or simply accept them as a gift, a way to know that she had been thinking of him, always, in his absence. They were narrative, not dialogue, and I couldn't tell where Thomas was, or why he couldn't receive letters. Even in prison, you can send and receive letters.

I folded them back up, retied the ribbon, then took the letters and the book of fairy tales back into the kitchen with me. Still distracted, but this was the kind of distraction I could make a story out of, at least once I had more coffee.

Ariel was spooning honey into a mug, last night's smeary eyeliner adding an air of debauchery to her cutoff grey sweats and well-worn Dresden Dolls T-shirt.

"You were amazing," I said.

"Thanks." Her voice was lower, grittier than usual. "You were a good crowd. A show's always better when people dance."

"I heard it's a big deal, getting asked to perform there. Congratulations." I poured milk into my coffee, passed her the carton.

"I tell you what, the whole audition process or whatever it was felt like something out of a spy movie. There was a letter in my studio one day, on top of the piano. I had to write my response on it, and leave it there. Gone the next day. Three days pass, and I don't hear anything.

"Yesterday morning, Angelica, my mentor, texts to tell me I'm confirmed, and that she has to walk me over to do my sound check. Which wasn't at the Commons, but this place in the woods, where I had to sing. Without being able to see who was watching. I'm pretty sure none of them danced. They definitely didn't cheer." She passed her hand through her hair, standing it in spikes.

"It was so bizarre. I thought it was a joke. If Angelica hadn't been there, I would have left."

"Weird. Did you send in an audition tape or something?"

"Angelica said they liked my application portfolio."

"That's so cool. Congratulations again. Send me a link where I can buy your stuff." I grabbed the book and my coffee.

"Absolutely. I'll send you the demo tracks for the new songs, too."

I was almost out of the kitchen when she spoke again.

"Hey, Imogen. Did you notice anything"—a pause, the sound of fingers drumming on the counter—"weird last night?"

An echo of a song she hadn't sung rang in my thoughts. "Weird how?"

"Like, toward the end of the set, I kept thinking that maybe there were people there in costumes or something?"

"So you saw them too?" I was half-relieved.

"I freaked out. Thought maybe I'd inhaled some smoke that I shouldn't have. But costumes makes sense." She rolled tension from her shoulders.

"They do, don't they. Or secondhand smoke. I had a beast of a headache." Both possibilities were logical.

"Most likely explanation."

I nodded, and we left it at that, neither of us making the point that the most likely explanation wasn't always the true one. It was just the thing that was most comfortable to believe.

7

Everything that could have gone wrong that day already had, so I wasn't surprised when the baking did, too. The second batch of still-watery egg whites slithered down the sink, and I clanged the empty bowl on top of the counter. "Fuck."

"Imogen?" Ariel asked. "What are you doing?"

"Failing at this, too, apparently." I stared blankly at the counter, covered in the detritus of unsuccessful cooking.

"Too?" She slid into a chair and tucked her feet beneath her.

"I'm having one of those days where I can't write for shit. I know I'm getting stuff wrong as soon as I put it on the page, and I can't see my way to fixing it. Which would be fine if it were just today, but yesterday and the day before were also one of those days. Plus I spilled a bottle of ink all over my favorite shirt and I cut myself shaving."

"And it's not even Friday the thirteenth," Ariel deadpanned.

"Exactly. So rather than sitting upstairs and sulking, I thought I'd come down here and make chocolate mousse."

"Seriously? You can just"—she waved her hands in the air like a wizard—"make that?"

I shrugged. "It's usually not hard. Except today, when I can't make anything get stiff."

Ariel snickered.

I stared.

"You heard what you just said, right?" she asked.

I paused, realized, and the two of us dissolved into laughter, far more than my inadvertent innuendo deserved, red-faced, tears streaming from our eyes. When we had gotten ahold of ourselves, Ariel stood up. "Right. I'm staging an intervention. For the both of us."

She poured two shots of whiskey, then handed one to me. "Here's to the losers."

"You too?" I asked.

"Me too."

We clinked glasses and downed the shots.

"I haven't ruined my clothing, but I've been writing like shit the past week or so myself," Ariel said. "It pisses me off. Here I am in this amazing place, with this prestigious opportunity, and I can't do a goddamned thing with it. And I'm sure that's part of why I can't write a decent song right now, because there's suddenly all this pressure to be worthy, to live up to being chosen to be here, to not waste my time, but knowing that is one thing and actually being able to not give a fuck and write songs is another."

"I thought it would be easier, being here," I said. "Like, all the things I told myself were getting in the way before would be gone. The only thing left to worry about would be my writing. Instead, I've picked up a whole new bunch of things to worry about. Like, what if I'm not taking enough advantage of working with Beth? Maybe I should be working on a collaborative project while I'm here. Am I somehow doing residency entirely wrong?"

"What if I'm good, but being here proves that I'll never be great?" Ariel said.

"And that's the big one." I pushed my glass to the side. "Good to know that insecurity keeps pace with ambition."

"It's weird, being here," Ariel said, sliding our glasses around the table like some version of a shell game that had our talent hiding beneath.

"Yes. Yes, it is. Good weird, but weird."

"I mean, I was giving piano lessons and working as a barista back home so I could pay rent. Grabbing gigs when and where I could, and being grateful if I got enough box office to pay the gas money. Here, I check a box for whether I want my dinner to be organic microgreens or a nice salmon risotto," Ariel said. "And I'm sure as fuck not complaining about that, but you know, I always told myself that if I could just succeed enough not to have to worry about whether I was going to be able to pay my bills each month, then I'd have the space in my head to stop hustling and really make something. Something great."

"And here we are, the luckiest of the lucky, with our organic microgreens, and what if we're still not good enough?" I said.

"Right. I have the space in my head, and instead of ideas, it's full of doubt. Everything they tell us about being here is how this is a place where we are meant to just focus on our art, to create for ourselves without worrying about anything else, but I have never in my life felt more like everyone is watching me work, and it's paralyzing."

"Like we're not making art for ourselves, but to represent Melete. All that tradition, everyone who came before us, and sometimes it's wonderful—look who I belong with!—and sometimes it just feels like a longer list of people to let down." I raised my empty glass, toasting Helena, who had just come in. She glared at us as she set the kettle on for tea.

"Also, I keep feeling like someone is literally watching me work," Ariel said. "I mean, obviously, they're not, because my studio has no windows, but I swear I feel eyes."

- 6 2 -

"Me too!" I said. "I've decided it's the weight of expectations and/or my own guilt manifesting."

Helena slammed the cupboard so hard it bounced open again.

"Do you have something you'd like to share with the class?" Ariel asked.

"You're both idiots. Of course you're being watched. We all are. You think they don't care about which one of us is the best, that you've made it to the top just because you got in?"

"I'm sure they do, Helena, but no one from Melete is going to be looking in my windows at night while I'm writing," I said.

"I wouldn't be so sure." She stared into her mug like she was using it to divine the future.

"Helena. I live on the third floor."

Ariel snorted out a laugh.

"Laugh all you want," Helena said. "But if you're smart, you'll pay attention to those feelings. Getting in here was only the beginning."

October had come to Melete, and brought apple cider weather with it. The air wasn't truly cold, but sharp and bright, the knife-edge promise of oncoming winter. The leaves were a quiet conflagration on the trees, but every day more and more dropped, baring the skeletons of branches to the darkening sky. The days were shorter, and slid through each other faster.

Melete was no longer new. This was our place now—we knew the paths under our feet, knew the sounds and the scents that surrounded us. It had become home, become very nearly ordinary. All of the strangeness, all of the things that astounded us, that we had exclaimed over when we first arrived, were now commonplace. As we began to see things as ordinary, we saw the cracks in the perfection, and the cracks in ourselves as well.

When you go somewhere to be alone with yourself and your art, the problem becomes that you are alone with yourself and your art. For some people, that aloneness becomes the abyss, staring back. It wasn't the kind of thing that got advertised in the promotional materials, but every year there were people who chose not to finish their residency, and left Melete early. We had our first in early October, a painter.

"I didn't know him, but Ali, the woman who has the studio next to mine, lived in the same house as he did, and she told me he spent, like, three days just walking around outside, not eating or showering or anything," Marin said. "Then he went back to his room, packed up everything except his paints and canvases and stuff, and declared he was unworthy of his muse."

"His muse?" I asked, shaking my head. Ridiculous.

"That's where things get really interesting," Marin said, leaning against the railing of the porch stairs. The late-morning sun was warm, casting gold over everything. "Because it seems like his muse was more than just metaphorical.

"Ali also said there was a woman—some utterly gorgeous super-model-type—who had been coming around at all hours to see him. And they had a fight. Like, a loud screaming fight. Ali overheard her calling him worthless and mediocre. She said his art was no use to her, and so he wasn't either."

"Ouch," I said.

"Right? Still, if you leave for no reason other than your maybe-girlfriend says you suck, you probably weren't going to have much of a career anyway. I mean, how do you get to the point of being good enough to get in here without also learning how to say 'fuck you' to the people who tell you you're not? Or did he just live in some magical world where he never got a rejection or a bad review?" She shook her head.

"Probably the latter," I said. "For those of us who don't audition, who work on our own when we want to, instead of in required classes, this may be the first time we've had to think about how good we are, and how much we'll have to work to get to where we want to be. Whether it's even going to be possible for us to work hard enough to get there.

"Maybe," I continued, "this was the first time someone had ever told him he wasn't a modern Michelangelo, and he couldn't take the criticism. You know, you find out that you're not perfect, and so instead of figuring out how to get better, you quit because you're not good enough."

"I guess that makes sense," she said. "I remember the first time I didn't get something I'd auditioned for. It was a couple of months after you left, an open call for Ballet New York." She set down her coffee mug and looked out into the forest. "I was so desperate for them to pick me."

This was a story I didn't know. Ballet New York was the company that Marin had been with from the time she left home to when she quit to come here. I'd always assumed she'd gotten in right away. "What happened?"

"To this day, I don't know. I even asked, after they did hire me and I'd been dancing there for a while, and they couldn't—or wouldn't—tell me.

"I'd had what I thought was a good audition, made it through to the last round of cuts, then 'wasn't what they were looking for.' No other reason. I almost quit dance."

"Really?" I couldn't imagine a Marin who didn't dance.

"I felt like, if they couldn't even tell me what was wrong with me, it obviously wasn't fixable. I just wasn't right." She looked lost, as if there was a part of her that still heard that voice.

"What made you keep dancing?"

She laughed, sharp and bitter. "Our mother. She had paid for classes, after all, and I was going to take them. So she wouldn't let me quit until she'd gotten her money's worth. And the next audition call was during that paid-up window, and I got it. It was the one time she's ever helped my career."

"I got fifty-three rejection letters before I sold my first story."

"Seriously?" She looked at me.

I nodded. "Fifty. Three. I probably have hundreds by now, if I were ever masochistic enough to count them all."

"Do you ever wonder why we do this to ourselves? Spend ninety percent of our lives being told we're not good enough?" Marin tied her hair back for practice, and picked up her bag.

"Sure," I said. "It's for the ten percent of the time we know that we are." I picked up my mug and went back inside to write.

Walking back from Beth's that afternoon, I cut across the Commons and through the studios, first wandering along the forest edge to see if Marin was in hers.

It had been an uncomfortable meeting. Beth had asked me for pages, even though we had agreed that she wouldn't. "Proof of work," she called it, and said she wanted to be sure I was pushing myself.

"What happened to protecting my art?" I asked. I had finished work, of course I did, but she had promised, and I had trusted her.

"That's fine, Imogen, but you also have to learn to accept feedback. If you wanted to work in an echo chamber, you didn't need to come here to do it. I'm not asking for everything, or for something that's still in draft. But I want to see two or three of your more polished sections. I can't help you if you don't show me what you're working on, and in case you've forgotten, the entire reason I am here is to help you."

"Fine," I said. "I'll do it when I get home." I had left then, cutting the meeting short. I had been on the verge of tears, and I didn't want her to see me cry. Part of me felt her request like a betrayal, like the rules had changed midgame.

But I was also angry at myself, because I knew better. I knew feedback was part of the process, and Beth had said during our first meeting that she wouldn't let me waste my time here. We had been in residence for six weeks now, and I hadn't shown her anything, hadn't taken advantage of her expertise. And not for any good reason, but because I couldn't shake the feeling that what she would tell me was that I wasn't good enough. Wasn't now, and never would be.

Marin wasn't in her studio, so I kept walking, curious to see if I could find Evan's. I was still too pissy to want to be alone with myself.

The studio buildings were loosely organized according to need, so the large, open ones for dancers were clustered together, separate from the musicians and the visual artists. Most people had decorated their doors or hung signs, some sort of expression of who was in there. Marin was tying all of her worn-out pointe shoes to the tree in front of her door. They danced like a corps de ballet of ghosts when the wind blew.

I circled past a door covered in painter's palettes and another with glass mosaicked on the front steps. The paths seemed to loop back on themselves, and even trying the labyrinth trick of only making right turns didn't work—I knew I had passed the same doorway three times now. It was covered in crinkled silver foil, reflecting the light, scattershot, everywhere. There was no one out working, no one I could ask for directions. My head ached with frustration.

- 6 7 -

I turned again, and there he was. I knew his walk, that shade of red-gold hair. "Evan!" I called, running after. But he kept walking, turned a corner.

And was gone. No one in front of me, and only the same shiny foil door. Again. I shook my head, pinched the bridge of my nose, hard. Home. Sleep. Coffee. All of these things would make it better, and make me brave enough to send Beth my pages, and to pretend that her response didn't matter.

Having decided that, my head cleared, and I found my way out of the maze of studios. Past the empty tables of There, and through the open Commons, dodging a game of what looked like musical tag—the players switching instruments when tagged, making a glorious cacophony. I waved away the offer of a spare trumpet, if I wanted to play, and made it home.

"Something weird happened while I was in my studio today." Marin's hair was still damp from her shower, and the heavy scent of her lilac lotion mixed with the menthol and eucalyptus from the oil she had slathered on her strained muscles. The combination should have been off-putting, but I found it strangely comforting instead. It smelled normal, companionable.

"Weird like how?" I asked.

"Like surreal, almost." She sat on the floor and folded herself into a stretch.

I turned away from my desk, from the night shining through the window. "Well, that sounds exciting. Tell me."

"I like to keep the windows uncovered in the studio when I'm working. When else am I going to get to dance in the middle of a forest, right? So I had them open tonight."

I didn't tell her that I already knew that she danced with the windows uncovered, that I had seen her, seen Gavin, through them. That moment was theirs.

"It's been long enough that most of what's outside of them is background noise. Like, I noticed the fox that went wandering by last week, but I don't jump every time a rabbit hops past, or the turkeys come to hang out, at least not anymore. Have you seen the turkeys? They're enormous."

"I saw them when I was running the other day. And detoured around them because, yes, enormous."

"Anyway, tonight, I kept catching movement in my peripheral vision. So I stop, and it's birds. A whole flock of them. Flocking back and forth, in unison, just outside my windows."

"That sounds beautiful," I said.

"It was, sort of. But also weird, because when I stopped to figure out what was going on, they took off into the trees. Then when I started dancing again, they came back."

"They wanted to dance with you." I laughed as I said it.

"I know it sounds crazy, Imogen, but that's kind of what it felt like." She shifted the pose again, walking her hands out in front of her.

"What did Gavin think?"

"He wasn't there. I work on my own at least once a week. I figure if I've come out here to get away from a company and the influence of other dancers, that I ought to take that part seriously." She bent herself flat to the floor, held the stretch.

"It's working better than I thought it would," she said. "There's this peace, clarity, to being in the studio by myself. I don't have to worry about the girl next to me having better extension or sharper turns. Like I'm figuring out how I see me as a dancer, instead of how everyone else does."

Confidence rang through her words. "That sounds great. And you're still happy you're working with Gavin?"

She sat up. "Is that a nosy big sister question, or a how's your art question?"

"Yes," I said.

"He's the best partner I've ever worked with. I can tell I'm dancing better, even when he's not there, because of what I've learned from him. Which is great. It's one of the things I was hoping for.

"I like being with him outside of the studio, too. He talks to me like I matter. We have fun." She smiled.

"I'm glad," I said.

"How's the writing going?" She sat up, leaned against the side of the bed.

"Good. I feel like I've got things figured out, at least for now." I had sent Beth the pages she wanted, and then obsessively checked my email until she responded. She'd said she was happy with their quality, that it seemed like I was truly pushing on the possibilities of the structure I had chosen, which had been enough praise to make me do a victory dance around my room. She had also given me a detailed list of things to think about to make them better, and that had been good, too. You don't tell someone how to get better if you don't think they can. "I may steal your audience of birds for it."

"If you're collecting weird stuff, you should talk to Ariel, too. Her studio was full of leaves the other day."

"Leaves?" It was so odd, I wasn't sure I had heard right.

"Everywhere. All over the floor. Even on her piano. It was a real mess. She had to call and have someone clean it out."

"I didn't realize we had wind bad enough to do that. Maybe I've been spending too much time up here." I hadn't asked for studio space, so it was easy to lose track of the world outside of my story and my room. Sometimes there were days that I didn't make it out of the house.

"That's where the weird comes in," Marin said, the undertone of excitement in her voice reminding me that she had devoured horror stories and unsolved mysteries growing up, the weirder the better. She always wanted to hear the scary parts.

"Ariel hates people overhearing her when she's writing songs, so her studio is one of the soundproof ones."

"Which means no windows," I said.

"Which means no windows. Which means that someone had to bring the leaves in there. So crazy, right?"

"Really crazy," I agreed. "But maybe good for a story."

Later that night, I looked up from my work, out of the window. The trees were full of birds, flocked velvet patches against the canvas of the sky. Maybe they watched, maybe they slept, tucked in convenient perches. Every time I looked up from my writing, they were there.

So I did what I had joked about. I stole the birds for a story, of a night that came in on feathers and covered everything around it, houses and rivers and trees. That perched, watching. Of a girl who grew wings to fly over and out of it, flying above those other wings, that feathered night, and all the watching eyes beneath.

Then I finished. Put my notebook away, saved files on the computer. Stood up from my chair and stretched, looking out once more to where the birds rested.

As one, they lifted from the trees, moving shadows that blended into the rest of the night's secrets.

8

Wood smoke curled in through my open window, rich, like burning leaves. I pushed the covers back, rubbed sleep from my eyes. The scent grew stronger. Curious, I looked out.

There was a fire in front of our house, and Helena was tossing things on it.

My right hand curved itself into a claw, and I felt the flames, felt the sick-sharp heat of them, the hunger that would turn even my bones to ash. Everything went black around the edges, and I swayed forward, catching myself on my desk. The crackle of the flames got louder, and I ran outside.

"Helena! What are you doing?" I stopped on the edge of the fire, close enough to grab her if I had to, far enough to feel almost safe.

She was soot-stained and covered in rage. "I'm not good enough. This fellowship was supposed to make me better, but the only thing I've learned is how inadequate I am. I quit. I'm done." She tossed another notebook, and watched, eyes hard, as the cover began to bubble and curl.

"Helena, I—" My stomach clenched, and my head was full of burning words. Sweat beaded up on my forehead. I was shaking. The words, the pages. My hand.

I bit the inside of my mouth until I tasted blood. I wasn't there. I was here.

I was here.

"Fine," I said. "Fine. You're right. I don't even need to have read your work to know that it's clearly the most facile, saccharine excuse for poetry ever written. It's not even good enough for greeting cards."

She stared at me, the final notebook loose in her hand. "You bitch."

"Pick one or the other, Helena. Either your work sucks and deserves to be burnt, or I'm a bitch who doesn't know what she's talking about. Which is it?"

She stepped back from the fire and clutched the notebook tighter in her hand. "I'm not good enough."

"Maybe you're not. That doesn't mean you should light your work on fire. On our lawn. Seriously, what the fuck?"

"You don't know what it's like."

"Don't know what what's like, Helena?"

The fire had mostly died down. Scraps of paper scattered across the lawn. My hand uncurled, no longer felt like it was burning, too.

When Helena next spoke, her voice was harsh and raw. "What if this is all I have? If I never get any better than I am, then I'm not good enough. I'm adequate. Competent. But not good. Not fucking good enough. And don't try to tell me there isn't a difference."

There was nothing I could say to that. She was right. There was a difference between competent and good. Talent wasn't the only thing you needed to succeed, but it was still needed. And the cruelest thing was, regular crises of ego aside, if you were competent, you could see the difference in your work. You knew how it stacked up, could measure the gaps between fine and good, and good and great. Not having enough talent seemed almost worse than not having any, because having a little meant having just enough to know what you lacked. I stood with her in silence, watching the flames burn to embers, then to ash. Watching her face, hard and lost.

When the last of the ashes had burned away, Helena walked up the stairs and back into the house, the one remaining notebook still in her hand.

It was impossible to settle back into my own work after that. Every time I opened my notebook I was sure I smelled smoke, even after closing the window. Even after going back downstairs, and filling the soup pot with water, and dumping it on the ashes.

The arts have their own version of the "your mom" joke. That you need more fans than just your mom. That just because your mom liked it, or put it on her refrigerator, or thinks you should be cast as Hamlet after seeing you as the second shepherd in the Christmas play, that it doesn't matter. That and three bucks will get you a ride on the subway.

The punchline is that of course your mom is your biggest fan. Everyone understands that. It's natural. The weird thing would be if she wasn't.

When my work got burned—when years of stories, everything I had written to that point, was thrown on the flames—it was my mother who threw them there. Who held my hand in the fire, burning me with them.

The most dangerous thing you could do in a fairy tale was to be a girl with a mother. Because that meant your mother would die, and that death would only be the beginning of things going very, very wrong. Your father would acquire a new wife, who would arrive with daughters of her own, and she would scheme to send you into a life of drudgery, or cast you out into the forest alone. Or, worse still, there would be no new mother, and your father would fall in love with you, forcing you to leave home and run far, far away to escape.

I couldn't imagine it, growing up. How a stepmother could be worse than my real mother, than this woman who was supposed to love me, and who so clearly did not. I envied the girls in the fairy tales, sent by stepmothers to sleep in the ashes, or in the barn with the beasts. The girls who ran.

Smart girls, brave girls. Girls who escaped. Girls who saw what they wanted their fate to be, and clawed for it. I couldn't imagine being that brave, not with a mother in the house. I made myself small and quiet, not even a whisper in a corner, and still she saw me. I kept all the secrets that she wielded like threats, that she stopped my mouth with, and still, I was not small and quiet enough. I think the only way I could have been small and quiet enough would have been to disappear completely.

At night, I would close my eyes and clench my fists, and wish that my mother would die. I couldn't see how I would survive growing up if she didn't.

She didn't die, and I did survive my childhood, but I think back on that wish, on those moments when I was curled in my bed, my faced buried in my pillow so Marin couldn't hear me crying, and remember how hard I wished. So hard I shook with the strength of it.

Even though I knew it was wrong, even though I knew it was terrible, that if I was in a story I was the monster for thinking such a thing, I never wished for anything else so hard in my life.

9

The wind blew strong enough to rattle the shutters on their hinges, and it howled like a chorus of lost souls. Rain spattered like stones against the windows. Trees snapped and cracked as the storm stole their branches.

"Are you working, or can I come in?" Marin stood in the doorway, sleep-tousled and wrapped in a robe I hadn't seen before.

I cocked my head, taking it in. "Does your robe seriously have—"

"Hippopotamuses wearing tutus? I just got it—isn't it great?" She twirled so I could appreciate its full glory.

"It is great. And I was working, but I can use the break, so make yourself at home."

She walked to the window, arms wrapped around herself.

"Trouble sleeping?" I asked.

"I was fine until the storm woke me up." A branch slammed into the window, shaking the glass in its frame. Marin flinched. "You don't happen to have any Star Princess stories lying around in your brain, do you?"

I took a breath. We had built enough of a bridge, I thought, that I could tell her now. Tell her I had written them out, made them for a Christmas that we'd never celebrated, that they were put away now. Maybe I could even ask her why it was she'd gone silent when I went away to school, what it was that I had done to make her not want to talk to me for years. Maybe we could finally say all those unsaid words.

"Though on second thought, you know what? I'd love to hear something new, something you've been working on here, if you don't mind sharing."

The moment slid through my fingers.

"Sure. Okay. Let me find something that's in non-embarrassing shape. One of the ones I sent to Beth."

While I sorted through papers, she dropped onto the bed, the side farthest from the windows, and tucked her robe around her, carefully covering her feet. "Okay, go."

"'Once upon a time,'" I began.

Once upon a time, there were two sisters, and there was a forest. The forest was, in the way of these things, full of secrets.

Not just the secrets of leaves and trees, of fur and feathers, of the shadowed spaces. Certainly it had all of those, but it had other secrets as well.

A tower, and at its height a woman singing a song that called the ocean in and out upon the sand.

A ruin of a castle, with ghost knights in spectral armour as guards for its crumbling hallways.

A maze of flowers that shifted depending on the day, with a pool that led to forever at its center.

And so the forest was a place of wonder for them, and they learned to love secrets and strangeness.

"Wait," Marin said. "Stop there."

"Why?"

"Because if you stop there, everything's fine. They're together, they're happy. They have a magic forest. If you keep reading, something bad will happen."

She wasn't wrong. "Even if I promise there's a happy ending?"

"Even then. I just want to skip the sad bits right now," she said.

"Okay. They lived long and happy lives together in their forest."

"Happily ever after." Marin smiled.

"Exactly," I said. "The end."

She yawned hugely. "Okay. I'm going back downstairs to hope that I can sleep through the storm this time. Good night."

"Good night," I said.

"Oh, and Imogen. I really liked what you read. Thanks."

And for a moment, I could have happily stopped time, my sister's words my own small happy ending.

"So, have you heard from Evan recently?" Ariel asked.

"Yesterday," I said. "He sent me a letter." With directions in it, precise ones, and a map. It gave me hope that this time I wouldn't get lost looking for his studio.

"Another on-paper letter? Not an email or a text?"

"I know. It would be so much easier. Sometimes I feel like I'm flirting with someone from a hundred years ago. But it is kind of sweet—he sketches on the envelopes for me." I opened the drawer in my desk and handed Evan's most recent letter to her.

"Okay, that moves it from ridiculous to romantic. Go on."

"He asked if I wanted to come and see his art."

"Oh, please tell me he said 'Come up and see my etchings.'" She passed the envelope back to me. "Because you know he wants to make out."

"The making out was implied."

"I'll bet. Have fun."

It would have been easier to walk to Evan's studio if the making out had been the primary purpose. I liked kissing Evan and wanted to do it again. Simple enough. It was the art that I was concerned about. There was the possibility that I would hate it, or worse yet, that it would leave me cold. It's one thing to talk about separating the artist from the art in the abstract, another when they're both standing in front of you. "That's . . . really interesting" only gets you so far, and usually in a direction that means that kissing won't happen.

Nerves singing under my skin, I stood in front of the door to Evan's studio and watched birds roost, black-feathered, in the trees. The leaves were more gold than green now, and the air smelled of stone and mineral, the first whispers of the winter to come.

I knocked.

"Imogen! Come in." Evan looked rumpled, soot or grease smudging his hands. He hugged me hello, and I breathed in the scent of burnt metal that clung to him. "Would you like the tour, or would you like to look around on your own?"

"To look on my own first, thanks." That way I wouldn't have to worry about keeping my face blank if I didn't like what I saw.

"Please." He stepped aside.

It was a forest, but a metal one. Trees of woven metal reaching through the air, up, as if the earth burned them and they would root themselves in the sky instead. There was something near-human about them, the branches outstretched like hands, the trunks elegant as dancers' bodies.

The metal was shaded, colored. Not the unrelieved black of iron, but other, richer shades—silvers and coppers, bronze and brass. Some rusted, some tarnished, some polished clean. I walked through them slowly, barely even breathing, turning in circles so I could see the detail. My fingers ached to reach out and touch them.

"I'm sorry," Evan said. "I was just going to leave you alone. I wasn't going to ask, but I have to know. What do you think?"

They made my heart hurt. "They're wonderful. Lonely and welcoming at the same time. Like a real forest."

I could see the tension slide off him. "I was more nervous than I expected to be," he said. "I got up early to work, and then I was so preoccupied, I couldn't do anything right all day.

"I haven't shown my work to anyone since—" He stopped. Looked away. "Sorry. Anyway, you're the first person to see these."

"So this isn't the commission for Gavin, then?"

His face was a careful blank.

"The one you mentioned when you guys"—acted so weird—"ran into each other at the Market?"

"No, this is something else. Though related, I suppose." He turned away, made a note on his drafting table.

I stepped forward and kissed him. "They're wonderful," I said again. "Would you mind if I stayed a bit longer, just to look?"

"Not if you don't mind that I'll be working."

"You don't need to entertain me." I wanted to be alone with the sculptures, to imagine the rest of this forest, the stories it held.

"Then stay as long as you like."

They were like lightning caught in metal, that same crackle and movement. Sitting among the trees, it was if I could feel people trapped in their shapes, longing, reaching out, transforming. There was nothing anthropomorphic about them, but still, I could feel the forest's broken heartbeat.

Late in the day, and the sun setting through the windows like stained glass, the colors of the sky broken by the metal branches. Magic. I wished I could see what the trees looked like out of doors, wished I could stay longer.

I went to find Evan, who was sketching at a desk in the back of the studio. "If I had known I could see your forest through the windows, maybe I wouldn't have gotten so lost when I was looking for this place."

"You got lost on your way here?" he asked, stroking his hand down the back of my hair. "I weep for my map skills. However can I make it up to you?"

I laughed, stepped closer. "No, the map was great. But last week I was walking by and wanted to visit."

His hands stilled. "And you got lost."

I had seen him that day. I was almost sure. Almost. Though, no. It couldn't have been him. If he had been there, he would have seen me, would have said something, wouldn't have walked away, leaving me more lost than when I began.

"Ridiculous, right?" I shook my head. "Underslept, or overcaffeinated, or my head lost in my writing. Something. At least I found my way here today." I wound my hands around his neck.

"And next time"—he brushed his lips against mine, once, twice, then kissed me again, deeper—"stay longer."

"I will," I said, and let myself out into the falling night.

The walk home was beautiful. The air crisp but not cold, the moon bright and heavy in the sky, and I was floating in a haze, near drunk on art and flirtation. So instead of working when I got back, I changed into running clothes.

Once I had laced up my shoes and clipped my lamp to my shirt, I texted Marin to let her know I was going for a run, and approximately when I thought I'd be back. My phone buzzed: *Have fun! Full moon! Watch out for werewolves.* The last was punctuated with a howling wolf emoji.

I headed off the path and into the forest, wanting the rustle and hush of living things. The moon was bright enough that I didn't turn on my lamp. It rimed the leaves with silver. Grass crunched beneath my feet.

I had run about three miles and was thinking of turning back for home when I heard the hoofbeats. Hoofbeats, and the crash and pressure of something heavy moving through the forest.

I clicked on my light to make myself more visible, and began to retrace my steps. The hoofbeats grew louder. All around me branches bent and cracked—sharp, shotgun breaks. My hair stood on end. The air pressure shifted, the sky turning green, as if there were a storm snapping at my heels.

I ran faster, no longer watching for the path, just running headlong, the fox before the hunt, gasping breath and panicked heartbeat.

Branches whipped at my arms and feet, and I slid on the ground, skinning my palms and knees. My lamp cracked and went out. As I was scrambling to my feet, the horse ran in front of me, close enough that I could feel the heat of its body. I flung myself backward.

Not just one horse. An entire parade of them—black, brown, grey, white. Masked riders. Galloping through the forest on some great rade. Lights like fireflies hovered around the heads of the horses, and of those who rode them.

The riders were impossible, unreal. Horned and feathered and winged, with eyes like the limitless dark. My mind gave them familiar faces—Gavin, Evan, a woman with eyes like rose petals. Impossible things. Too much to believe, or to bear.

It probably took less than a minute for them to pass in front of me, but I was shaking when they finished. From cold, and from something between exhilaration and terror. I stayed where I was, crouched in the undergrowth, until the sound of the hoofbeats faded, until I was certain they wouldn't turn back and pursue me.

I fled home like a hunted thing.

Once there, I ran to my room, locking as many doors behind me as I could—the door to the house, then the door to my room, then the door to my bathroom, where I set the shower running. Stood, holding myself up on the sink, breath rattling like chains through my lungs.

I looked like a wild woman in the mirror—arms and legs scratched and muddy, black hair tangled in knots down my back and snagged with broken twigs and leaves, skin so pale my eyes looked black, too. Smudges on the sharp lines of my cheekbones and jaw. Visibly shaking.

It wasn't real. It couldn't have been.

A rattling at the door.

I bared my teeth in a hiss, lips curling back as I flattened myself against the wall.

"How was your run?"

Marin. My sister. Her voice.

I wheezed out air in response.

"Imogen?"

I cleared my throat. "Good. Just getting a shower now." Bent over, my head between my knees, until the shaking stopped.

"Sounds good. You forgot to text, so I wanted to be sure you got in all right."

"Fine." I stepped into the shower, watched as blood and dirt ran down my skin and into the tub.

No. It had been real. Very real. Horses from a nearby farm and a nighttime ride for a party. The moonlight and shadows blending to make it strange. Real things. Things that made sense. I was fine.

Just fine.

Instead of sleeping that night, I stood at the window, looking for the shadows of pursuing horses, waiting for them to run past. I watched until the sun rose.

10

A couple of days after Helena burned her notebooks, I had sent an email to Janet Thomas, her mentor. I'd hesitated, as it seemed like tattling, a betrayal of Helena, somehow. But I couldn't let it pass without saying anything. Helena was obviously stressed, yes, but we all got stressed. Dealing with bad days and doubts were part of life.

Helena's stress had caused her to build a fire on our front lawn. A housemate who thought "burn it down" was a good solution to her problems was not someone I could comfortably live with.

Janet had emailed back this morning, and told me she had an opening this afternoon "to discuss the situation." Exhausted from standing at my window all night, I'd suggested a different time. She countered with her suspicion that perhaps I wasn't concerned about Helena at all if I could so cavalierly reschedule, and that she would speak to me today or not at all.

So here I was. Her house was small, and closer to the forest than the other mentors' houses, like it had quarreled with them and then picked up its foundation and walked away in a huff. Its grey stones pressed tight to each other. There was a weeping cherry planted near the front door, and a yew tree opposite it. Over the door was a panel of stained glass, a woman in a green dress riding a white horse.

I knocked, and the door swung open. "Come in."

Janet was tall—about six feet, I thought, and in low-heeled brogues. Lean and silver-haired, eyes the same green as the tweed suit she wore. Both the shoes and the suit seemed from a different era, but her gaze was as sharp as her gestures.

"I haven't told her that I had plans to speak with you. I'm not certain if I will. Helena sees you as a rival, and the fact that we are speaking might upset her," she said.

Not exactly the most promising opening.

"If my being here is going to upset her, then I should go."

Her eyes narrowed. "I think you should stay."

"Why?"

"Curiosity." She handed me a plate of cookies, thin and peppery.

"What do you want to know?" I set the plate down on the table next to me.

"Why do you care if Helena burns her work? Do you not draw lines through your own writing, hit delete when it is necessary, consigning the words to the ether? How are those losses any less to be concerned about?" She sat so straight in her chair her jacket might have been corseted with steel. Her speech was somehow off—too precise, like she was counterfeiting a posher accent than she actually had. Everything about her seemed calculated, but I couldn't parse the desired effect. It was just . . . weird. Uncomfortable and weird, and I was beginning to understand why Helena had felt so desperate that she had burned her work.

"When I delete something, yes, it's gone, but that's part of the writing process, not something angry or destructive. The purpose of doing so is to improve the work that remains. And even if I were to erase an entire file, hitting the delete key doesn't risk the other people I'm living with."

"So, had Helena torn years of work to pieces while sitting quietly in her room, you would not be here." She gave a small nod, confirming something to herself.

I felt as if I were sitting for an exam, one that I was failing, even though I had a cheat sheet right in front of me. I wasn't going to use it. "No. I wouldn't. I probably wouldn't have even known that she had done that. As you said, she doesn't like me. She doesn't confide in me. We're not friends. I've never read her poetry, but even if I had, it wouldn't be my business if she tried to destroy it, and I seriously doubt she would have told me if she did.

"Our house has a fireplace. I'm guessing Helena has a trash can. But she burned her notebooks outside. In front of the house. It was really hard to miss. So I think she wanted someone to know, and to stop her. Maybe even for someone to be concerned about her, because setting things on fire strikes me as an extreme reaction to a bad day's writing."

"Indeed," Janet said. She ate a cookie, and then another. "You really should have one. I find it's always best to take a gift when it's offered."

She wasn't offering Turkish delight from a winter sledge, but I was pretty sure the cookies would still have tasted of betrayal. "I'm still not sure what I'm doing here. You talking to me about what I think about hitting the delete key doesn't do Helena any good."

"And that keeps you from eating?" She shook her head. "As I said, I was curious. Now, I am less so.

"The structure at Melete, or lack of it, prevents me from monitoring Helena. She has no obligation to me as a student, nor do we have the kind of professional relationship where I might call upon her socially. She does not, I believe, like me very much either. We are not close, and we don't need to be. I am her mentor, not her friend, and my duty is to her art. All the same, thank you for telling me of her distress."

"Is there anything else?" I asked.

"No," Janet said.

"Then I'll see myself out." I did not have a cookie.

I was sorry I had gone, and fairly sure that nothing I had said to Janet would be used to help Helena. All I could do was hope that I hadn't made things worse.

"Well, that is a little unusual," Beth said, after I had described the meeting with Janet. "I know I would feel very awkward and inappropriate discussing you with any of the other fellows. In fact, I wouldn't do it at all, unless something dire had happened."

"Janet didn't act like she thought it was dire. More like it was something she thought was curious, and she wanted a closer glimpse of the event." Like she was a child with a magnifying glass. I wasn't sure if I had been the ant smoldering beneath, or if Helena was.

"Do you know her at all?" I asked. "Janet, I mean."

Beth sipped her tea. A different cup this time, with some sort of spidery-looking purple flower, and a matching saucer. I remained deeply grateful that she offered me coffee, and solid mugs to put it in, when we met. "A bit," she said.

"We've spoken to each other at events for Melete, of course, and she's always been perfectly civil to me, but I find her very affected. She strikes me as someone who is both extremely snobbish and trying to hide something she's insecure about. To be frank, what you've said about this situation with Helena makes me wonder whether she should be allowed to be a mentor anymore." Beth shook her head. "That's beside the point for now. It's far too late to assign Helena to another mentor.

"How is your work going? You haven't lit anything on fire recently, I hope."

I forced out a laugh, using the reaction to cover up the shudder that ran through me, the ghost pain that sparked through my hand. "No."

I didn't want to say it, to jinx myself by speaking the words, even to Beth, but things were going well. After a few false starts, and some pieces I would fix in revision, I had found the voice of my stories, and the themes that would unite them into a whole, a novel, rather than just a collection. It was the best work I had ever done, and writing them felt like running a full-out sprint along a tightrope. I'd be fine as long as I didn't look down.

"Good. Destruction of your work is rarely the solution to difficulties with it."

"Have you ever hated your writing that much?" I asked.

"That I wanted to destroy it?" She shook her head. "There are things I would write differently, were I to write them now. That's not embarrassment, that's simply the nature of the profession. I've been at this for more than thirty years, and it would be dishonest to say that there's nothing I'd change, that I wouldn't be able to say things better now, than I did when I originally wrote them.

"And there are works of mine I prefer not to look back at, because remembering the time when they were written, the person I was when I was writing them, is not pleasant."

She paused, collecting herself, and I looked away from her memories.

"That doesn't mean that I would destroy those works, or that I'm not proud of having come out the other side. Our past art makes our present art as much as our past life makes us who we are now. In the end, if the art stands up, that's what matters.

"Which reminds me." She stood. "I have something for you."

"You do?" My eyes immediately went to her bookshelves.

"There is a secondary award system here at Melete, once you've become a fellow. Mentors nominate particular people whose talent they feel is exceptional, outstanding even for here. You've been chosen as one of them."

"I have?" I pressed my hand hard against my chest, as if that could keep my fizzing heart closed behind my ribs.

"The stories you sent me, when I was so rude as to break our bargain and ask you for pages, were spectacular. Even in draft. It was my honor to recommend you. Here." She handed me a tiny box, wrapped in paper embossed with the Greek letter *mu*, the first letter in Melete. Inside was a necklace, an hourglass pendant on a silver chain. "I hope you'll forgive me now for breaking our agreement and demanding to see your work. I needed to judge where you were, and have something to turn in with your nomination."

Overwhelmed, I nodded, then blinked away the tears that threatened. "I do. Of course. Thank you."

"It gives you extra time here, if you want it. You can stay through the summer, in addition to the nine months of your original fellowship. There are other benefits as well, so wear the charm while you're here.

"I'm so proud of you, Imogen."

Proud of you. I played the words in my head over and over again as I walked back home. It wasn't the first time I'd been complimented on my writing. I'd sold stories, gotten good reviews. Hell, I'd gotten into Melete. I knew that I had achieved a certain level of competence, enough to know I wasn't wasting my time with my work.

If I had been asked, I could have said that I was proud of myself, because I had worked hard to make all of those things happen.

But, growing up, writing had been something I had to keep secret. My mother didn't want me hiding in my room and "making up lies," and there had been consequences when I did. So this was the first time that I had been told that someone was proud of me because of something I wrote. For those words to come from Beth, whose own work meant so much to me, made it matter even more.

I wanted to write her words down, tape them above my desk, make them a talisman against the days when my own words didn't come, or were facile and flat. To hold them as a shield against bad reviews and rejection letters. I held the charm around my neck hard, hard, until the metal embossed itself on my skin.

Once I got home I braced myself, then knocked on Helena's door. She let it open only the thinnest sliver. "What?"

This was going well already. "I need to talk to you."

"About what? I'm not really in the mood for another lecture on believing in my art."

"I saw Janet today."

"Why would you do that?" Horror in her voice.

I could only see part of her face through the door, but she looked worried. No, not worried. Like she was braced for a blow. My stomach clenched.

"I was worried. So I told her about your notebooks. The fire. She asked me to come and speak to her. It . . . it was strange, so I thought I should tell"—warn—"you."

Helena closed her eyes, whispered, "No."

"I know," I said. "I'm so sorry. I wish I had never said anything."

"Me too." She leaned her head into the door frame. "Is there something else?"

"Look, Helena, if you need anything—"

"You mean beyond what you've already done? Yeah, thanks, I'll remember that." She shut the door.

When I was halfway down the hall, I heard something crash and shatter. I paused, and then kept walking. She had made clear that I had done more than enough already.

11

Marin was still in her practice clothes, face flushed, her hair a tangled knot at the back of her head, when she knocked on my door later that night. "Did you get an email from Mommy Dearest, too, or am I the only lucky one?"

I clicked on the icon for my email program, then loosed a breath in relief that there was no new mail. I'd learned not to read them, but just seeing her name in my inbox messed with my head, made me feel trapped, panicked. Like it was the start of a countdown that ended with her appearing. "Nope. Just you this time. Did you read it?"

"It was really informative. You see, I'm wasting my time—how did she put it?—'languishing in obscurity' out here in the middle of nowhere while my company is doing *Giselle*, and how I'll never get to perform the role now, and everyone will have forgotten about me by June when the fellowship is over, plus I'll be a year older, and we all know what time does to a dancer's career, don't we?" Marin paced the room as she spoke, striking exaggerated poses for emphasis.

"About the only thing she left out is her certainty that I'm getting fat, though she probably didn't think it was worth mentioning this time, considering I'm going to be an old, obscure dancer without a career to go back to."

"She was on a tear, even for her. Are you okay?" Our mother's specialty was the poisoned paper cut, the wound that started out as an annoyance but then lingered, festering. She had a knack for knowing exactly where they'd hurt the most, too.

"I'll be fine. She is what she is, and I've long since stopped expecting anything different from her. I just—she's not wrong, you know? I might not have a career to go back to at the end of this. I will be a year older and have spent a year away from the stage. Closer to a year and a half, actually, because of performance schedules. Which is basically forever, in dance terms. I'm glad I'm here, I am, but I also realize that I might have completely screwed myself." She dropped backward onto my bed. "If I don't find a job for when this fellowship is over, then I've already danced my last role."

I flopped down next to her. "Have you asked Gavin what he thinks about your career prospects?"

"Gavin said he thinks NBT would hire me, especially if they see us dance together. Which would be a huge step up from where I was. A dream come true, actually. Logically, I agree with him—I've never danced this well in my life, and I can feel myself getting better. It's just, you know. Her. It's like she knew I was happy, and she had to put an end to it." Marin pressed her fingers to her temples.

It was when she moved her arms back down that I saw the silver glint around her neck. "You have one, too," I said, pulling my hourglass charm from under my shirt.

Marin's hand pressed against her charm. "'Too'? Oh, that's great. I'd hoped you'd get the chance.

"Still, right now, I'm not sure if I'm delighted, because getting one means I'm good, or if it makes things even more stressful, because that's even more time away from the stage, if I decide to take it. Which—I want to. Mostly. I love training on my own, in my own headspace. I've even started working on developing some of my own choreography, which I never thought I would be able to do, and would be a way to extend my career. But I can't shake the feeling that there is a clock winding down on me."

"Like you said, you know how she is—don't let her take this from you," I said. "Trust Gavin. If he thought being here would be a risk to your career, he'd tell you to leave. It doesn't do his reputation any good if you study with him for a year and then can't get work."

"You're right," Marin said. "You're right. I wish I didn't let her get to me like that. I mean, I know there's nothing she can actually do to me, but still."

A phantom ache ghosted through my hand. "Still."

She looked at the ceiling. "Hey. You really did put your stars up."

"Of course I did," I said.

"I thought maybe you just said so, to make me happy. I'm glad they're really there," she said. And we stayed there, together, watching the unmoving stars.

Once upon a time, there were two sisters. The older was dark, and sharp as a knife; the younger warm and golden as the sun.

The younger sister had been given a pair of magic shoes by their mother. When she put them on and danced, she was more beautiful than the stars in the sky. But, like all magic, the shoes came with a cost, and it was paid in the red salt of blood and the white salt of tears.

The mother told the younger sister that she was only beautiful when she danced. Her words dripped poison, but the girl wanted to be beautiful, and she loved her shoes, and did not wish to take them off.

And so. And so.

The older sister took her sharp edges and her knives and she turned them on herself, dissecting until she found her own truths. She spoke story after story until their mother, who had little time

- 9 3 -

for such things, beat her so that she would be silent. She was not. True stories will not abide silence, and they will speak, even though you bleed for it.

Red salt. White salt.

The younger sister danced and the older sister spoke stories for her, and in time, the shoes were no longer painful. And the younger sister danced the older sister's stories into being, and they had already paid in salt, red and white, and so what remained was magic. With that magic, they escaped from their mother, and went where she no longer had power over them.

And they lived.

I set the pen down, pushed back from my desk, from the memories I was painting over with fiction.

I've never asked Marin what she told herself to stay sane, what her fairy tale ending to our lives growing up would have been.

Maybe I could have asked her, if I had stayed. Maybe I could have told her mine, if there hadn't been the years of silence between us. But there are some truths that don't just cut you when you speak them, they stab the person listening, too. Better to not open the wounds.

Survival was the only thing that mattered, for me. Happily ever after, the traditional close, those weren't words that even came into it.

My fairy tale ending was to live.

The day was Bradburyesque and golden, late summer dropped into fall's calendar. I packed a bag and went outside to write. There wouldn't be that many more days when that was possible, and I wanted to take advantage of the time now.

I wandered through campus, away from the forest that I usually ran in, and toward the Mourning River. Bracketed in bridges, it ran swift between its banks, sweeping the fallen leaves of autumn with it. Wind plucked at the trees, sending more leaves tumbling through the air.

Through the branches I could see a bridge less fanciful than the others. It seemed an ideal place to work, one where I'd be less likely to be interrupted than, say, the replica of the Kissing Bridge, where every couple at Melete felt obliged to visit and seal their love with kisses lipsticked onto the stones, or the replica of the Pont du Gard aqueducts, spanning the Mourning's widest point. That one had been renamed the Wishing Bridge, because it was where residents went with their most secret desires written on paper boats, to be lit on fire and cast into the water below. Tradition held they would only come true if the boat burned completely before anyone saw you or it.

I walked along the Mourning's banks, toward what looked like a stone ruin, heaping itself out of the ground. It was tucked at a bend in the river, set back in the shadows of the trees.

The old stones rose gently out of the bank of the river, as if they had grown there over some long-unwinding stretch of time. At what should have been its apex, the bridge stopped. Not cleanly— the edge was uneven, as if what had once been there had crumbled, but there were no ruins in the river beneath, no pieces of a fallen structure on the opposite shore. Just a stretch to halfway, and then a stop.

The wind picked up, whipping the river to white. Leaves tore from the trees, all of autumn's fall happening at once. I shrugged into the sweatshirt I had stuffed in my bag, and for a second, shaking myself free of the hood, I thought I saw the other half of the bridge. An entire other forest at the end of it, the trees still dark with green, instead of licked by the flames of autumn. My pulse quickened in recognition—they were a memory I hadn't yet seen, those trees. The echoes of hoofbeats thundered in my head.

A man's figure on the end, his expression that of surprise at his own sudden appearance.

Evan.

I called out to him.

The wind whipped past me again, blurring my vision. I blinked my eyes against it, and everything was as it had been. Melete in the fall, and only me, standing on one side of a bridge that was only half there. Nothing on the other side but the forest, dressed in autumn. The leaves still clung to their branches. Evan was nowhere. I walked carefully up, then to the bridge's edge. Put my fingers on the stones, then crept them forward.

Air. Nothing.

I made my way carefully off the bridge. At its foot, I looked back to the other side, but it was still empty and unchanged.

The wind picked up and the sky greyed, but I risked the storm to detour through the studios on the way home. Evan's trees were darker shadows against the windows, but there were no lights on, no answer to my knock. I wasn't quite bold enough to try the door uninvited. Or to begin a conversation with "Hi, I maybe just hallucinated you in the woods, how's your Tuesday?" if it turned out he was inside.

Rain pelted down, near-sleet and spiteful. I closed my bag more tightly over my notebook and walked headlong into the wind toward home.

There was a letter from Evan when I got there, smudged, and slightly damp from the rain.

He had drawn a forest on the envelope again, a couple holding hands as they walked through it.

> Dear Imogen,
>
> My forest will be exhibited at the Night Market the day before Halloween. I hope you will be my guest there.
>
> And after.
> Evan

Evan had to be at the Night Market early to supervise the setup of his work, so I asked Marin if she wanted to walk over with me.

"I'm working with Gavin that evening, so we're going together. But I'll see you there.

"Oh, and Gavin says wear your charm where people can see it. Especially at the Market," Marin said, pulling her own hourglass out so it was visible over her shirt.

"Why?"

"It's like some kind of secret sign. People will 'treat us well' because of it, whatever that means."

"Fun. I always wanted to be in a secret club. I'll see you there."

When I got ready that evening, I made sure my charm dangled over the scarf wrapped around my neck. The air was cool enough to flush my cheeks as I walked across Melete's darkening grounds, and I arranged my scarf more securely. The stars winked into place above me, and bats skittered across the tops of the trees. I stopped, stood, and let the night, all its possibilities, fill me.

I heard the music before I saw the Night Market's lights.

Old-fashioned, calliope-style. The kind you'd hear at a carousel. There were more fire pits along the paths this time, and the fairy lights strung through the trees glowed orange, making everything flame-kissed and autumnal. The air shimmered, a shook foil, as I walked into the Night Market.

There was a booth at the front selling maple sugar candy formed into shapes more likely to be found in a fantastic bestiary than in a candy store—I picked a gryphon, a basilisk, and a unicorn.

"How much do I owe you?" I asked the woman, a chain of flames tattooed across her collarbone, who handed me my bag.

"Nothing."

"I don't understand."

"You wear the hourglass, and so it's a gift to you."

My hand went to my throat where the charm hung. This was what Gavin meant. "Thank you," I said.

She nodded, watching after me as I left.

It seemed I wasn't going to be allowed to pay for anything. The perfumery that had been at the previous Market was there again, and I was given a vial that smelled like autumn distilled—the rich darkness of loam and leaf mold, the warm spice of the harvest, the metallic hint of winter to come. "It would be our honor if you accepted this as a gift," the man working there said. His hair was the same riot of flames as the leaves on the trees.

"Are you sure?" I asked.

"Please." He placed the bottle in my hand and folded my fingers around it.

I hesitated before deciding to get hot chocolate. It felt awkward, to be given things like this. Undeserved. Like I shouldn't look at anything with interest, because then someone would feel obliged to give it to me. But at least with the hot chocolate, I could leave a tip, assuage some of the awkwardness I felt that way.

But the chocolatier set her hand over the tip jar. "We don't take any of your money. Not if you wear the hourglass. Bad luck to those who do."

"Bad luck?" I asked.

She nodded. "We're paid in other ways. Don't leave your money here."

"Thank you, then." I'd have to ask Gavin about what exactly the charms meant when I saw him. It was obviously something more than just the extra time that Beth had told me about.

The calliope had grown louder the farther I walked into the Market. There were more vendors here this time—it took up more space in the Commons than before, so much so that I half-expected to see booths tucked next to the studios. I wound through the crowds of people, some already costumed for Halloween, looking for the source of the music.

The first of Evan's trees stood close to the Market's center. The others stretched out from it—the forest walking in among the people. They looked wilder out in the night, illuminated by flame and fairy lights. Like the ancient skeletons of a forest, twisting and reaching toward the sky, the shadows cast by the flames part of the artwork, too.

The trees had been arranged to form a path, leading away from the lights and people of the Market proper. Walking through was like walking into someplace secret, the glimpses of other people like scenes from a play, figures from someone else's imaginings. A walk into Narnia, or Wonderland, or some other fantastic place, tucked away just out of sight of the real. Velvet gowns looked like dresses made of rose petals, and wings climbed from backs, so cleverly attached that it was impossible to see the joins. Everything was one drop more, one shade closer to the fantastic.

The path drew in on itself, and then opened up into a grove of metal and light and shadow. In the center of the grove, a carousel spun.

It hovered on the edge of impossible. Metal animals, rearing horses, prowling cats, a dragon, serpentine and clever. Like the trees, but not, more living than skeleton, metal hearts beating inside their bodies. The lights played over them, and they looked almost as if they breathed as they turned in slow circles. I watched in awe.

"Do you like it?" Evan asked.

I had been so entranced by the carousel, I hadn't noticed him until he was next to me. "This is what you made?"

Pride on his mouth as he nodded.

"It's extraordinary. The only way I could like it better is if I could ride it."

"Once Gavin's here, you can."

"Are you serious?" I grinned like a child.

"Completely." Evan smiled, and oh, I was glad I was a grown-up.

"This is the project you were working on? The one he commissioned?" I tried to fit the bestiary brought to life with what I knew of Gavin.

"It's part of it, yes." He kept his eyes on what he had made, watching.

"What is he going to do with it?" Gavin lived in New York, where the National Ballet Theater was based, when he wasn't here. The carousel was not the sort of thing that would fit in a city apartment.

"I cannot spill his secrets, even to you."

"So formal," I teased.

Evan held my gaze, solemn and silent.

Then Gavin and Marin arrived. Gavin walked around the carousel, then stopped in front of Evan. "It's even more than I'd hoped. Very well done."

Evan nodded, accepting the praise. A man wearing a Green Man mask lifted the chain, the guardian of the forest granting us passage, and Evan handed me onto the back of one of those wild, rearing horses. The reins were heavy red silk, and I held them as the carousel spun. Slowly at first, then faster and faster, just to the edge of dizziness. The whirl turned the other riders into blurs, painting them with impossibility, until we all looked like something from a fairy tale.

The spinning continued after the music stopped, after we had climbed down, but that was because Evan's hands were tangled in my hair, tangled in the chain around my neck, and his mouth was on mine. The wildness, the heat of him, and the magic of the night.

But he, he wasn't magic. He was solid and real under my hands and I craved that realness. I broke the kiss just long enough to say "Come home with me, now," and to hear him answer "yes."

The walk back to my house took forever, and I wanted to grab Evan's hand and run, or throw him down on the grass and press myself on top of him.

I didn't.

We walked. Like people who weren't ready to burst from our skin with lust. Like it was nothing, this air that we walked through, that made a night so silent I could feel its weight on my skin, and even that didn't muffle the thunder in my racing heart. Like we had forever, like there was no rush, like you couldn't strike sparks from the heat that burned in my blood.

We walked through my front door, locking it behind us, and quietly up three twisting flights of stairs to my door.

The door closed.

I pressed Evan against the wall, kissing him as if he were my breath. Our hands tore at each other's clothing. No finesse, just speed. Then his skin was hot against mine and his fingers were inside me and I bit into his shoulder so that he cried out when I came.

The sheets on the bed rumpled beneath us, and I traced the scars his art had left on his skin with my mouth. We rolled over, and his hands spanned my ribs, tight, tighter as I took him inside me. I moved over him, arched back. He reached between us and pressed rough fingers against my clit and I came again, trembling.

We collapsed into each other and, still tangled, fell asleep.

Dawn was pinking the edges of the sky when he kissed me awake. "I have to go." He was already dressed.

"I can't convince you to be late?" I sat up, the sheets pooling around my waist.

He closed his eyes, and a muscle flickered along his jawline. "If only."

"Well," I said. "Good morning, then."

"Good morning, Imogen." He closed the door behind him.

12

Ariel was in the kitchen when I finally made it downstairs for coffee. "That is some truly spectacular sex hair you have going on, Imogen."

My hand went to the back of my head, which was simultaneously fuzzy and knotted. I could feel myself turn strawberry red. Didn't matter that I was neither ashamed nor embarrassed, my complexion thought I should be a blushing virgin. I poured coffee. "It was some spectacular sex."

"Good for you," Ariel said. "So are you going to let him scare your pants off again for Halloween tonight?"

"No, I've got a thing."

She snickered. "I just bet you do."

I did, though, and not what Ariel thought. The letter had arrived the week before Halloween, the stationery embossed with the same stylized version of the Greek letter *mu* that had been on the paper that Beth had wrapped my hourglass charm in. It had given instructions for a meeting Halloween night, on the Commons. For those of us who had been chosen, the letter said. After the reactions of the people at the Night Market to the charm, I felt even more like we were all going to be inducted into some secret society. Which, honestly, seemed kind of great.

As the day went on, I was less and less able to focus. Eventually, I resigned myself to the probable necessity of rewriting every word I had managed to get on paper, and I went to find Marin.

"Are you ready?" Marin asked.

"As I'm going to be," I said. The letter had been cryptic, not offering much in the way of detail except when and where. I didn't particularly like surprises.

Mourning the chance to wear my planned Susan Pevensie costume for Halloween—I had put together a full-out Narnian queen outfit, and accessorized with lipstick, nylons, and a fan made of party invitations—I had dressed for practicality. Jeans, boots, jacket. Marin looked much the same, though her coat was fleece and mine was leather. At least we looked like we were going to the same place.

As we walked across the grounds, we could see traces of Halloween celebrations. Some people had gone all out. "Oh, look, it's Isaac!" Marin waved to a genial-looking patchwork of a man, strapped to what looked like a laboratory table on the roof of a house. Occasional flashes of light strobed across him. Isaac waved back, and blew her a kiss.

"You look great!" she called.

We walked through a graveyard that had managed to generate its own eerie fog, and stood far back as a Headless Horseman galloped down the path.

"I think he's letting the horse navigate," I said.

"I think you're right." Marin laughed. "Speaking of horses, I was going to say hi to you and Evan last night, tell him how much I loved the carousel, but you two seemed a little preoccupied. And then a lot gone. Things are good?"

"Really good." I smiled.

"I'm glad," she said. "I eagerly await Helena's scandalized pronouncements on your behavior and morals."

"Yes, but I'm up on the third floor."

"Details, details."

I laughed. We spent the rest of the walk catching up. Normal conversation. Trivia. The kind of things you share when you live with someone, and so the peripheries of your lives overlap, but there are still secrets and unknown pieces. It was wonderful. I felt warm, perfectly happy.

"This is exactly what I wanted when I came here," I said. "To be able to talk to you again. To have things feel normal."

Marin nodded. "We should maybe think about getting a place together. When we're done. I mean, if you want."

"I'd like that," I said. Then: "Marin."

We were at the Commons, and it was changed utterly from the night before. All traces of the Night Market were gone. The lights in the trees were the cold white of the stars.

Evan's carousel stood at the center of the Commons, surrounded by horses. For a moment I flashed back to my run through the woods, the great crash of horses across the path before me, the feeling of being pursued. Of being prey. I shook my head to clear it, and looked again.

"There's Helena," Marin said. "I didn't expect to see her here."

I hadn't either. She had given me her publishing credits in the same breath as her name when we first met. If the hourglass was, as Beth said, a way to acknowledge the most talented residents, I couldn't believe she hadn't made sure we all knew she had a charm. She was already horsed, and looked unhappy about it. Beth and Janet were there, too. Beth smiled and nodded when she saw us. Janet's gaze passed over me without acknowledgment.

Evan met us at the edge of the gathering, dressed like a prince from a fairy tale. There was even a circlet of tarnished silver around his head. "I hadn't known we could wear costumes," I said, smiling at him.

"I need to see your charms," he said, stiff and formal, as if we hardly knew each other, as if he hadn't nearly torn mine from my neck the night before. He looked at each of the hourglasses carefully, then let us pass. He led us each to horses, mine as black as night, and Marin's as pale as the moon. They were saddled in leather and bridled in silver, with reins of thick bands of blood red silk.

"What is going on?" I asked.

"You'll know when it's time." His face was blank, and there were no clues in his voice. He helped me up into the saddle, then turned and walked away.

"Evan!" I called after him. I saw him flinch against the sound of my voice. He heard me, but he didn't turn around, didn't answer.

Confused, hurt, I tried to get to Marin, but couldn't navigate the press of people and horses. My horse danced in place, flicking its ears and snorting, as unhappy as I was.

More and more people arrived. The Commons was full of horses, and nearly all had riders. It was remarkably hushed for such a gathering, as if each of us was afraid to break the silence. People didn't gossip, joke. I looked around to see if I recognized anyone else. There was Angelica, Ariel's mentor, though I didn't see Ariel. Off by himself, Gavin stood on the edge of the crowd. He watched Marin, and only her.

People were there in costumes, fabulous and grotesque and hideous and strange. The Green Man who had let us onto the carousel last night, and this time not just wearing a mask, but his entire body leafed and vined, and in boots made of bark. Someone beautiful, arrayed in pieces of broken things, mirrors and teacups and clocks. A woman whose skin was covered in illuminated script. "Do not read me," she said, kneeing her horse to make it walk on. "Your eyes will change the ending." The letters shifted as she rode away.

My head reeled, and I felt dizzy, drunk in my saddle.

Evan was horsed now, too, a horse as white as bone. A horn blew, low and long, echoing toward us from someplace out of time. Gavin walked through the parting horses and stepped onto the carousel. I saw then what I hadn't the night before—there was no motor, no gears, no mechanics to turn the carousel. It should have been static, unmoving.

It wasn't.

It spun slowly, in the opposite direction that Gavin walked. Shadows clung to the metal of the sculptures, filling them out, making them whole. Our horses began to move, a spiral outside that of the spinning carousel.

Faster.

The horn again, and the carousel spinning faster now. Gavin still walking, a procession of one, against its turning, and the shadows built themselves around him, too—a cape that fell from his shoulders, and a horned crown that reached up from his head.

Our horses were running now, moving faster with each circle, and with each circle the night became less recognizable. We rode in a dream of pale kings and princes.

A crack like lightning in the air, but shadowed, not bright. Gavin pulled himself up on one of those spinning metal horses, and it broke from the carousel, leaping over our heads. They landed next to Evan, one horse white and one horse dark, Evan crowned in silver and Gavin crowned in horns that grew like a stag's from his temples, cloaked in shadows and magic.

The air shuddered. The horn sounded again, and the spiral of horses broke, too.

Faster.

We followed Gavin, followed that impossible horse made of art and shadows as they ran, headlong and faster than the wind. With the reins wrapped around my hands, I twisted my fingers in my horse's mane and clung to its back as we tore through the bounds of Melete. Lights hung in the trees to guide us, and I heard bells ringing clear even above the thunder of so many hooves, the thunder of my heart.

We raced through the woods and down the banks of the Mourning, past bridge upon bridge. With the night streaming out behind him, Gavin urged his horse toward a bridge—a bridge that was only half there.

Panicked, I heaved back in the saddle, yanking on my horse's reins. They burned across my palms, abrading the skin, as it took the bit in its teeth and kept running.

"Ride, fool!" The imperative voice of the woman covered in stories. She urged her horse closer to mine, making it impossible to turn. Their hooves clattered across stone, across a bridge that continued over what had so recently been only empty space.

On the bridge's other side, the stars above us changed.

The lights grew brighter. There were people among the deep green of the trees. They reached out, beckoning as we rode by, and I realized: what stood in the forest, what cried out and called as we passed, was beautiful, was strange, was not human.

They were made of the same otherness, eerie and compelling, as the masked and costumed riders, but in this light it was clear they weren't masked and costumed at all. These were their true shapes, unglamoured. Bones at sharpened angles, pressing closer beneath the skin. Eyes without irises. Feathers for hair and teeth fanged as serpents'. From all of them a sense of longing, of desire made heavy, of want with hands and claws, that nearly knocked me from the back of my horse.

If I had fallen, I would have stayed.

I knew where I was, even if my thoughts raced away from the word. It was Halloween, Samhain, the end of one year, the beginning of the next, the walls between one world and the other the thinnest until the season's next turn.

We had ridden into Faerie.

The horses did not check their speed. If anything, they ran faster still; we passed through the trees like a hurricane. The seeds of Evan's trees grew all around me in this forest, like and unlike the ones I knew. Their shapes stark and almost human, as if there were souls trapped inside those reaching branches. I knew better than to reach back, but it was a near thing.

Faerie, like the Fae, was beautiful enough to seduce, but it was a seduction with nails and teeth, it was passion with blood. My skin felt electrified; desire scorched across it. I wanted to stay.

I wanted to stay.

Then the stars shifted again, and we were back in the known universe of Melete. Over the bridge again, and as they cleared it, the horses shied and scattered, running away from something heaped on the ground.

Marin. Moonlit, pale on the cold hillside.

I screamed, hauled on my horse's reins, and this time it obeyed, tossing its head in protest as it came, dancing, to a halt. I slid, weak-kneed, from the saddle. "Marin! Marin, are you all right?"

"I have her." Gavin, antlers crowning his head, scooped Marin into his arms. "I will see her safely back."

"Will you?" His eyes, endless black, met mine. The air around him shook like smoke, and I could taste the burnt ozone of a lightning strike, of magic, at the back of my throat. He did not look anything like safety.

"I'm fine, Imogen. Just dizzy." Her voice was quiet, but not panicked. "I fell. That's all."

There was tenderness in Gavin's hands as he held Marin. He cradled her as if he would be her shield, and she didn't look at anything but him. "All right," I said, and took her horse's reins along with mine, walked them both back toward the Commons.

The plain, ordinary Commons. Being back was like being in mourning for something. My eyes ached for what I wasn't seeing. My heart echoed in a hollowed-out place in my chest. Everyone here looked faded. Human.

I shook my head, blinked, tried to make reality sit easier in my eyes.

"I'm not," Evan said, behind me. "What they are."

"Then what are you?" I turned to him as I loosed the horses back into the teeming crowd, watched as faces shifted from starlit and strange into ordinary, known. Though not his. Even though it was a face I had kissed, that had rested on my naked skin. He was, it seemed, not something I knew.

"What you are. Human. An artist, which is something they prize."

"They," I said. It wasn't a question. I flung the word at him like a gauntlet at the opening of a duel.

"They," he said. "The Fae. You know what you saw."

"I know where I saw, not what." His hand, tangling in the chain that I had needed to wear tonight, before it moved over my body. "And why you?"

"Because every seven years, Melete pays a tithe to Faerie. One of us. And almost seven years ago, it was me."

13

Once upon a time.

Once upon a time, there was a girl who was given a wish. One wish, just one, but it would grant her anything she wanted, the truest desire of her heart, the one she kept closest, locked away, barely taking it out to whisper its name.

"But," she was told, "you must be very, very careful what you wish for. Be certain you ask for precisely what you want, else you will be disappointed. Or worse."

The girl was the sort of girl who read books, and so she knew well the perils of wishing. Wish for the return of a beloved pet, now dead, and a rotting corpse walks into the yard to play fetch. Wish for everything you touch to turn to gold, and with a hug you've made your best friend a statue, and murdered her besides. Wish casually, and you waste whatever the possibility might have been.

So the girl was careful. She did not speak a wish, but waited and thought. Every time a desire formed itself in her head, she thought of how she might wish for it. Even then, she could imagine the wish turning in on itself, growing teeth. And so each time, she remained silent, and worked for what she wanted. Sometimes, what she would have wished for happened anyway, and she was glad, and clutched her wish close, like a secret, like a shield.

But one day she spoke. She spoke in haste, and without thinking, and she spoke in passion. She said, "I wish you could love me."

There is a cruelty in a wish that comes true. It is weighed, it is measured, it is absolute. No less than the words that invoked it, but no more, neither.

This is the first thing she learned: Just because someone can love you doesn't mean they will. This is the second: It is worse to know that someone can love you, and that they have chosen not to.

I wish, I wish, I wish.

I hugged my arms to myself as I walked with Evan back to his studio, the cold not from the night, but from inside me. Evan had offered his jacket, but I stepped away.

He unlocked the door. "Just, give me a minute, please." He jammed his hands through his hair, so it was even more disheveled, opened his mouth to speak, then walked to the back of the building. The click and low hum of space heaters, the snap and sulfur flame of matches. "Electric lights hurt my eyes, after."

I nodded, as if that were normal, as if everyone's eyes should hurt when they came back from Faerie, as if there was nothing strange about going to Faerie in the first place. My hand clutched at my hourglass charm, hard enough to press its edges against the bones of my fingers, to crack the raw places on my palms open. The sharp pain was comfort.

I knew it was real.

"Look, never mind. We can talk later. Or not. I need to go home, be with Marin." I turned back for the door.

"She won't be there."

"What do you mean?" Panic's claws around my heart.

"She'll be with Gavin. He swore he would take care of her, and so he will. At the very least, he doesn't break his promises."

"She might need me. At least I could be there."

He laughed, sharp and brittle. "Do you really think you can do anything for her that he can't?"

"I'm her sister."

"And Gavin, in case you didn't notice, Imogen, is the King of Faerie. Which, in this case, counts for rather more."

"Fine. Then let's talk about that. Explain to me," I said, proud that my voice didn't stumble, didn't break, "what the tithe is, and how it's you." I would start my questions here, with something small. Something I could talk myself into believing the answer to. Something that would sit lightly on my churning brain.

He leaned against the wall, closed his shadowed eyes. We sat on the floor, far enough away from each other that we couldn't touch.

"There's a bargain," Evan said. "Faerie takes a tithe from the residents at Melete. Every seven years, a human goes, and remains there. Stays in Faerie for seven years. When the tithe returns, they get success. Guaranteed. Beyond your wildest dreams kind of stuff. You become a person whose art lives forever."

"Forever," I said.

"Think of the great names. Not just the ones still in galleries or on bookshelves after ten years. But the ones we still talk about, the works that still move us one hundred, two hundred years later," he said, envy raw in his words. "You know the ones."

"What's the catch?" There had to be one. There always was.

"The seven years, for one. For some people who might be chosen, that's enough to make them say no. There's a lover, a life, a child— something that matters more to them than what would come after. Something that matters more to them than their art.

"I don't understand those people," he said.

"The catch," I said.

"Faerie is a difficult place for a human. Think of what you felt tonight when we crossed over."

That longing. That terrible need that had threatened to pull me from my horse, that reached up and grabbed at me even now. Marin, ghostlike, on the ground. I shuddered, and pulled my knees closer to my chest.

Evan nodded. "Yes. Exactly that. That's the catch. It will feel like that, and worse, while you're there. Always. Constantly. They feed on that emotion."

"How long have you been back?" I asked.

His head dropped against the wall, his eyes on the ceiling. Somewhere else. "I'm not. Not all the way.

"Are you familiar with the work of Tania Arden?"

I blinked at the apparent non sequitur. "She's a glass artist, right? Very precise sculptures. Mathematical, almost. Intricate, and very colorful. And . . ." My words slowed. "She died. A little over seven years ago." A car accident, I thought. Something tragic and sudden.

"She was my mentor, when I first came here as a fellow. My mentor, and we became lovers, while I was here. Also, she was the Queen of Faerie."

Jealousy sank its green and bitter fangs into me. His lost dead love—a gifted artist, and the Queen of Faerie. And I knew I shouldn't let it hurt, let it matter, but it did.

"She was the one who told me about the tithe. I knew I wanted to go from the first moment I heard about it, but after she died, I wanted it even more. Living in Faerie would be like a tribute to her, I thought.

"I had thought being there, her home, being around what she was, would make her death easier for me to bear. It didn't. You can't go blank when you're there, can't turn off your emotions, can't deaden them, or cope by drinking, or exercising, or sleeping around. Emotions are what the Fae want, so every part of them becomes more. Heightened. What you feel, it turns back on itself, intensifies.

"Eventually, it became difficult for the Fae to be around me. My grief, my inability to feel anything else, was like a poison to them. They wouldn't have cared if I died of grief, but after enough years around me, they were getting sick. So this year, Gavin allowed me a temporary and restricted sort of parole. I'm allowed to be here, on Melete's grounds, for a certain number of hours in the day—more if I'm with him, or if I'm working on his behalf."

"The commission," I said. The carousel that had spun out a road before us, turned its figures into something eldritch, a horse for the King of Faerie. The trees, stretched and twisted in the close air of his studio, the moving shadows of the candleflames, making it look as if they moved in some faraway wind.

Faerie wind.

No. I pinched the inside of my wrist, reminding myself of where I was. Here. Not there.

"But wait. That makes no sense." I paced across the room, walking farther away from him. "How can you be working in metal for him? The Fae can't bear metal, cold iron is like poison to them."

Evan shook his head. "In case you haven't noticed, Gavin has no problem functioning in the modern world, as full of iron and technology as it is."

"But it's in all the stories."

"And I'm sure there was someone, somewhere, with the Fae equivalent of an allergy. Tania used to laugh about that stuff, all the ridiculous things humans believed, like needing to call them the Fair Folk and whatnot. She said it helped them hide, because no one believed anything that was true." He leaned forward, wincing, closing his eyes against the light.

Then continued: "My working on the carousel, having it there tonight—it was a way for Gavin to bend the rules that he's bound by. But it's difficult for me to be here, even with his help. The tithe doesn't like being worked against. There are consequences. I get pulled back."

"That was you, then. On the other side of the bridge."

He nodded. "It's where I usually wind up, coming or going."

"And the day I got lost?"

"That wasn't me. But they wouldn't have wanted you in here, would think nothing of trying to keep you away from me—it would have been a game to them. They don't like my being distracted by lesser emotions."

Lesser emotions. He had left my bed early this morning. "That's why you write me letters. Not because it's romantic, but because you can't call while you're there."

"Yes."

"Could you have told me about this, if I had asked?"

"Yes." Quiet. As if the word were nothing.

"Bastard." My hands fisted at my sides, and tears threatened to choke me. I swallowed hard. He didn't deserve them.

"Why didn't you tell me any of this before?" I finally let myself ask the question.

"I didn't know until last night when I felt the chain around your neck that it would matter. Not everyone who gets into Melete can be the tithe. Something about the power in the art—I don't know, exactly. If you need to know the specifics, ask someone else."

"Another thing you didn't care about?"

"Yes, Imogen. Yes. The most important thing to me was that being the tithe would help my art, would make it great. Even thinking that it would be a way to mourn Tania came far after that. I already knew I wanted it when she died. I didn't care about the fine print. Any of it."

"But you could have. Told me. There's no rule." Because of course asking again changes the answer.

"I could have told you. From the first day we met, yes. Though you should ask yourself exactly when you would have believed me."

All of the things I had seen, and had talked myself out of believing. Again and again, until belief had no longer been a choice.

"And last night?" I asked, pinning myself, wriggling, on the blade, waiting for the words that would push it further.

"I wanted to feel again. Something real. I wanted you. Your emotion, your response. Can you imagine how overwhelming you were to me, after Faerie?"

"Maybe I could have. If you had told me."

I pushed myself to my feet, held on to the wall for a moment to steady myself. "I need to go. I can't be near you right now."

If you look carefully at what we call fairy tales, there are very few characters in them who are actually fairies. None in Red Riding Hood, none in Rumpelstiltskin or Rapunzel, even the fairy godmother in Cinderella is, in older versions, a hazel tree planted on her mother's grave, and watered by Cinderella's tears. There are wonders and oddnesses, certainly, but fairies are rare.

It's easy not to notice this. The stories begin as they ought—once upon a time—and end as we know they are supposed to, with everyone living happily ever after. And in a story with a witch, and a house made of gingerbread and candy, who will notice that no fairy appears? It's not the sort of thing that even matters, except for the name we give to the stories.

Stories that have fairies in them, they're crueler, more frightening. You're cautioned not to say the word "fairy," but to call them the Fair Folk, like pacifying the Furies by only speaking of the Kindly Ones. The Fair Folk won't tell you their names, and you should never, ever, give them yours. They steal the things you value, even people, especially people who are bright, who are beautiful, who are talented. They take the best of us, and leave in return a bundle of leaves and sticks, or leave nothing, and return the person taken in seven years, or in one hundred, or able to speak only cold truths. They are beautiful and without mercy. Cruel.

Not just cruel. Capricious. They violate laws of guesthood and hospitality, with their food that entraps and money that turns to leaves or to dust in the night. They plague lovers for the sake of sowing discord between them, and lead travelers off the safer paths and to their deaths in the darkness.

Stories of the Fair Folk are not at all then what we think of as fairy tales, those moralistic stories wherein evil is punished and virtue triumphs, that were set safely in once upon a time, and had happy endings guaranteed. True fairy tales are horror stories.

I barely recognized the Melete that I walked home through in the early morning's breaking hours. Every piece of it seemed strange to me again, some fantastical, impossible place, and I had been left in it without a map. The glamour of Faerie clogged my eyes, gritting like sand.

That same sand gritted in my thoughts. Faerie, the Fae, were here the whole time. Even though I had ridden through it, seen them—had drinks with Gavin, who apparently normally had horns on his head, for fuck's sake—even though I had spent most of my childhood wishing I was in a fairy tale, the reality of it was too large to hold in my head. Which felt like my shock and disbelief had taken form inside of it, and were trying to bash their way out.

I shouldn't have been surprised. Of all people, I should have known. Fairy tales were what I had thought I knew, the thing I had thought I was an expert in. And yet.

We had lived next to them in these strange half-shared spaces ever since the day we moved in. I had stood on that broken bridge and looked across its border, and yet. As much as I thought I knew, I hadn't put any of it together. I hadn't seen. Hadn't let myself see. Every time something had bled through, I had explained it away. Made it normal. Real, I had told myself, not knowing how much larger real was.

People ran by, laughing and shrieking, winged and horned, capes trailing behind them, and I froze. The gallop of hooves. My heart raced in my chest. I tensed to run.

The Headless Horseman, his costume slipping to the point where he was only Mostly Headless, whooped after them.

The end of the Halloween celebrations. Still the same day. Not Faerie. Melete.

Shaking, I heaved out a breath. Another.

In the stories, when people are stolen away to Faerie, they wake after one hundred years, certain that only one night has passed. They return home, shocked at the passage of time.

Dawn hadn't even broken on the new day, and I felt a decade older than I had been only a few hours ago.

I went to Marin's room first. It was empty, the bed neatly made. She was fine, I told myself. Gavin would take care of her.

When I finally got to my own room, I was trembling from exhaustion and felt sick, like poison ran through my veins. The last thing I wanted at that moment was to sleep on the same sheets where I had slept with Evan the night before. Didn't want to remind myself of the scent of his skin, or the rough scratch of his stubble, or the sound of his voice when he gasped my name.

I ripped the sheets from the bed and curled up on the mattress with blankets piled on top of me. After an hour of wide-eyed sleeplessness, aching joints and itchy skin, I gave up. I would go do laundry, something I could pretend was normal.

On the way down, I checked Marin's room again. This time, it was clear she had been back—her dance bag was open, its detritus scattered about the bed.

She was in the laundry room, hanging tights and leotards to dry. Perfectly composed, normal looking.

"Are you all right?" I asked.

She waved away the concern. "Totally fine. I wasn't even thrown. My horse got jostled, and I just sort of slid off. I'd had a hard enough time staying on anyway—you know I'm rubbish around horses."

That much was true. For all her grace onstage, she had fallen off a pony ride when we were kids, one of the kind that spring up in hardware store parking lots in the summer, the ponies tethered in a slow circle. When she poofed into the sawdust at his feet, the pony looked as shocked as everyone else.

"Really," she said, "I'm fine."

She seemed like she was. There was color in her cheeks and no shadows under her eyes. And she thought I was asking about the fall, and not the rest of it.

"How much of last night was a surprise to you?" I asked, stuffing my bedding in the washing machine.

"I didn't know we were actually going into Faerie, but otherwise, nothing."

"Even about Gavin?"

"He told me everything when he gave me the charm. It would

have been kind of ridiculous if he hadn't." She answered, like all of this was normal, ordinary. As if we hadn't ridden through an imaginary place by way of a bridge that only partially existed. As if the world hadn't been knocked sideways.

As if her boyfriend wasn't the King of Faerie.

"You couldn't tell, before? I mean, about him?"

"Imogen." She shook out a leotard with a snap. "It's not like he does magic when we're together."

"Why didn't you tell me? I mean, not about him, specifically, but about the tithe?"

"Because I thought Beth had told you. You didn't even blink when you saw my necklace. You were even dressed for riding last night." She hung the last pair of tights and looked at me. "You didn't know."

"Nothing. About any of it. Not Faerie, not the tithe. Well done me and all my fairy tales." I leaned against the washing machine, exhaustion a weight in my bones. "I thought all the hourglass meant was extra time, a few nice things at the Market."

"You can refuse it," Marin said. "No one has to go."

I almost asked what would happen to Faerie, if there were no tithe, but realized it was a ridiculous question. There would always be people willing to make that bargain.

I was.

For all I felt turned inside out by the last few hours, that was the one thing I knew. If I had the chance, I would go. Like Evan, the fine print didn't really matter, and any consequences paled in the face of what it meant for my art.

"Will you go?" I asked. "If you're the one chosen."

"Yes," she said. No hesitation.

"But—seven years of not dancing, Marin." I hadn't realized how much stress one year off to be here would cause her, but even I knew that a dance career couldn't survive a seven-year hiatus. The loss of training, and the merciless toll that time takes. It would be impossible. I couldn't understand how she could even consider it.

"Gavin says the time won't matter while I'm there. It's part of the magic. And when I come back, I'll finally be able to save us. I'll be able to make sure Mom never comes near us again."

"Marin, what are you talking about? How would she be part of this?"

Her voice was low and harsh. "What do you think success—real, true, top of the profession, your name lives forever success—means, Imogen? It's not just fame. It's everything that goes with it. Including money and power."

"Great. I still don't understand how that keeps our mother away. You're talking about the woman who always managed to talk herself backstage, and past dorm security, no matter how hard either of us tried to keep her out."

This was how it would start, every time. She'd start by telling nice stories. It was my birthday, and she was there as a surprise. When I let people know that was one of her favorite lies, she'd try penitence and crocodile tears—she knew she had hurt me, she had so much to apologize for. There was always someone willing to believe her, and open the door.

"I know she did the same thing to you," I said.

"Yes, but when I'm the one paying the security, or the doorman, when I can have them fired if she gets in, it will be different."

I wanted so much to believe her, but I had thought I was free before, and been wrong every single time. Our mother had always managed to find us, to be there, waiting. Some days I felt like we'd never be truly safe unless she was dead.

"It will be," Marin said again. She reached out, took my hand. Her scars were so faded, I could only see them because I knew they were there. Mine were stark against them. As I held her hand, I could feel mine burning.

That afternoon, I knocked on Beth's front door, then shoved my hands in my pockets against the early November chill.

"Imogen. I thought I might see you today. Come in."

I had been braced for her house to look different, to be able to see the smears of Fae glamour that still clung to her. But no. Nothing had changed, even though everything had. "Your first book, the one that won the Orange Prize—it came out just over seven years after your residency here." I knew her bibliography, had read everything she'd published, and I'd never noticed the gap before.

"You've done your research, I see. Yes, I served as the tithe for seven years after my fellowship. Coffee? You must be exhausted. The ride takes so much out of us, especially the first time you pass through. I know some people decide not to go after that."

"No. No coffee."

"And you're angry with me. You think I should have told you. You think I owe you answers now, and Imogen, I'm happy to give them to you." She spooned Earl Grey into a teapot that looked like a pink piglet. "But think: What would you have said if, when I had given you that necklace, I'd told you it might be your ticket to fairyland?"

"I wouldn't have believed you." I leaned against her counter, trying not to fall over.

"Good. You shouldn't have, then. But now you do, and now you have some idea of the stakes, so it's time for you to think seriously about how much your writing means to you. Is it enough to accept the bargain, and go to Faerie? More important, is it enough for you to push yourself to be better than your sister so that you're the one who gets there?"

Hearing things actually spoken, even when you already know what's going to be said, makes them more real, more absolute. Because of course that was the flip side—if I were the tithe, Marin wouldn't be, and she wanted it, too, at least as much as I did. My stomach clenched.

Beth pushed a steaming mug into my hands. "I know you drink coffee, but the way you look right now, you'd bring that right back up. This is mint tea. It will settle you."

The tea tasted like liquid breath mints, but it did calm the roiling in my stomach. "Do I have to do anything about it now?"

"You'll have until spring to decide. Though, if you're considering it, you should move the timeline for finishing your book forward, because you'll need that to be in good shape.

"There is an audition process." Her gaze went very far away then, before it refocused on me. "But we'll deal with that then.

"This opportunity isn't any different from anything else at the end. The only thing you can control is your writing, so make that as strong as you can, and let the rest go."

My hands cramped around the cup, so hard I couldn't set it down. I shook, and my vision greyed.

Beth put one arm around my waist and carefully took the cup away from me. "Come on now. Let's get you over to the couch. You're tired, and you've had some shocks."

She guided me over to the couch, helped undo my boots when my hands were too clumsy to unknot the laces. She tucked a blanket around me, soft and hand-knit.

"Get some rest. Sleep. Stay as long as you want."

I tucked myself deeper into the blanket and closed my eyes. The simple quiet comfort of it was like a fairy tale—or at least what I thought they had been like, before I knew better.

14

Let the rest go, Beth had said. As if the tithe, Faerie, everything I ever wanted, were all the same sort of thing as wondering if an editor would like my writing style, or as having a day where my words were flat enough to make me doubt myself. I couldn't let the rest go; I lived in a house right next to it.

So I ran, as hard and as fast as I could, through Melete's forest. Through trees gone skeletal and a marble-grey sky. Through the snow that fell like fat, white feathers. Not sticking to the ground, not yet, but chilling everything. Through the branches that whipped at my arms and plucked at my hair, through the burning in my lungs and thighs as I ran away, away, away.

But the Melete I ran through looked strange to me, and I was compelled to look for the places where Faerie overlapped. The trees, the grounds, the river looked unchanged, everything the same as it had always been, and the sameness haunted me, because I knew it was a lie. I couldn't trust it, and I couldn't trust myself, because I had been blind to the truth of what was all around me.

This Faerie tale was nothing like the ones I'd read.

I was also running away from the knowledge that I looked strange to myself. I spent too much time thinking, trying to see what it was in my words that had translated into a chained hourglass, wondered what would be the thing that would or wouldn't mean that I was chosen. I didn't know the rules, suspected it wouldn't make a difference even if I did, but I still wanted to know them, wanted a list of what to do, to make the Fae choose me.

But in all the strangeness, the feeling that I had stepped through the looking glass instead of stopping at the reflection in it, I knew that it was only my perspective that had changed. The lie was only there because I knew what I wasn't seeing.

The grass beneath my feet was still Melete. My writing was still my own, and I had still come here to try to change my life with it. I could still do that. That part hadn't changed. Even if I hadn't seen Faerie all around me, I could still write my fairy tales—mine might not be real, but I could still write them true.

I said those words to myself, but I didn't believe them.

Everything had changed.

The wind picked up and the snow fell harder, sticking to the ground. The hourglass charm bounced against my breastbone as I ran past the mentors' houses, through the falling light. The first days here had seemed to stretch out forever, but darkness came early now, even the sky helping to keep the secrets.

Past the dancers' studios, and I looked for the light in Marin's. I couldn't outrun the ugly voice that told me I needed to be twice as good if I wanted to be chosen, because being Gavin's girlfriend gave her an advantage. I could smash it to the back of my head, tell it to shut up, ignore it, but I couldn't keep it from speaking, and I hated that about myself.

My being the tithe meant that Marin wouldn't be. Never mind the other fellows—they didn't fit into jealousy's calculus that told me there was one place, and two sisters, and that all of this would come down to the two of us. One would speak diamonds, the other, toads. Never mind that both were uncomfortable and a curse—one was still better.

I felt like I should want Marin to be chosen—if I were truly the good sister, I would yank the chain from my neck and step out of her way. I knew she wanted the chance. She'd had time to think about it, to weigh the loss of seven years against the gain of absolute freedom, and it was a freedom she offered to share with me. *Keep us safe,* she had said. Us. I loved my sister. I felt like I should want this for her. And I did. But only if it couldn't be me.

Then, at the forest's edge—feathers spinning and twisting in the wind. It wouldn't have even been a strange thing, not something to notice at all, except the rest of the day was windless and still.

More feathers, different shapes and sizes, colors from an entire aviary of birds, until the air was thick with them, until they were all around me, blanketing me, shutting out the sun.

Between one heartbeat and the next, all of the feathers fell to the ground.

A woman stood, looked at me. Her eyes banded, yellow like an owl's. A close crop of feathers rather than hair on her head.

Words formed just behind my teeth, and then—

She exploded into a flock of birds.

I swallowed everything I might have said.

Echoes of wings faded across the sky and one feather—iridescent grey, almost silver—floated to the ground at my feet.

I picked it up and turned away from the studio lights, ran home. There was no escape from the strangeness, there was no putting Faerie and the complications of the tithe aside. The world had changed.

Today, the bridge was only halfway there. A crumbling arch that stopped midpoint, leaving only air to cross to the other side of the river. For the space of a breath, I thought about running across it, throwing myself into Faerie with nothing more than the belief it would be there, waiting to catch me, if I just ran fast enough. Hands in a theater, clapping to bring Tinker Bell back to life. I do believe, I do.

But it hadn't been speed that had gotten that headlong rush of horses into Faerie. It had been that night, the tick of midnight's clock. It had been Gavin riding at the head of the mad gallop of horses. The horned and crowned magic he held had thrown open the doors of his hidden country, and given us a path to enter it.

The rush of the Mourning below me was rapid and deep, the air cold. Without magic, I wouldn't run into Faerie—I would fall from the bridge, soak myself, and freeze.

"It won't work. You can't get there like this." Evan's voice.

"Oh, I see you've decided to start telling me things now. Even before I ask. Lucky me."

"I'm sorry I hurt you, Imogen. I didn't mean to."

I believed him. It didn't help. I was sure he hadn't even considered the possibility it would hurt me. He probably hadn't considered me at all, which was pretty much the problem.

"Look, I'm a big girl, Evan. I'm not going to sit alone in my room and pine if it turns out that what we had was nothing more than one really hot fuck. It doesn't need to be anything more. But if you think you want it to be, you need to know that I won't be with someone who lies to me, who is casual with me. If you want it to be more, you're going to need to treat me as if I matter. I don't want to be your everything, but I need to matter or you're not worth my time."

He was so close. I could smell the burnt metal scent that clung to him, remnants of his art. I took a step back.

"All right," he said. "I'll try."

He had to go, soon after. To Faerie. He tried, he said, to keep to a regular schedule. It reduced the chances he'd be pulled away in the middle of something, let him make plans, sometimes, that needed to happen at a certain time and place.

"Like meeting me at the Market," I said. "That was why Gavin was so weird that first night there. Not because he thought you should be working, but because he expected you to be in Faerie."

Evan nodded. "It's his kingdom, his people. My being there feeds it. He makes sure I'm not gone too long."

"What does it feel like," I asked, "when it's time to go back?"

"Like a hook in my heart, pulling. It's not pleasant, and gets worse if I ignore it. So I don't."

I watched him leave, expecting that it would have some extraordinary component, some ritual or magic word. But he simply walked to the end of the bridge, and then, between one step and the next, was gone.

Ariel and I were walking back from the world's worst bar. There had, if anything, gotten worse since the previous time I'd visited.

"It's like someone made a deal with the devil," she said. "Like, Melete can exist, and can be this perfect refuge for art and artists, but in order for this to be possible, a balance must be maintained. And so never can a drink order be served properly on the first attempt, nor shall it ever take less than twenty minutes to get a gin and tonic."

"Also, you can't ever get edible food," I said. "That grilled cheese they brought you was—"

"Neither. I know. Bread and tomatoes. Cold."

Our breath puffed out in white clouds as we walked back home, the grass crunching beneath our feet. The Mourning flowed fast beside us, cold and dark as it raced over the rocks.

"Thanks for enduring it, though, Ariel. I just, I needed to get out of the house, and vent to someone about Evan."

"No problem. You owe me a better class of drink at some point, though. When we're both rich and—

"Imogen." She grabbed my arm, stopped walking. "What the fuck is that?"

A naked woman sat in the river, combing her long hair. Her skin was pale as ice, and her eyes glowed green fire. She smiled at us, and her teeth were thin and pointed needles.

"That's really happening, right? She's actually there?" Ariel's hand was tight on my arm, her fingers digging in.

My hand went to my neck, to the hourglass charm around it. "Yes. She's really there."

"Come in, come in," the woman said, and her voice was water on rocks, was ice in a river, was peaceful drowning. "Come in, and I will comb the dreams from your hair."

"Is that where they come from?" Ariel asked.

"Where else would you find dreams? They need nets to tangle in."

"Right. Of course. Well, maybe another time. When it's warmer," Ariel said. "Have a good night."

"And you." The woman disappeared beneath the rushing water.

"They're real," Ariel said. "The Fae."

"They're real." We stood, shivering, on the edge of the river. "I didn't know you knew. Do you have an hourglass?"

"Not yet, although Angelica informs me it's not that I'm untalented, it's just that she thinks I want to be a rock star more than I want to be an artist, and so giving me one right now would be a waste.

"There's still time for me to earn one, though, if I sort out my priorities when it comes to my art."

"That's . . . rude."

"Considering that she knew exactly the kind of art I wanted to make when she chose to work with me? Yes." Still holding my arm, she started walking back. "And Gavin really is the king? Of Faerie?"

"He is."

"Huh," she said. "And yet still grumpy before he gets his morning coffee. Maybe some things are universal."

"I can't imagine the woman we just saw sitting down to morning coffee," I said.

"Neither can I. What was it like to go there?"

"Beautiful. Terrifying. I want to go back, and I want to never see it again. And yes, I'd go as the tithe if I were picked. That's how it was."

"Well," she said. "I guess I'm sorry I missed it. Because I'm pretty sure I wouldn't."

She was the first person I had heard say that. "Why not?"

"Seven years without performing? Are you fucking kidding me?"

I laughed. "Do you miss it that much?"

She nodded. "I want the charm and the chance, not because I want to go to Faerie—which does not get any less ridiculous when I say it out loud—but because I want to be the one who rejects them, rather than thinking that they've rejected me. I think seven years with no applause might actually break me.

"Plus, I want to succeed on my terms."

"What do you mean?" We were back home now, on the safety of recognizable stairs, our own front porch.

Ariel unlocked the door. "Wouldn't you always wonder? You get back and you make the *New York Times* bestseller list and your book gets made into a movie, or whatever it is that's the signal of super-ultimate writer success. Wouldn't you wonder if it was because you were actually good enough, or if it was just because of the Fae, holding up their end of this weird-ass bargain?

"I don't want to walk through the rest of my career thinking that

I didn't earn my own success, wondering if my art really had been as amazing as people claimed it was, or if they had just magicked people into thinking I mattered."

"But you would have earned it. That's what the seven years is," I said.

"I'd rather spend seven years making art," Ariel said. "If you have the talent, if you make something amazing, the success will happen anyway. If you don't believe that, working as hard as we do makes no sense."

15

"Someone annoying is at the door for you, Imogen," Helena called.

"Okay, I'll go right down and take care of that," I said.

There was a paint-spattered woman pacing back and forth on our front porch. "Can I help you?"

"Are you Imogen? You look like Marin said you would—tall, with long black hair. But I've been wrong about people before, so maybe you're not." Her words ran together like rain.

"I'm Imogen," I said cautiously.

"Good. Okay, good. I'm Michelle. Marin said you were good at fairy tales, like, good enough to write your own. And I have one of these"—she dangled a silver hourglass from her hand, then stuffed it back into a pocket—"but, like, I barely know anything beyond Hansel and Gretel, and this isn't really a candy house sort of thing, is it?"

"I'm pretty sure not."

She was literally wringing her hands, squeezing the stress from one set of fingers to the next. "So what do I do? I looked on the Internet, and it said stuff about leaving out bread and milk, and not speaking their names unless you want to attract their attention, but I do want their attention, so how do I make something good enough that they pick me?"

It was an excellent question.

"Look, um, Michelle."

She stopped pacing, stared, laser-like. I resisted the urge to step back, out of range.

"Here's the thing. The fairy tales I know about, they're in books. I don't know anything about actual Fae. I didn't know that's what Gavin was, when I met him. I didn't know that Faerie was right across the river. I don't know why the Fae are here, or what they want from us, or how to get their attention, though I'd say you can probably skip the milk and bread deal. I'm pretty sure Gavin drinks whiskey."

"Are you making fun of me?"

I sighed, scrubbed my hands over my eyes. "I'm really not. But I don't know anything more about how any of this works than the rest of you."

"Are you sure?" Her voice cracked, and she looked like she might cry.

"Look, give me your email, and I'll send you a list of my favorite fairy tale collections. Maybe there's something in one of them that will help you."

"Okay." She nodded vigorously. "It's just so stressful, you know? Like, every little bit helps."

"You're right," I said, thinking of demanding answers from Evan, from Marin, from Beth. "It does. I'll send you the email. If you can't find the books, come back—we've got at least some in the library here."

I knocked on Marin's door.

"Come in," she called. She was sitting on the floor, folded into lotus position, and breaking in a new pair of pointe shoes, reshaping them to better fit her feet.

"So, I just ran into your friend Michelle outside."

She winced, slammed her shoe into the ground. "Sorry about that.

She has a studio just a couple spaces away from me, and she's really been freaking out. You're the closest thing to an expert on this stuff I know."

"Well, if I'm the expert, we're all fucked. I mean, I haven't come across any stories that look like what's going on here. Believe me, you'd be the first person I told if I had."

She paused. "Really? You don't have any ideas?"

"Marin, I've spent most of my life thinking that fairy tales were, you know, fairy tales. Plus, all the stuff in them about how you'll be fine if you're just pure of heart and virtuous, and kind to the white cat that follows you through the woods or to the little old lady at the fork in the path—well, I don't really think any of that applies. So no, I don't have any ideas."

I paused. "I mean, you're dating Gavin. Have been almost since we got here. Do you have any insights, any ideas into how to impress the King of the Fae?"

"That's not who he is when he's with me."

"Good," I said, meaning it.

She set one shoe aside, picked up the second, whacked it against the floor. "Still, point taken. I won't offer you up as a consultant again."

"Thanks. Like I said, I couldn't help her anyway." I walked over to her window, watched the river run past.

"So, for something completely different, what do you want to do for Thanksgiving this year?" I asked.

"Besides the obvious part where we stay the hell away from our mother?"

I shuddered. "When did she stop asking you?"

"Oh, she still does. It's random now—she only invites me to one of the major holidays each year. I've never gone to any of them."

Holidays had always been even more awful than everything else when we were growing up. Our mother had seen them as performances, meant to showcase her.

When I was nine, I had been reading, and I hadn't noticed the buzzer for the pumpkin pie going off until I smelled it burning. There hadn't been time or ingredients to make another, so I had spent that Thanksgiving locked in my room, the visiting relatives told that I had the chicken pox. Marin had smuggled me a roll and a slice of turkey, both covered in blue fuzz from being stuffed in her pockets. I had eaten it all, even the fuzz. It had been the only food I had gotten that day.

"Why not cook here? Something nice, something not turkey and dressing. And invite any other orphans to eat with us," Marin said.

"Like who? I mean, besides Gavin, obviously."

"Ariel and Helena." Marin rolled her eyes as she said Helena's name. "We can't ask one and not the other. Beth, if you want."

"She has plans already. Visiting family."

"What about Evan?" Marin asked.

"I think so." I had meant what I'd said—if he was willing to behave like I mattered, I was willing to give things between us another chance. The couple of times we'd seen each other since, he'd seemed like he was trying.

"What happened? Do I need to kick him for you?" She wiggled her feet.

I laughed. "No, but I'll let you know if that changes. I remember what you did to Brian O'Neal."

"He deserved it, kissing that what's-her-face when he was supposed to be your boyfriend."

"To be fair, she was a grade ahead of me. The allure of the older woman."

"Hey, a cheating bastard at eleven is no different than a cheating bastard now. And if a guy needs to be kicked, I will kick him." Marin leaned in and gave me a hug. It was good, normal. She was my sister, not my rival. Better to remember that.

We hadn't talked about the tithe since the morning after the ride through Faerie. I was afraid to bring it up—it would feel like declaring opposition. I tried to tell myself that it was no different than applying to Melete. There had always been the chance that one of us would get in and the other wouldn't. But I knew that was a lie. This was different. There was only one spot. It was obvious from the beginning that one of us wouldn't get it.

She still wore her charm, so she hadn't changed her mind about wanting it. But then, I still wore mine, too.

As it turned out, Ariel was going home for the long weekend. "Which I will regret to some extent, because they'll all call me Arabella, which I hate and have hated my whole life, and which hasn't been my name since I legally dropped it and started going by Ariel—which is actually my middle name—so it's not like I suddenly asked everyone to call me Starchild or something random, but they don't see what the point was, and so they ignore it, because Arabella is what they're used to." She stuffed another T-shirt into the suitcase I had loaned her.

"Arabella Ariel?"

"I know, right? There will be at least one conversation, probably started by Aunt Ida, about when I think I am going to grow up and get a real job instead of showing myself off onstage, and at least two offers to set me up with 'a nice boy.' Now, I do like boys, but the ones on offer won't, let me assure you, be nice. In either instance. And one of the so-called nice boys will be there, and at some point he will grab my ass and I will punch him. Plus, you know, I already have a girlfriend.

"But I miss my mom, who likes my girlfriend, and will have invited her as a surprise for me, and who will secretly appreciate the fact that I punched the ass-grabber, and I really miss her bourbon pecan pie, so I'm off."

"Oddly enough," I said, "I can totally understand why you're going. Have a great time."

"I'm hoping that being away will help me clear out my thinking on the whole should I stay or should I go thing, too," she said, zipping the suitcase shut. "Have fun with the cooking."

"Thanks. Travel safe."

Helena was staying at Melete, and once she realized we weren't planning the traditional turkey dinner, she said she'd join us. "Pumpkin pie is an abomination. I'll get the wine."

Marin and I made boeuf bourguignon, because it was the kind of thing that would cook all day and make the house smell warm and welcoming. Helena brought her work down to the library instead of staying up in her room, and joined us in the kitchen for a glass of wine as we cooked. It was the most social she'd been since we arrived, and the first time I'd thought she looked relaxed.

Evan had sent me a letter saying he would be here. And so I stood in front of my closet, like a teenager getting ready for her first date, rejected articles of clothing scattered across my bed and dropped at my feet. Everything was too something, and I wondered how it was that even though I had bought every item hanging in my closet, all of them were wrong. "You're an idiot, Imogen," I told myself. "It doesn't matter what you wear. He's already seen you naked, and if you don't put on some clothes soon, everyone else will too."

I glanced at the clock on my phone. "Fuck." I shimmied back

into the black dress I had taken off twice, put on my favorite red lipstick, and got downstairs at the same time as the knock on the front door.

"Happy Thanksgiving." Gavin held a cake box, and Evan an armful of roses, reds and golds.

"Come in," I said. "Gavin, you can put that in the kitchen. Here, Evan, let me take those." Their fragrance burst like glory into the air.

"Thank you for inviting me," Evan said, so close that when I breathed, my arm brushed his.

"I'm glad you're here," I said, filling the vase with water.

"I'm hoping we have some time alone. Later." His voice was low, secret, a shiver over my skin.

"I—ouch." I winced. Blood welled around the thorn broken off in the pad of my finger.

The oven timer rang, and Helena came in to pour the wine. "Are those from the rose garden? I love that place. I'm surprised there's anything still in bloom there, though."

"They're not," Evan said. "I love the rose garden, too, but these are from a florist."

It was one of the best Thanksgivings I'd ever had. No holiday pressure or baggage, just a meal among friends, food, wine, and conversation. The most common of magics, an alchemy of people and place, transmuted into happiness.

Gavin and Marin sat across the table from me, and I watched them. Evan had said that the Fae weren't good at emotions, that they didn't love. But Gavin looked at Marin as if she were a miracle. It looked like love to me, or at least what I hoped love was.

"I'll go get the dessert," he said, gesturing Marin and me back into our seats when we protested. "You made dinner, and I'm sure I can find plates without trouble."

"I'll help," Helena said.

Marin widened her eyes at Helena's departing back. We waited and waited. "I'm just going to go see if they need any help. You know how tricky the coffeemaker is," I said, lying through my teeth.

I opened the pocket doors.

"She said you promised." Helena looked furious.

"I can't make that promise," Gavin said. "You know what the rules are."

"You owe—" Helena began.

"Do you guys need any help?" I said, overly brightly. The dessert, chocolate ganache cake, draped in a dark red sauce, was already plated. "I'll just start taking these in."

"Thank you," Gavin said under his breath as I picked up two plates. "Nothing I could have said was going to be the right thing."

Helena clattered her way through dessert, stabbing her fork into her cake as if it was Gavin's heart she expected to see pierced on the tines. Once she finished, she went back upstairs without saying good night.

Evan and I took our coffee into the library. A fire crackled and glowed in the fireplace. Romantic golden light and the pleasant smell of wood smoke. "I feel like there's an invisible neon sign blinking 'make out now,'" I said.

"An invisible neon sign?" Evan curled his hand around the back of my head and stroked up and down my neck with his thumb. "Sounds complicated."

He leaned in and kissed me, and even though I didn't move any closer, I kissed him back. His mouth was bitter like coffee and sweet like chocolate, and it would have been so easy to sink into the taste and feel of him. To not think about secrets and tithes and complications.

"When I'm in Faerie, all I can hold in my head is Tania," Evan said. "It doesn't matter that it's been seven years now. I go back there, and it's like traveling in time. Everything is raw, immense."

As seductions went, this one was failing on a number of levels.

"Then I come back," he continued, his hand stroking up and down my back. "And you're here, and you're real. I can feel you under my hands, and taste you on my lips, and it's overwhelming. I breathe, and there you are." He closed his eyes, spoke the next words into my hair. "I get lost in you."

And so, for the moment, I let myself be overwhelmed. I didn't ask questions, didn't consider the complications. I wove my fingers into his hair, pressed against him, and kissed him hard in the dying light.

Ariel got back late Monday night. She still had her bags with her when she knocked on my door. "Thank God you're still up."

"What happened?"

"Actually, will you come downstairs? Because downstairs is where the whiskey is, and I really want a drink with this conversation."

"Sure, of course. Let me just make sure that I've backed up my work."

"I'll drop these in my room and meet you down there."

She poured us both generous glasses, then drank off half of hers in the first sip. "So, have you talked to anyone about that magic charm?"

"This?" I pulled the hourglass necklace from under my shirt. I'd gotten so used to wearing it, I hardly noticed it anymore.

Ariel nodded.

"Sure. You, Marin, Beth. Evan, sort of. I mean, we talked about the tithe, but not the charm, specifically. No one said not to. Which is weird, now that I think of it." It seemed like a thing you'd be warned against discussing: By the way, Faerie is real and also a significant percentage of the world's most successful artists served time there, and that is part of why they're successful. But there hadn't been a warning, and somehow the tithe was a thing that there weren't even whispers of rumors about—no underground gossip about the events of every seven years.

"They don't need to tell you not to. Try it with anyone who's physically not here, and you can't."

"What do you mean?"

"I mean you literally can't. I went out with my girlfriend on Friday. After we reacquainted ourselves, we started talking about whether or not I'm going to stay here. And even though it sucks being apart, she's totally supportive of me staying, if that's what I want." Her eyes flicked to the windows, her fingers playing along the rim of her glass.

"So I decide I'm going to joke a bit, ask how she'd feel if I were gone for seven years. And I can't. Literally can't. My throat starts closing up like I'm having an allergic reaction to the words every time I try to say something."

"That must have been terrifying," I said.

"It was. And it gets worse. Because after that, I can't leave it alone. I try to tell everyone. Every single way I can think of. Nothing works. Not only can I not talk, my email messages bounce. My cell phone turns into the Ninth Circle of Autocorrect. Even the fucking pen I try to use bursts open in my hand."

She refilled her glass and drank. "Then I get back here. I'm on the shuttle, and we pass through the gates, and everything just comes bursting out of my mouth, and I'm babbling away about the Fae and tithes and all this magic shit, and the driver just nods and says 'yes, miss' like I'm talking about the fucking weather."

"Are you okay?" I asked.

"No, I'm really not. I couldn't speak, Imogen. I'm not even part of this. I don't have an hourglass, and I wouldn't go to Faerie even if I had one. All I did was agree to come to Melete, and still they got in my head and made it so I couldn't talk.

"My voice is who I am, and they can take it from me. I don't know how to feel okay."

I gave her my hand, and she held on tight.

"Are you here just to pack your things and go, then?" I asked.

"No, because the sick thing is, leaving doesn't help with this. The part that's weird and scary just gets worse if I leave, because there will be no one I can talk to. I won't even be able to say why I left.

"So no, I'm not leaving. I am here to the end, because if they can do that to me, if they can take my voice, then I am taking everything I can from them by way of payment. I will stay in this house and eat the food and use the time that I have to make something brilliant, and in the end, they will have paid for all of those things." Cold fury in her voice.

"So what will you do?"

"I'm thinking of changing my project," she said.

"No more Joan of Arc?"

She finished her drink and smiled, and there were teeth in her smile, sharpness. "Suddenly I find I'm more interested in exploring ideas of silence, rather than of voices. And from sources that aren't necessarily divine. I think I'm going to work on something that might speak for me a little better when I do leave here."

"Be careful, Ariel."

"Come on now, Imogen. You know how this works. No one ever made great art by being careful."

16

I reached into the drawer of my desk for a new notebook, and my hand brushed against the packet of letters—*My Thomas, True, Your own, J*—that I had found in the library. So much had happened since then, I had forgotten about them. The scent of rosemary crackled into the room as I took the letters out of the drawer. I unwrapped the ribbon and read them again.

This time, I caught what I hadn't known was there before. Woven among the promises of love and fidelity was the ongoing refrain of seven years. I sat up straighter in my chair and read them again, slowly. *When your seven years are over . . . When these seven years have passed . . . I would wait even seven times seven years.* She told him she was writing a book of poetry to decrease the hours until he returned. When he returned, he would have her love, and all of his dreams. It was never made explicit, but the evidence was there. Whoever Thomas was, he had been the tithe. J was writing love letters to him while he was away in Faerie.

I tied them back up in ribbon and seal, then went downstairs.

"Hey, Imogen," Ariel said. "Come outside and look at this."

She opened the front door. A large box filled with batteries and candles and blankets had appeared on the front porch, a sign reading BLIZZARD SAFETY KIT on top of it. Extra firewood was stacked along the side of the house. The dull iron scent of snow filled the air.

"So, are they serious with this, or is this like a 'be prepared' sort of care package?" Ariel asked. "Because honestly, all of this stuff seems a bit much. It's just snow."

I pulled up the weather report on my phone. "I think they're serious. This says possible blizzard conditions, over a foot of snow expected by tomorrow morning." I hugged my arms to myself, bouncing on the balls of my feet for warmth. The wood of the porch snapped and groaned, almost as loud as the trees. Our breath puffed out. The sky was grey and flat, but the only things blowing across it were leaves, the tattered ends of fall that cartwheeled and dipped.

Marin rushed up the steps, cheeks pink. "It's freezing. What are you two doing out here?"

"Looking for snow. Apparently we're due for a big storm." Ariel looked excited.

"I wouldn't be surprised. My hip is killing me," Marin said, pressing her hand to her left side. She had taken a bad fall in a pas de deux class when she was twenty, and cracked the cartilage in her hip socket. It ached in cold and stormy weather.

The text alert sounded on all of our phones then, confirming the blizzard warning, and that supplies were being delivered to all of the residences.

"I've always wanted to get snowed in by a blizzard. Snow angels and hot chocolate. This is going to be so great," Ariel said.

"Ariel, sweetie, where are you from again?" Marin asked.

"Miami. I've never seen snow fall in real life."

"You just keep believing that the storm will be fun, then," Marin said, and went inside.

"I will," Ariel said. "My enthusiasm renders me immune to cold and to snark."

I started a pot of soup that we could keep simmering on the

stove. Ariel lit a fire in the fireplace, and we went outside with her when the first flakes began drifting through the sky. She grinned and caught the snow on her tongue, spinning in circles until her hair was dotted with white.

"Can you do the Snow Queen dance from *Nutcracker*?" she asked Marin.

Marin closed her eyes and moaned in mock agony. "In my sleep, probably. Why would you ask a question like that? I thought you were my friend."

"What's wrong with *Nutcracker*? I love that ballet. I go every year."

"You and everyone else in the world. For the entire month of December. Every. Fucking. Year. Hence the problem. I'm convinced hell is actually an eternity of being a snowflake in *Nutcracker*."

"So you're saying I just asked you to sing 'My Heart Will Go On.'"

Marin nodded. "I will if you will."

"Fuck no." They looked at each other and shuddered. I laughed.

The sky grew darker and the snow fell heavier as the day went on. We lit candles throughout the house and set flashlights in every room.

Helena wandered into the kitchen and got out a bowl. "I'm trying Imogen's stress-baking idea. I hate this weather." She baked a tray of flatbread crackers to go with the soup, and the four of us sat down to dinner.

A gust of wind slammed against the house, rattling the windows and howling under the door. Another. Helena cringed. With the third, the lights went out.

"I think this is maybe when I stop being excited about blizzards," Ariel said. She snuggled into the scarf that was still wrapped around her neck.

"It'll be okay," Marin said. "We have lots of firewood, and there are extra blankets in the closet. We have warm food—the crackers are really good, Helena—and we'll be fine."

The wind gusted again.

"I hate this," Helena said. "Storms like this make me feel like I'm being buried alive."

"So, we need a distraction," Marin said.

"I have one, actually. Hang on." I grabbed a flashlight and went upstairs to get the letters.

"I found these back in September, right after we moved in." I set the packet on the table. "At first I thought they were just interesting, but I figured out today that whoever this J was, the Thomas she was writing to was the tithe."

I unwrapped them and handed them around. There was a rustle of paper, and then: "No. No, it can't be. Oh, fuck."

"Helena, what is it?" I asked.

"I know this handwriting. I know exactly who these people are. My parents. Fuck." Her expression shattered like glass.

"Give me the rest of those," she said.

Ariel, Marin, and I passed her the letters that were no longer a fun distraction, were not clues to the mystery in a party game.

Helena bit her lip as she was reading, so hard it bled. She scrubbed the back of her hand across her mouth, leaving behind a gory lipstick smear, near-black in the candlelight. "*J* stands for Janet. Janet Thomas is my mother."

That was the first unexpected thing. There were more.

"I've never met my father. He abandoned her while she was pregnant. Well, maybe not abandoned. She was away in Faerie, as the tithe."

"Wait," I said. "The letters. They were both there? Two tithes?"

"He went first," Helena said, "and even though she had waited for him when he was there, he didn't wait the seven years for her to come back."

"But—" Ariel began.

"Look. This sucks already. Let me tell it my way, and then you can ask your questions.

"He was a glass artist. Now he's more like a general sculptor. You've heard of him—Thomas Greene. My mom changed her last name to Thomas after I was born. To remind him of us, I guess, but it didn't work out. He's a dick. Whatever."

We had heard of him. He was one of those artists that had a name people recognized, even if they didn't particularly care about art. He'd done a famous memorial. Designed a museum people were still arguing about. Huge spears of glass that caught the light and reflected it like some kind of alien spaceship. Won a genius grant. His third wife was a supermodel. And only two years older than Helena.

"They met during his fellowship year. This was the house he lived in, up in the tower room, so my guess is that's why the letters are here. Anyway. Doesn't matter.

"He was looking for a model. She answered the ad. The glass over the front door of her house. It's an early piece of his, from before he changed his style. The woman in it, that's her. They had a relationship. Fell in love, I guess. This is when the story changes from what you're expecting, because she didn't get pregnant then. She got pregnant seven years later. When he got back. Right before she left."

"Oh God," Marin said. "You grew up there."

Feral. Like she didn't know quite how to be human. And of course, she didn't. The ride through Faerie and the greedy emptiness of it. Not all of the tithes survived their seven years. I couldn't imagine what it had been like for a child.

"For almost the first seven years of my life." Helena's face was splotched with red and streaked with tears. I passed her a napkin, but she ignored it.

"What was—" Marin's voice cracked. "What was it like?"

"I don't know," Helena said. "I don't remember.

"I need a drink." She got up, poured herself a glass of bourbon, and brought it and the bottle back to the table. None of the rest of us moved.

"Janet worked her ass off after he went. She wanted the same deal he got, so she decided to be a poet, and she wrote, and she wrote, and she got good enough to get published, and she got good enough to get in here, and she got good enough to be one of the shining ones who get offered the deal with Faerie. Which she took.

"She hadn't been planning for me to get in the way, but I didn't really. She was already there. She had what she wanted, so I didn't matter."

Ariel was crying, too, silent tears streaking her face, and Marin looked like she wanted to be sick.

Helena continued. "Seven years later, we came back. And Melete gave us a nice little cottage in the woods, some kind of backhanded apology, because while Janet bargained herself into Faerie fair and square and Melete is just fine with that, I got screwed.

"And I got screwed again, because the deal Janet made didn't cover me. Janet's famous. She's won a fucking Pulitzer, a National Book Award. I don't have any of that. I'm not even good enough to get one of those fucking necklaces."

"But you were there, on Halloween. You rode with us into Faerie," I said. "I thought—"

"If you're here at Melete on the Halloween before the tithe, and you've ever dwelt in Faerie, you must ride in the rade on Samhain night. Seeing the old year out, bringing in the new possibility, blah blah. So I have to ride, every time."

"Even though you never lived in Faerie by choice," I said.

"They do love their rules." Bitterness dripped from her words.

"You sound like you hate it," Ariel said.

"I do. Hate it, and all of them." She spat the words like a curse.

"Then why do you want to be the tithe?" I asked. "Hell, why are you even here at Melete? Why not go as far away from here as you can, and never look back?"

"Because being the tithe means being the best, and I want to be the fucking best. Because after I came back from Faerie, I would have power, and then I could leave and never look back, and everybody who mattered would know that I didn't crawl away because I wasn't good enough, I left because I was better.

"Because if I'm the one chosen, Gavin has to give Janet back my father."

"What?" Marin's voice was a whip crack.

"When he was in Faerie, the Queen of Faerie stole his love for Janet. It's why he didn't wait for her, why he can't love anyone now. I mean, look at the way he is," she sneered. "But if I go, it redeems him. He'll remember that he loves Janet. Loves me."

"Helena, that's not how this works," Marin said.

"I'm sure that's what Gavin's told you. I'm sure he's told you a lot of things." Helena's mouth twisted around the words. "Just think about what he would get, having you there, with no one else but him to rely on, for seven years."

The wind howled again, the wail of something ending. Branches rattled against the windows like questing hands trying to get in.

"They can't lie," I said.

"There's a big difference between someone lying, and someone not telling all of the truth," Helena said.

"Here's the thing that I don't understand," Ariel said. "Even after hearing Helena talk about it, say she hates them, all you—any of you—can see is the end. The thing that happens when you come back. I mean, sure, hurrah for success, but come on. Did it occur to any of you that you're good enough on your own? Or that the seven years might not be worth it?

"Do you really think you—or your art—come back the same after the time you spend there? Think about what you're really giving up, because seriously, you all sound like a cult." She got up, started clearing the dishes.

"It's easy to think a choice looks simple when you're not the one who has to make it," Marin said.

"Thanks for that little reminder," Ariel said. "And that's not what I'm saying. I'm just saying that maybe you ought to consider that not everything about this bargain is good."

"Of course it's not," Helena said. "We know it's not, and we want it anyway. That's why it works." She took the bottle of bourbon and the letters, and went upstairs.

I write when I don't know what else to do. When I don't know what to think. To deal with the pieces of life that are too hard, too painful to think about otherwise.

That was pretty much why I started writing in the first place, to deal with the things I could only stand to look at out of the corner of my eye. Now, I can write for other reasons, too—for the joy of it, for the challenge—but that first reason is still there, beneath all the others.

So I took a candle and went to my room, high in the dark, the storm spinning past my windows in a haze of white, and I wrote.

———◆———

Once upon a time.

Once upon a time, the Queen of the Fairies met a mortal knight as they both rode out one morning. He was a comely man, well-formed and well-spoken, and so she took him as her own, there on the green hillside. He pleased her so, she took him back to Fairy with her.

And he went, and he was pleased to do so, for he thought the time he spent there to be only seven days and seven nights, and oh, the nights paid for all. But at the end of those days and nights, she put him from her, and he discovered that they were not days and nights that had passed, but years. He left her, lost. Lost from her side, and lost from the life that had been his before, and lost from all but his memories.

Once upon a time, as a knight rode out, he met the Queen of the Fairies. He wove flowers into her hair and kissed her moonlit skin, and she kissed him back, and made him her own. And when they finished, and when he slept, she sent him dreams, and in those dreams were death. Pale kings, pale princes, all cold and dead. And when he woke, he too was pale and cold, a shadow to haunt that wild hillside. Some of those he haunted fled into Fairy, and some of those returned, cold, to the world of that hill. But she never returned to him, nor he to what he had once called life.

Once upon a time, the King of the Fairies met a woman. She was beautiful and kind, and she danced as if the wind itself had blessed her feet. And he loved her, because that is the way of these things, and he took her to Fairy to dance with her forever, because that is what you do, when you are a king and you fall in love.

And the woman went away to Fairy and she danced with the king, and she danced, and she danced, until one day she did not rise to slip her graceful feet into her slippers. That, too, is the way of things.

These are not stories with happily ever afters, all of the different once upon a times.

Except they weren't only once. They were always.

"I know Thomas a bit." The scent of lavender rose into the air as Beth poured her tea into a cup the color of a cloudless sky. "He's talented, certainly, and genuinely charming. But I've never met a man more driven by his libido. I have no doubt that he would have told Janet whatever he thought was most likely to get him laid, regardless of the truth.

"Especially as he had just gotten back from Faerie. Because you spend so much time being nothing more than a creature of constant emotion while you're there, physical sensation is incredibly heightened when you return. My first day back, I spent an hour under the shower because I could feel every drop of water on my skin. It was almost a week before I could bear even the loosest of clothing comfortably."

You made me feel real, Evan had said. I thought I had understood what he meant, but maybe I had only gotten part of it.

Beth continued. "I also have no doubt that nearly everyone would rather believe that the Queen of Faerie stole their lover from them, than think he was quite happy to walk away and not look back."

"You knew Tania, too," I said.

"Oh, yes. She was the queen when I served, had been for a small eternity before. She was still dwelling almost entirely in Faerie when I knew her—she hadn't yet decided to come out and play at being a human, an artist. And for her, it was play. An amusing distraction. Gavin is, from what I know of him, quite different than she was.

"Do I think she could have made Thomas love her? Absolutely.

Either by glamour or by more carnal means. It would have been no more to her than a snap of her fingers. If she had cared.

"But if Tania ever had a great love, Thomas wasn't it, and Janet would have been less than nothing to her. So no, I don't think she would have bothered to make Janet miserable. Janet was more than capable of doing that all on her own."

"Here's the thing I still don't get, though," I said. "If Janet is so desperate for Helena to have a chance to be the tithe, why doesn't she just give her one of the charms, and then let her be judged with the rest of us?"

"Because that's not how it works. I didn't place an order for yours, or pick it up at the admin building. The day I gave it to you, I found it."

"Found it?" I echoed.

"Bookmarking my calendar, so that when I turned the day over, there it was between the pages. I wanted to give you the chance, but I wasn't the one who decided you'd earned it. That was why I needed your pages. To read them myself, yes, but also to pass them on to the Fae. They were the ones who made the decision. Much like they will make the decision in the spring, as to which one of you is chosen."

The feelings of being watched that we had all had when we first moved in. Had they ever gone away, I wondered now, or had we just gotten used to the sensation?

"How long does Helena have?" I asked. "For someone to decide she's earned her chance?"

"The charms can be given at any moment up until the selection is made at the equinox. But they don't tend to be given late. I would say that if Helena doesn't have one by the new year, she won't get one at all.

"Still, if it were me, I wouldn't want to go back."

"Helena says she doesn't remember it, from before."

"Well." Beth closed her eyes. "That's probably for the best."

"Did you know that Helena was Janet's daughter?" I asked.

"No. This is my third time back as a mentor since they would have returned, if I can trust my math and my memory. So, two years besides this one that I could have seen Helena on the grounds.

"Which isn't as noteworthy as it sounds—mentors may bring families with them, and unless you are in someone else's house, you may well see a child without realizing to whom they belong. But I don't believe I've ever seen Helena before, and I certainly didn't know that Janet had a child."

"I can't imagine what things were like for her, growing up," I said.

I had seen kids playing on the grounds. Soccer or football or some variety of game that involved shrieking and running on the Commons. Riding bicycles. Running along the paths. Doing kid things. With friends. It was possible to come here and have a normal life in this very not-normal place.

Unless your mother locked you away like a secret in a tower.

Practically raised by wolves, we had joked. The monster and the metaphor, and the way they match up that makes the double-edged sword of wit. And then you realize what your words have done, and you weep because you're both bleeding.

Once upon a time, there was a Fairy Queen with a heart made of flesh. Such a thing seems impossible, I know, but I have promised not to lie.

No one's heart begins as a stone. Hearts are things that beat like birds in a cage, fluttering about, flying away from us at the least provocation. But once a crown is placed on a head, in that moment, the queen is dead and long live the queen. So a heart must be taken out, and all its love placed into something unbreakable. Into stone, because one cannot love and rule, not without things even more valuable than hearts breaking.

You know this. This is why there are stories about the tears of a cold and marble-pale queen, each drop a miracle, a doorway large enough to let the dead walk living out of hell. Because for such a heart to love enough to weep, what else but resurrection could follow?

When she first changed her heart, the Fairy Queen liked the stone weight of it in her chest. The stone heart was strong. It would last forever. Changing a heart of flesh to one of stone was better even than hiding a life in an emerald, in a bird, in a tree. She did not worry that her heart would be stolen, that some accident would befall her.

And truly, she told herself, it was not as if she had lost anything. There are all sorts of things that look like love, that have its pleasures, that offer its heat and its tastes, and the queen enjoyed all of these things, her heart kept safe.

But sometimes. Sometimes even a stone heart can beat. Love, when it is true, is a force upon which even stone can shatter.

And so the stone-hearted queen looked, and loved. And she gave of herself, and even gave her heart. Her heart of stone, that beat once more in her chest.

Even a heart of stone can break.

He was her love and her beloved, and she would have plucked the sun from the sky and given it to him for the sheer joy of seeing it in his hands.

But to be loved in such a fashion is not a comfortable thing, and there are hands that will not bear such heat as a sun, casually given.

And so the beloved turned from her. He told her that her stone heart was cold, and that he craved a heart of warmth. He told her that love was not a queen set above him, but someone who would look at him as if he ruled.

And she was proud, and she was a queen, and she would not do those things, even for something called love, for to do so meant unbecoming who she was.

He walked away and did not look back. He thought nothing of her ever again, for who can break a heart of stone?

The queen made a vow: that her heart was hers, and that she would never again give it. It was a vow she kept all her days, though she kept always by her side one who would play, for her sake, at love. Not the same one, of course, never that. She changed them after a night, after a season, after seven years.

After and after, the stone-hearted queen died. And her heart of stone was taken from the opened cage of her body, so that it might be a monument to her passing. But when it was picked up, it shattered into a thousand, thousand pieces, as if it were tears, or uncountable grains of sand.

17

Snow blanketed Melete. Drifts heaped against the walls of the houses. The onion-domed red roof looked even more like it grew there after a photograph of Russia had been planted in New Hampshire.

When I stepped off the path, I sank deep enough that snow threatened to crest the tops of my boots. I wobbled as I walked, holding my arms out for balance. Once I got closer to Evan's studio, there was a partially broken trail, and I shuffled my way through that.

I stomped the excess snow from my boots on his doorstep, and looked up to see orange-berried branches hanging from the gutters. "Is that some weird version of mistletoe?"

"No, but I'm happy to kiss you under it," he said, dropping me back in an exaggerated swoon of a kiss. Flushed and laughing, I followed him inside.

The air in the studio smelled scorched, and I looked around to see if there was something new he was working on. There were shapes, obscured with drop cloths, impossible to discern.

He tracked my gaze. "I thought you were interested in seeing my older work."

"Don't worry, I wasn't going to ask. I don't love letting people see works in progress, either." And I was here to see his older work, the art he had made before going to Faerie.

What Ariel said, about being there changing a person's art, had been a hitch in my thoughts. Beth hadn't published anything before the book she started while she was here and finished in Faerie, and I had no desire to read Janet's poetry. But I liked Evan's art, and he was still in the same studio that he'd been assigned when he arrived as a fellow. So I could compare.

He led me through the trees I had seen before, and I was struck again by the lonely beauty of them. Then further, into the back of the studio, where drop cloths had been undraped and pushed aside. "Here they are."

They weren't metal. Marble sculpture, creatures emerging half-formed, as if in the process of birthing themselves from that cool, unforgiving stone. A falcon in spread-winged flight, an uncoiling serpent, a herd of horses rising from the foam of a wave. All of them small scale, a feast of detail.

"Why the change?" I asked.

"I wanted something barer. Stripped down, more essential. Plus, I wanted to let my art take up space."

I could see that. The newer pieces, the metal ones, had no softness to them, nothing extra. They stood in front of you and forced you to feel. The marble pieces could simply be seen as beauty. The emotion was there, but it required the viewer to put her own story— escape, birth, emergence—on top of them.

The older pieces were beautiful; the new ones were alive.

"Do you ever think you'd go back to your old style?"

"I'm not that person anymore. And yes, I'm sure being in Faerie changed me. Just like Tania's death did. And so did all the small things that have happened over the course of nearly seven years. It might not have shown up as drastically in my art, but things would still be different even if I hadn't gone. Do you want to be writing the same thing in seven years as you are now?"

"Of course not," I said. "I want to be better."

"Exactly. And better means pushing yourself. Trying new things. I know you were hoping for a clear answer, but I can't tell you what kind of art I'd be making if I had been somewhere other than Faerie for the past seven years, Imogen. I'd have to be able to erase them to do that."

That was always the catch. Your past came with you to your art whether you wanted it to or not. It haunted you. If you had a fraught past, it was the question you always considered, and always had asked of you—would you change it, if you could? Would you trade bad for good, or even for normal, knowing that if you did, the things that mattered to you now might disappear along with the evils of the past?

I started writing as an escape, as an act of defiance. If I hadn't had a childhood that had driven me so far into stories, that might never have happened. But I liked who I had become, and I was proud of my writing. Take away one thing, and maybe I don't get the other. I couldn't answer the question of who I would be without my past. So I had part of my answer.

Then there were the questions I couldn't ask Evan, like what kind of a person he had been before Faerie. Though, in a way, his answer would be the same. Seven years different from the person he was now, and the time in Faerie was only part of the reason why.

For now, that was enough. I reached up and kissed him. Evan pulled me closer, fisting his hands in my shirt, and deepened the kiss. I sank into it, losing myself in the sensations. "I've missed you, too," I said. "Come stay with me tonight."

"Stay with me now," he said. "Let me show you how much I want you." His hands moved over my skin, and he kissed his way down the cord of my neck.

"Yes," I breathed into his mouth. We took each other in the shadows of the forest he had made.

I didn't feel the cold as I walked home.

I opened the front door to the warm vanilla-cinnamon smell of cookies baking. Music played. Ariel hit the high notes in "All I Want for Christmas Is You." The mixer whirred. In the time I had been gone, someone had wound a garland of silver tinsel, gaudy and sparkling, around the banister, and decorated it with red and green glass balls. I hung my coat on a hook next to the door and wandered into the kitchen.

It wasn't just Ariel baking—Helena was there as well, a Santa Claus hat providing a terrific contrast to the bright fuchsia of her hair.

"Give me a job," I said, while washing my hands, "I'm ready to help. Helena, I love your hat."

She jerked away from whatever she had been stirring, looked at me. "You're serious. Okay. I wasn't sure if we were dressing up, so I just got a hat. I've never done something like this. Janet doesn't care for holidays."

"I'm serious. It's great." I rolled the dough Ariel passed me into balls, then dented the cookies, so there was a place for the chocolate kiss that would be baked on top.

Baking together had been Ariel's idea. Her family had done it growing up. "Because there were always like twenty cousins wandering around, and my mom figured she might as well put us to work. Harder to get in trouble if you're rolling dough or spreading frosting. And she gave cookies to everyone—the delivery guys, our teachers, our priest—so she always had a ton that needed baking. End of the day, we'd all be flour-covered messes, but it was fun. The four of us need fun."

She was right. The ocean of unrelieved white through the windows looked more like an alien landscape than a Currier and Ives print. The blizzard had socked us in the house and made everything tight and claustrophobic. For the first few days after, we hadn't been able to escape the house, or each other. Tempers had frayed.

Marin was sure that Janet was lying to Helena about the tithe. "I asked Gavin. He told me things don't work like that, that it can't be used to bargain for anything beyond success. Even if it could, Faerie would have had no reason to mess around in Thomas and Janet's relationship, because there was no gain in it."

It was a cold way of putting things, but the calculatedness of it was also why I believed Gavin. "Beth said something similar. I'm starting to think that Janet could give our mother a run for the money in the awful-parent department."

"Seriously. She never even asked if Helena could be sent out of Faerie after she was born, or if there was some way to protect her while she was there. I get that maybe Janet never wanted to be pregnant, but the Fae could have undone that, if she had asked. She just didn't care. I don't think she's ever started caring."

Marin came in wearing red and green parti-colored tights. "Helena! I love your hat."

"Everyone does, I guess."

Ariel caught my eye and shook her head at Helena's response. Prickly as usual, but she was here, and cooking, and not starting fights with anyone, and I even heard her singing along under her breath to a couple of the carols.

It was a good day. Five kinds of cookies and two kinds of fudge dissipated the tension that had filled the house since the night of the blizzard. Helena had even smiled at Marin, and laughed when

Ariel pronounced the event "a Christmas miracle." It wasn't a miracle, but it was, quietly, enough.

Beth was going to be away from Melete over the holidays. "I apologize for abandoning you like this—usually I stay all the way through once I've made the commitment, but my daughter just had a daughter. This is her first child, and my first grandchild, so I'm going to stay with them, to help out and celebrate."

"Oh, that's lovely. Congratulations." Strange to say the words and mean them, to think of a family visit as something associated with celebration, but Beth's face was full of joy. There were piles of completed knitting—blankets, beanies—stacked up around the room, ready to be packed. I shoved aside my envy, and the thought that if I ever had a child, I would do everything in my power to make sure that my mother never got near her.

"Please don't hesitate to get in touch if you need anything. I mean that. Same email and cell phone as when I'm here. The holidays always bring their own complications with them, and sometimes remaining in residence can aggravate those complications. It's okay if you change your mind and go home."

My hand clenched into a claw at my side. I breathed in, out, willing myself to relax. Picked up my mug of coffee, drank. Beth and I didn't discuss my life outside of Melete. As far as I was concerned, there was no need to unless some part of it turned into something that interfered with my work here. So I didn't tell her that I knew all about the fraughtness of the holidays, and Christmas in particular. I had been eleven the year my mother took my Christmas kitten back to the shelter, telling me she had them put it to sleep immediately, because I hadn't gotten dressed in my Christmas dress. She hadn't bought me a new one, and the previous year's had been a size too small. The zipper burst when I put it on for dinner, and so I had put on a dress that fit, knowing it was the wrong decision, and also knowing that there wasn't a right one.

Marin had looked up the phone number for the shelter, held my hand while I called, while I wept out the story on the phone to the kind woman who told me, "No, dear, of course we don't put down healthy kittens. That ball of fuzz went to a good home today." I still cried myself to sleep that night, but at least I stopped feeling like a murderer.

When I was a freshman in high school, thirteen, I had the lead in the local Christmas program. It was the first time my mother had ever told me she was proud of me. She couldn't wait until I was on the stage, where everyone would be able to see that she had two talented daughters. "And you both get it from me," she had simpered.

I was so terrified that I would somehow do something wrong and make her angry, that I had a panic attack and collapsed onstage. When we got back to the house, she threw all of the notebooks of stories I had written onto the fire. If I hadn't spent all my time making things up, she said, maybe I would have been prepared for the play, and I wouldn't have embarrassed her.

I cried out as they burned, and Marin reached in, trying to save them. She burned her hand, and my mother had slapped her, for "interfering in something your sister has brought on herself." It was the one time I had ever seen her strike Marin.

As we both stood in shock, our mother grabbed my hand, my right hand, the one that I wrote with, and held it in the fire. Holding it as it burned, as I screamed. "You have to learn to do as I say. I've told you and told you, and obviously that hasn't made an impression. I'm only doing this for your own good."

Red. Blisters. An agony of pain. My breath whistled in gasps. I couldn't speak.

She let go.

"Now, Marin, let's get you to the hospital, where they can take care of the damage your sister caused. We don't want you to scar—that wouldn't look right onstage." Our mother gathered her keys, her purse. "Let's go."

"But Imogen—she needs to go, too. More than me."

"Your sister is going to stay here and think about what she's done."

"But—"

"Marin." I swallowed down a sob. "Just go."

That was the year I started looking for boarding schools, and saving my babysitting money to pay the application fees. I worried about leaving Marin, but I thought it might actually kill me if I stayed.

It was the year I learned to write left-handed, and to get even better at hiding things, and keeping secrets.

My hand clenched harder, shook, and coffee spilled over the rim of the mug. Breath hissed out through my teeth.

"Imogen! Are you all right?" Beth leaned forward, her knitting loose in her hands. "I didn't realize the coffee was so hot."

I breathed out again, setting the mug on the floor before my trembling made the spill worse. "No, it's fine. Scar tissue is just more sensitive. I wasn't paying attention." There was nothing she needed to know. More to the point, there was nothing the Fae needed to know.

Cutting off the questions I could see forming on her face, I shook my hand out, smiled. "But there's no need for me to go home this year. Marin and I are staying—we'll have Christmas together. I'm really looking forward to a quiet holiday."

"Well, that does sound lovely." She let the questions go, leaned back, her knitting needles moving again.

"Is that a stocking for your granddaughter?" I could stay. We could finish the conversation. Most of the pain was in the past, not in my hand. I stretched my fingers along the outside of my thigh, steadying the shaking.

"Silly, I know. But I couldn't resist. Family and the holidays." She looked at me.

I smiled. "That's why I'm staying with Marin."

"You know, Imogen, I wasn't sure how it would work out, the two of you here together. I'm glad you're so close, such a support for each other. But there's something I'd like you to think about: If you're chosen as the tithe, will you be able to leave Marin and go?"

The pain in my hand was almost bearable. "Of course," I said. "She'd want me to."

I was, at least, certain about the first part.

The Night Market returned at the winter solstice, darkly glittering in its beauty. The trees were hung with silver bells that chimed when the wind brushed against them, sending the night singing. A fire burned in the center of the Commons, the Yule fire, to chase away the long darkness, and welcome back the sun.

The air was fragrant with the warmth of roasting chestnuts, the resin green of pine, the smoke of incense rich beneath it. Under the moon, the snow sparkled like fragments of a mirror, and crunched beneath my feet as I walked through booths draped in greens, the brilliant red of holly berries, the waxen white of mistletoe.

"For you."

I turned toward the voice, and out of the corner of my eye I glimpsed feathers falling through the air like snowflakes, eyes as sharp as an owl's. I breathed in the cinnamon and spice of the cup she held out, and the illusion melted away. A dark-haired woman wearing a feathery white scarf stood in front of me.

"A toast to the season," she said.

I sipped at the cider. "Thank you."

The cup was warm in my hands as I walked through carved sculptures of snow and ice. They made me think of the residents of Narnia, turned into statues in the endless winter. I had read the entire series to Marin when she had the chicken pox. Always winter, and never Christmas. But this was winter frozen in beauty, and I didn't want to break its spell. For all the glory of Aslan's reign, his return is when Narnia's death begins.

Sleigh bells rang in the distance, and a group of people sang carols in front of the Yule fire. I thought I recognized Ariel's voice in the harmonies, one of the angels, chorusing on high.

I walked into a booth shining with crystal and glass. Figures and fantasies, carved and spun and captured. Ice made unmelting, tears preserved. A constellation of stars, hung from ribbons of blue velvet, shading from the pale almost-white of thin milk to the richness of the midnight sky.

"How much for these?" I asked.

The man tending the booth lifted them down with wrinkled hands. "Nothing for you."

"Please. They're a gift."

"Bad luck to those who take your money." He spread them out on a black cloth. Each star was different in size and radiance. I stretched my hand toward them, then pulled it back and shook my head.

"Let her pay," Gavin said behind me. "The prohibition is lifted for this."

The older man bowed to Gavin, and named a price. Dear, but worth it. I gave him the money.

"Thank you," I said to Gavin. "They're for Marin. It wouldn't have felt right to give them to her, if they had been free."

"I understand," he said. "Some things matter more when there's a cost."

The bells rang again, louder this time. Not just the silver jingles, or the motion of sleigh bells. Church bells, deep and sacred. Warning bells, hung from the heights of walls of ancient cities. Ringing in time, and out of it.

Clear and crystalline as the air, deep as the darkness, reverberating through the night. The sound pulled, a hook in my heart. I longed to follow it, to walk into the night and the snow until I could surround myself in the music. It wasn't until the bells went silent and I felt frost on my cheeks that I realized I had been weeping.

"It's a powerful thing," Gavin said. "The turning of the year, and the return of the sun." He handed me the package I had forgotten in the echoes of the bells. "Marin's gift."

I nodded my thanks, not trusting my voice. The bells hadn't only been proclaiming the return of the sun, but the end of something, too. The past, burned away in the Yule fire. I hadn't heard celebration in their ringing. I had heard an elegy.

There was a letter from Evan when I got home, wrapped with mistletoe, its berries waxen white. Promises of kisses, and a gift for the season. Promises for when we would see each other, the next time Faerie loosed him from its grip. Words that made me wish for him as I climbed into the winter-cold sheets of my bed.

Wakefulness drove me from it later. Piled under blankets, I was drenched in sweat, and when I sat up, the walls of my room pressed too close. I put my jacket on over my pajamas and went outside to the porch.

Through the night, a horse galloped—whiter than the snow, whiter than the moon. Snow heaved up from his strides and fell again like stardust. Holly was braided into his mane, deep green leaves and berries red as blood. I felt the same ache in my heart as I had listening to the solstice bells, and longed to run after the horse, to follow. To ride once more along the bounds of Faerie and pay the tithe so that I might pass through them.

18

Melete ushered in the new year with an enormous glitter of a party. Black-tie and champagne, cut-glass chandeliers, and mirrored walls to reflect every sharp-edged sparkle back on the attendees. Lavish enough to remind us that we weren't just some sort of pocket outpost for Faerie, but also a place that had been home to a deep pool of artistic talent—talent that had very wealthy friends.

I embraced the invitation to glamour and slunk into a silver shimmer of a dress, lined my eyes black, and painted my lips wine-red. When I saw Evan, I was glad I had gone to the effort.

He was wearing a tuxedo, but his shirt was embroidered all over, white on starker white, with a pattern that shifted and changed beneath my gaze. On his head, the coronet of tarnished silver he had been wearing on Halloween, bent and curved like thorns. There was a sort of haze around him, making him look backlit, carved in relief.

"You look . . . ," I said, searching for words the rightness of which seemed peculiarly to matter.

"Yes?"

"Like a sacrifice." The truth fell from my mouth like a stone.

"Ah. Gavin has dropped the glamour. This should be an interesting night." Evan held out his hand, and I put mine in it.

I understood what he meant when we walked into the party. All of the impossibility of the ride through Faerie brought together in a ballroom. All pretense that the Fae were human had been let fall like veils. It was quite clear that they were anything but. We had stepped sideways from the mundane, moved elsewhere from the ordinary.

Eyes like the darkness and bones too sharp. Horns that spiraled from brows and hair made of feathers, made of flowers, made of butterfly wings. Skin scaled like a serpent's. Still beautiful, even when they weren't. The Fae drew the eye until looking away was the pain of heartbreak, a pool of loss.

Everything looked dull, contrasted with their wild glory. Even Melete looked less than golden and perfect. The cracks in the paint, the scratches on the floors glared, as if the presence of the Fae was too great to bear. For the first time since I arrived, Melete seemed pale, ordinary. Mortal. The Fae were impossible, and they were the most real piece of the night.

Even knowing what I did about the tithe, about what dwelling too long in Faerie could do to a person, I understood why the world was full of stories of people who had worn themselves into nothingness, into death, in search of the thing that would let them stay in Faerie forever. Who had tasted Faerie food and starved themselves to death waiting for a second bite. It would be so easy to let myself go, and do the same.

Beneath the voices, beneath the music, beneath the champagne fizz and crystal chime of glass, the ticking of a clock. A counting down. Change. Ending.

"Will you dance with me?" Evan asked.

I nodded, and he pulled me into his arms. For a minute, two, three, that dance was all there was. His hands guiding as we turned across the floor, my feet in steps so old they could have been a ritual, a conjuring. The awareness of skin and the distance between it. I wanted him like breath.

The song changed, and the enchantment broke. Somewhere, a clock grew louder.

As we danced, I looked around at all the unfamiliar faces, women and men, polished and groomed and in elegant clothes. Melete's donors. The gallery owners and the angels of the theater. Editors of white-shoe presses that spent their summer Fridays in the Hamptons. The ordinary ones, though not a one of them would have thought themselves such. "What will they remember tomorrow?"

"Some will convince themselves this was a masked ball," Evan said. "Others will half-remember what they saw, and laugh about the eccentricities of artists. There will be those who remember the entire thing clearly, but blame it on an excess of drink or drugs. One or two will see it for what it truly is. They will never forget, and they will never speak of it."

He spun me out, back in, dizzying turns.

"The rest of us," he added, "will simply have a good time."

"Do they remember Gavin, what he is, when they see him dance?"

"It's part of the glamour. He's larger than life onstage, not himself. The people who meet him, either here or there, they already expect him to be half-magic, so they don't think about whether he might be more than that."

We turned again, and I stopped, gasped. "Oh my God, is that Davina Harrison?" The tiny dark-haired woman talking to Gavin was enough of a presence to distract even from the Fae. Which was only to be expected from someone who'd won three Oscars and two Tonys in the past decade. No, I realized as I did the math. Not quite a decade.

"It is, and I should say hello. She was the tithe before me. Here— I'll introduce you."

Davina's eyes landed on my necklace during Evan's introductions.

"A writer," she said. "How lovely. Come tell me a story." She tucked my arm in hers and stepped away from Evan, away from the periphery of people trying to catch her eye.

"Will you go?" she asked.

No need to ask where. "Yes."

"Good. Time is always too short not to grab onto anything that brings what you want closer. And there's no sin in ambition, just denying it." Her voice like honey, like whiskey, and no wonder people wrote plays as prayers that she would star in them.

"Are you glad you went? I've heard it can be hard."

"Anything in life worth having is hard to earn." She plucked glasses off of a passing tray. "Even for someone like her."

I followed her glance. Marin was all in red, the firebird, the phoenix's flame. As she and Gavin danced, the shadows of antlers branched over his head. When they moved together, it was like magic. Not the magic of Faerie, or of spells and incantations, but the magic of art, which transmutes difficulty into ease, which steals the eye and breaks the heart. The magic that gives the lie to reality. Already half-magic, Evan had said of Gavin, but even without being Fae, Marin was, too.

"She's my sister."

There was pity, then, in Davina's eyes. "Well, I wish you both the best of luck."

The clock, louder still, its count the echo of a great hidden heart.

I danced with Ariel, who was looking Dietrichesque in a tux that clung to her like honey. "I'll give the Fae this," she said. "They throw a hell of a party."

"Do you know—"

She laid her finger on my lips, silencing my question. "Haven't decided. I'm not thinking about any of that tonight. Tonight is for champagne and dancing with pretty girls and gorgeous boys and the fabulous Fae. It's for celebrating, and for stealing kisses."

Smiling, she leaned in and kissed me, and I could taste the champagne on her mouth. "Happy New Year, Imogen."

"Happy New Year, Ariel."

Still the clock. Something ending. Almost. Not yet.

The candleflames crept higher, and the shadows deepened.

"I would dance with you, if you will." The man wore unrelieved black, his hands covered by gloves of smooth leather. His eyes were black too, entirely so. Fae.

"Of course," I said, and put my hands in his.

He moved like coiled shadows, and his touch burned my skin like ice, even through the gloves. He was all I could see as we danced, him and the lights reflected in the drowning pools of his eyes. My feet followed his steps as though all other paths were barred to me.

"I have always wondered why you humans celebrate time's passing, when you yourselves have so little of it," he said.

"Maybe that's why we celebrate," I said. "Because we're still here."

He cocked his head, a snake watching prey. The nerves at the back of my skull told me to flee before that regard. My heart fluttered like a dying bird.

"Or maybe we just like the champagne."

He laughed, and his laughter echoed in my head. "I like the shape your words make. You are such a little piece of time. I can make you take up more of it."

The floor spun from under me. I was falling, falling, falling.

The room, the lights, the party were gone.

Only black as I fell, a veil spun from nothing wrapping me like cerements. Spinning into emptiness, unmoored from myself, slipping out of my skin. Coldness crept, ice-like, into the gaps in me, crackling along the emptiness, hoarfrost, and desolation.

Falling. Forever.

Ice in my blood. In my soul.

Curling through the darkness, the scent of a forest. Sharp and green, bright resin and rich loam. A white stag, horns climbing from its brow. Spring sending shoots through my veins.

The call of a horn, and the blackness split and cracked.

Floor, solid, beneath my feet.

Words in a language I did not speak, burning the air. Hands pulling me back into my skin, into a body needled with frostbite.

I opened my eyes.

"If you kept us better fed, we would not hunger so on our own." He spat the words at Gavin, blood the color of tarnish dripping from his mouth.

"And I have told you that you will not cross out of our bounds unless you control your hunger. You will go from this place, now, and you will not return." Gavin was something dread and terrible, his bones electric beneath his skin.

A clock chimed. The air vibrated like lightning had passed through unseen, and all around the smell of leaf mold and pine needles, the mineral coldness of river waters foaming white over rocks, the musk of running animals.

A burst of rot and a smear across the air and lights so bright against my eyes that I stumbled.

And my hands were caught in Gavin's, and the room was only music and the clink of glasses and the song of a hundred small conversations. Candleflames and champagne and dancing. "You are well?" he asked.

My feet followed his through the turn of a waltz. "Yes," I said, and in saying it, I was, the word a spell of its own.

"Forgive me," he said, bowing his head, the horns still reaching like a crown. "That should not have happened."

Brushing it off meant everything was fine. "It would hardly be a party if at least one of the guests didn't misbehave."

He smiled, but there was tightness in it, and his eyes were dark and far away.

The music slowed, and I danced with Evan again, holding on, leaning in to him, letting the warmth of his body call to me. For the small eternity of the song, he was all there was, his heartbeat beneath my own, the cedar and sandalwood scent of his skin surrounding me. Here, now, real.

The clock ticked forward. All of the clocks, an echo of time itself.

Clocks were everywhere—fixed on the walls, set in the centers of tables, hanging on the very air. There was no escape from the marked time, no way to avert eyes from its passing.

Trays glided through the crowd, carrying glasses full of champagne, a universe of effervescing stars. A hand, red-gloved, plucked a glass, and then the rest of the woman bloomed out of the air in front of me. The scent of roses was everywhere. I tasted it on my tongue like liquor. "Are you having a good time?" she asked, voice lingering over the last word.

"I'm certainly having an interesting one," I said.

"You hold your truth as if you were one of us, weighing its value in scales so as not to spend too much of it." Words bloomed like ink over her skin as she spoke. "I had an artist before. A painter. Mediocre. You, though." She stroked her hand down my throat. "You might be more useful. Would you like to be my artist?"

A painter before. The story Marin had told me months ago,

about the painter who had left Melete, unworthy of his muse. I didn't want to be anyone's, but I also didn't want to piss her off. "You do me great honor."

"I know." She clinked the rim of her glass to mine. "Think on it. Anything written can be changed."

She walked away, and I felt like I had escaped.

Janet stood separate, like a shadow, her dress the same medieval green gown as the stained-glass woman hanging over the door of her house. She had wrapped herself in reserve, but her eyes watched the Fae like they were holy and she had come here on pilgrimage.

I bumped into her on my way out of the restroom, and she grabbed my arm, hard enough to leave bruises. "They would give you such power over them, and you don't even see it. You are as much of a failure as my daughter."

She yanked her hand back and pushed past me, but she was the least of what I cared about, so I didn't ask, didn't follow. I slid back into the glamoured shine of the party.

Helena and Gavin danced, her hair the only bright spot atop a dress that was a column of stark black. Her face was so pale as to be nearly translucent, and I thought I saw tears sparkle on her cheeks. But she danced with him until the end of the song, and did not look at Janet as she walked away from her, after.

The clocks became more insistent, and the people in the crowd called out numbers, encouraging the new year in. As if, without our voices, time might stop.

Three.

Two.

One.

The striking of the clock and the kisses and the golden sparkle of the wine. Glasses smashed to the floor and the mirrored reflection of the night stretching on until forever. Faces bright and wild. Skin flushed with lust and alcohol. Cheers and celebration and loss beneath it. The death of one time, to usher in the next. The Fae, feral and beautiful. And hungry.

Waiting.

A new year.

19

Bleary-eyed and still recovering from the New Year's celebrations, I stumbled into the kitchen. Water was running, and the air smelled like sulfur and soap. Helena stood hunched over the sink.

She shut the water off. "I didn't burn the eggs on purpose, if that's what you were wondering."

I hadn't been. Her eyes were red, last night's makeup raccooned around them. "Helena, are you okay?"

"She named me that because of *A Midsummer Night's Dream*, you know." Her voice was harsh and cracked.

"I didn't," I said. "Can I make you coffee? I'm desperate for some."

She nodded, sat down. "Because Helena was the one of the four mortal lovers who caught Oberon's eye. He felt sorry for her, so he told Puck to help her. It all goes wrong, of course—Janet didn't think about that part, I guess—but that was what I was supposed to be. Someone who would be pathetic enough that the Fae would offer to help."

I set a mug down in front of her. She didn't touch it.

"I was almost fourteen the first time we rode into Faerie. I thought it would be an adventure. All the books at Janet's have stories about Faerie in them. She's obsessed. With them. With the place. But, like, not with the stories where the fairies will rip your heart out for breathing wrong. The ones where they're the most

- 1 7 9 -

beautiful, and the most perfect, and just waiting to share their gifts with the chosen one. You know how those stories are."

I did know. Full of happily ever afters and fairies who could be tamed with a dish of milk left out overnight or by speaking their true name. Pretty stories. Easy ones. Nothing helpful, nothing true. "So I'm guessing no Angela Carter."

A laugh tore from her throat. "No. Not so much. I didn't even know those stories existed until after I'd been to Faerie.

"So I thought Faerie would be great. The best. I wanted to go. By that point, I knew I had been born there, and so I'd built up this story in my head that my dad was Fae. Told myself that was the reason that I'd never met him. Because he couldn't live here. I thought maybe he'd recognize me that night, tell me I could stay, live with him. Learn magic. All the stuff you think when you're thirteen, and stuck with a mom who doesn't love you.

"Once I got there . . ." She closed her eyes, swallowed. "Well. It's not like the stories. Not the nice ones, anyway."

Helena went silent. I reached out, pulled my hand back when she continued. "But we got back, and Janet explained to me about how the beautiful woman I met that night, the one at the head of the riders, was the Faerie Queen, and she had stolen my dad away. That she had made a bargain with Janet, and that I was the key to winning him back.

"I believed her."

"Of course you did," I said. "You were a teenager. She's your mom."

She reached for her mug, and it skidded from her hand. "Then she told me how I could get him back, what I had to do. Be the tithe, prove myself, and it would break Tania's spell.

"I've been trying all my life to be able to do that, to make it so he can love Janet again, and come back, and I can get to know him, and it turns out that I'm an idiot, and pretty much everything she's told me is a lie."

"That's what you and Gavin were talking about?" I asked. "You know what, I'm hungry. Let me see what I can make."

I wasn't. Even the idea of food was enough to make my stomach contemplate rebellion, but Helena was pulled in on herself and shaking, and I thought food might help. "French toast?"

"Yeah, okay."

I beat the eggs and milk together. "What made you believe him?"

"Oh, he wasn't the one who told me. She did. While you were dancing with that creepy guy who almost—what did happen?"

"Awful." I shuddered. "Don't ask." Back home in my room, I hadn't been able to bear the darkness. Every time I closed my eyes, I was falling again. Slipping away into nothing. I'd put all the lights on, slept in fits and starts.

"Anyway. She was watching, and said that I needed to be more like you and your 'whore sister'—sorry, I don't think that about Marin anymore, but it's what Janet said—and put myself in their way. Flirt. Whatever. Look how Gavin had come to your rescue when you needed it. My talent clearly wasn't enough to make me anything other than mediocre, and being mediocre wouldn't break the Faerie Queen's curse."

"That's really gross," I said, and set the french toast on the table. "Here's the syrup."

"There was a Fae woman near us, who had been one of Tania's best friends. She was furious at Janet for what she said about Tania, and said the tithe didn't work like that, that it couldn't, and that Tania wouldn't have needed magic to take any man she wanted, certainly not from someone like Janet.

"Then she did something to Janet that made her have to speak the truth. All of the truth. The whole thing about me being able to save Thomas, break the curse—it was a lie. She lied to me, she said, because she knew from the beginning that I was untalented and worthless, a waste of her time.

"She said she was trying to motivate me, to make me something other than ordinary, and she thought if she gave me a nice story, maybe I'd try harder. But as it had turned out, even with two parents who had been good enough to live in Faerie for seven years, I was still nothing.

"And don't tell me that was a lie, too, because all of that was forced out of her. So." She stabbed at her french toast, set her fork down without eating.

"Just because she believes it, doesn't make it true, Helena."

"That's what Gavin said, too." Helena smiled, but her eyes were blank, lost. "Thing is, it also doesn't mean it's not. Because that was the other thing I asked him. About the hourglasses. Why she couldn't just give me one. So now I know that if I were good enough, as good as you or Marin, it wouldn't matter what Janet thought.

"I'd have one."

Once upon a time, there was a girl who lived in a house made of mirrors. Every surface showed her reflection: the walls, the floors, the ceiling. She lived there alone, but never felt as if she were, surrounded by so many copies of herself.

With so many selves around, the girl did not notice at first when they began changing. Small things, at the start. A reflection that moved a blink before she did, or one that turned left when she turned right.

Even when she did notice, when the reflections began to walk into a room before she did, when they sat still as she moved, or

ROSES AND ROT

moved when she did not, the girl was not concerned. Reflections, after all, are lies, not true selves. These were just lying more than they had in the past.

The girl knew that she was true. She was real. Blood and bone and breath, not just someone else's reflection, light and air, only visible if someone else was looking.

But air is the same as breath, and who is to say who is seen, and who is not?

But then. But then.

The reflections began to leave the house of mirrors. To walk away from rooms the girl was in, and never to come back. They left, they disappeared, and yet she was still there.

The girl began to feel diminished. To feel as if she was the lie that was cast by the reflections. She felt alone, uncertain of what to do.

She wanted them to come back, those other selves, even changed as they were. To return with the pieces of her that might change their hair, or wear a different color, or dance when everyone in the room was sitting. She once had all of those pieces inside of her, she knew it.

But without her reflections, the girl felt unseen. And so she sat, very small and very still, in the corner of a room, watching as she disappeared from all the mirrors in it. Watching as she disappeared.

Once upon a time, there was a reflection who finally broke free of her mirrors. Perhaps that story ended with a happily ever after.

Perhaps.

Perhaps the only happily ever after is to survive to tell the story.

- 183 -

20

I sat next to the window in the train, a silver snake winding its way through the dingy white that was late January in the Northeast. Stark skeletons of trees and near-untouched woods alternated with parking lots and industrial equipment as the train churned on.

Evan had a gallery show in New York. Someone from Drowned Meadow had been at Melete and seen the carousel he had made. The gallery had been established a hundred years ago, and only three other artists had ever had their premiere solo show there, he told me.

"This is it, Imogen—it's beginning. Everything I've worked for. Will you come down? I want you to see it."

I said I would, of course; borrowed Ariel's leather pants to wear to the opening, packed an overnight bag, and got on a train.

It crossed a bridge, concrete and rusting metal, the water moving sluggishly beneath. Nothing at all like the fantasies of bridges guarding the Mourning River's clear, dark waters. This was a bridge connected to a city, not to a fairy tale.

I watched the other people on the train. Men and women in dark suits, arranging their faces in expressions of seriousness as they checked the screens of electronic devices. A teenage girl with tiny braids dyed the entire spectrum of the rainbow and glitter on her eyelids danced in her seat to whatever music she heard through her headphones. A harried young woman—older sister or nanny,

I thought—tried to keep two boys from menacing the rest of the passengers with their superhero action figures, and was told "You can't put Batman in time-out!" It seemed a valid point.

The other passengers seemed strange to me, almost unreal, all so far removed from the bubble of art I had been living in for the past few months. I wondered what they would sacrifice to have a different life, what they would trade seven years for. There's always a shinier office, a bigger promotion, a more prestigious title. Ambition and talent dress themselves up in all sorts of clothes—a dancer's pointe shoes, a doctor's white coat, a CEO's Louboutins.

The train rumbled through the city, and the car filled with reminders to take all children and belongings with you when you disembarked. People clutched bags, shrugged back into coats, arranged faces into the careful blank stare best suited to negotiating the crowds of New York City, a place where the Fae could gallop through Times Square and only the tourists would blink.

The train pulled into the stench and grime and chaos of Penn Station. There would be a car, Evan had said, sent by the gallery to bring me to the hotel. "They're hinting at offering an exclusive contract, not just one show, but long-term, so they're trying to impress me, and I'm fine with letting them." On the way to the exit, I stopped.

There was a girl dancing. Her skin was dark, rich against the red fabric that she wore, tank and pants and wrapped around her head. She turned fouettés as if her pointe shoe was nailed to the floor, as the boy sitting next to her tore through a cello rendition of "Smells Like Teen Spirit."

Entertain us.

I watched until the song finished, then dropped a couple of dollars in the open cello case. They were already moving into the next song, but she caught my eye, and nodded slightly. I wondered again—what would they trade, if offered the chance? Or maybe being there, New York Penn Station, getting paid for their art, was itself a piece of a dream that had come true.

The car was waiting, and I slid into the lush quiet of it, already a different world from the stink and closeness of the train station, from the snaking line of business travelers and tourists waiting for cabs, hoping to snag one before the threatened rain became actual.

The car stopped in front of an elegant building a few blocks from the New York Public Library. "You're already checked in, miss. Key and room number are inside this folder, and my card if you find you want to go anywhere or you need anything. I'll be back to pick you up for the opening later this evening. You're a guest of Drowned Meadow while you're here, and I'm pleased to be at your service."

They really were trying to woo Evan. For a mad moment, I wanted to ask for something truly outrageous—the address of an underground nightclub, or the most expensive drink in the city, delivered to me in under an hour. A couture gown and shoes that would outsparkle Cinderella's. Something magic. But then I recovered myself, tipped the driver, and walked through the hotel's discreetly opened front doors.

As a gallery, Drowned Meadow went for tradition and subtlety. No polished concrete, no exposed ductwork, no hot-and-cold-running beautiful people passing drinks and ornate food. Instead, it was all dark wood and burgundy accents, precise lighting and plushness. Quiet, restrained, and, like a vampire, confident in its own power and immortality.

I was brought straight to Evan when I arrived. He kissed me once, hard. "Let me show you the sculptures."

There wasn't the space to set them up in the full carousel, so they were scattered through the different rooms of the gallery. A couple of new pieces, too—birds in flight, a phoenix rising. "Some of them have already sold." Evan's eyes glittered, his color high.

"Congratulations," I said, watching the people who angled themselves away from the art to watch the artist walk through. Sharp-cut suits and architectural dresses, all high-shine polish, their eyes almost as hungry as the Fae in Faerie. "Though, if your commission was from Gavin, how can the work be sold?"

"A percentage goes to Melete, and of course, the publicity is very good for them. He said it helped maintain the balance of things, with my being elsewhere."

I nodded as if all freelance work had magical elements that needed negotiating. "Well, Drowned Meadow has certainly done a gorgeous job with the presentation. You'll sign with them?" It seemed a logical choice. The gallery had turned the building into a stage, illuminating Evan's work. The people in attendance reeked of influence.

"Maybe. I have other options. People have been calling and setting up meetings. Even if I do sign here, I might be able to leverage something."

"Must be nice to be so wanted." I smiled.

"It is."

A woman cut across our path, her dress pleated and gathered at the precise angles of origami folds. "Evan, you said that if the dragon sold, you wanted to meet the buyer."

"Excuse me, Imogen." He kissed my cheek and walked away, the woman walking just in front of him as they passed through the gallery, a herald announcing a king.

"It's not just him they're wooing, you know."

"Excuse me?" I didn't turn from the sculpture to see who was speaking.

"This. The excess. The success. It's not just for him. He's already theirs. They're trying to impress you, too."

"I'm sorry, I don't know what you're talking about."

"You do. Because it was me in your shoes, say about twenty-eight years ago."

I did turn then, and I recognized him. The man who had designed the museum that people were still arguing over. Thomas Greene. Helena's father. Not in a suit, but in the artist's uniform of expensive black T-shirt and jeans. He wore his charisma casually, the lines in his face and silver at his temples adding interest. Helena had his smile.

"But how?" My hand went to my throat, closing around words I couldn't speak.

"Pronouns, darling. They can refer to a gallery and its minions just as easily as"—he reached out, traced his finger under the chain around my neck, the dangling hourglass—"something else.

"So, are you this year's girl?"

"I'm sorry. I hadn't realized you'd gotten divorced again."

He grinned. "A palpable hit! But you know that's not what I meant."

I knew. "Maybe. Maybe it's someone else. Like, I don't know, your daughter."

"Now if that one was supposed to wound, you need to take better aim. Why should I be anything but happy for Helena if she gets an opportunity to have this?" He turned slowly, taking in the room, all its secrets, all its power.

"I didn't think you cared about her, one way or the other."

Thomas looked at me, then shook his head. "Come on. Let's walk over to the bar and get drinks, so we can stand in the corner while you tell me what a monster I am. That way you'll have something to throw in my face later if you decide you're right after we talk."

He was not at all what I had expected, so I walked with him to the bar. "Vodka gimlet, please."

After we had our drinks, we tucked ourselves into velvet slipper chairs in a semiprivate corner, where we could still watch the people pass through, preening, and where they paid us precisely the kind of sideways-glanced attention Thomas had said they would. Close enough to watch, enough distance to make clear that they didn't dare to eavesdrop.

"So. You want the whole story of how I'm awful and selfish and abandoned my daughter."

"Can't hardly wait," I said over the rim of my glass.

"Things being what they were," he began, "I didn't know Helena even existed until she was almost seven, and a letter from Janet showed up in my mailbox. I never wanted to be anyone's dad, and I wanted it even less, then. I was the hot new thing, and it wasn't only my art people wanted to collect. I'm not going to lie to you and say I didn't love it, didn't take full advantage.

"But while I may be selfish, I'm not a complete asshole, and I knew being born wasn't the kid's fault. So I wrote back to Janet, told her she could have custody, I'd pay support, pay for college— hell, I'd pay for a pony if the kid wanted one, all that kind of stuff— and Helena could decide if she wanted to know me or not."

I took a long sip of my drink, holding the tart lime against the inside of my mouth. "None of that sounds even remotely like what I've heard." Though I wondered, now, how much of that past Janet had changed to fit with her made-up narrative. Hard to tell some- one their father is under a curse if he's just sent them a pony.

"I'd be shocked if it did. After I wrote, I heard nothing. Months went by. Enough months that I noticed, and wondered if maybe something happened to the kid. Janet wasn't answering my calls, and the only address I had for her was Melete, so I went there.

"And found out she'd rewritten the entire story." Thomas passed his hand over his eyes. "She went on and on about our perfect love and how—" His face twisted as he was forced to swallow the words he almost spoke. "How we were interfered with, by Tania, who was . . . you know."

I nodded.

"Janet continued that way. She knew I'd come back once the curse was broken, all this stuff. And she was calm about it, like it was perfectly sane, like we really had some kind of love for the ages that was magicked away from us.

"I tried to explain that I didn't love her, I never had, that we were friends who'd had a great time together, but that I didn't want to be with her like that. That I was just there for the kid, to try and do right by her."

As we spoke, glasses were raised in salute to Thomas from across the room, kisses blown. He didn't react. I wondered if he was immune to everyone's desire for a piece of him after all this time, or if his focus was part of his charm: *All these people want me, and I want only you.*

"Another drink?" he asked.

"Please."

On his way to and from the bar he said hellos, kissed cheeks, strode through the social hierarchy. Heads turned in my direction as he walked back. I fought not to fidget under the smiles, the whispers.

He handed me the fresh glass and continued.

"Janet wouldn't have any of it. If I didn't want to be with her, I couldn't see the kid. She wouldn't budge. Wouldn't even step out of the doorway and let me into the house.

"So I opened the accounts that I said I would, left the passbooks on Janet's doorstep the next day, and got out of there. I hoped that maybe if I left and stayed gone, Janet would get her head on straight."

"You left Helena there. With Janet. Who hasn't changed, by the way. She's still convinced that the two of you have some great thwarted love.

"If anything," I said, "she made it worse, telling Helena that the only way you could be saved is if she went"—I paused, considered— "where you did, for the same reason."

Thomas finished his martini. "Helena knows that's not how it works, right? I mean, if she wants it for herself, good on her, and I hope she gets it. But even if that were true, I wouldn't ask anyone to go there for me. You get what you get because being there isn't a relaxing vacation."

"She knows now," I said. "She didn't before. It might do her some good to hear from you."

"Can I have your phone?"

I handed it to him, and he programmed in his information. "Still her choice, I'm not going to force myself into her life, but if there's anything I can do, she should get in touch. I mean that." For a second, he looked uncertain. Not the smooth, professional flirt. Just someone who hoped for something he didn't know how to ask for.

"And you can call, too, if he doesn't work out." Thomas nodded in the direction of Evan, who was laughing as he and Gavin cut through the crowd.

"I'll be sure to keep that in mind." But I smiled when I said it.

Thomas grinned. "Good luck with whatever I'll be hearing

about from you in seven years." He intercepted Gavin. I walked to the bar for a glass of water, and Evan met me there.

"Enjoying the evening?" I asked.

"I really am. A lot of decisions to make," he said. "I'm going to stay an extra day to deal with them, but Gavin said he'd take you back to Melete tomorrow. He's got a car, so you won't have to fuss with the train."

Gavin was deep in conversation with Thomas, and I idly wondered if the ban on speaking about the tithe outside of Melete applied when it was the King of Faerie you were talking to.

As the evening went on, more people—polished, elegant, subtle—came to pay court to Evan, to exclaim over his art, to promise calls from one agent to the next to discuss future projects, interviews, drinks. I stood at his side, smiling and silent, a forgotten accessory, and then, when the ache of keeping up the politely interested façade began to feel false and feral, like I might bite the next hand that reached past me to grab a piece of him, I excused myself.

I splashed cold water on my face and over my wrists in the fluorescent quiet of the bathroom, the door locked against the hard flash of want, of ego, outside. Head aching from the constant hum of voices, arches screaming in my heels, I went back into the gallery, looking for Evan, to see if he'd mind if I went back to the hotel early.

The heart foreshadows things very well. Even before you find the mostly closed door with the slice of light at the bottom, even before you hear the gasps and the wet slick of flesh meeting flesh, you know. You know that you have been looking too long, you know that the side-eyed glances from the people you pass are no longer envy, but pity. Your heart stutters with the knowledge of what will be on the other side, but like Bluebeard's wife, you open the door anyway.

The woman's head was tossed back, her artful hair disheveled, her coral-pink lips gasping out her orgasm. I closed my eyes and pulled the door shut before I could see Evan's face.

Everything he ever wanted.

I leaned against the wall, pulling myself together, biting the inside of my cheek until I was certain no tear would fall. Checked my makeup and repainted my mouth blood red, because there was no way I was walking back into the crowd looking less than perfectly composed.

The purposeful click of heels. "Ah. I'd hoped this wouldn't happen."

The assistant from before, in her beautifully folded dress. Of course she knew. She was, I was certain, very good at her job.

"I'd like to go back to the hotel," I said. "Can you call ahead and book me into a new room, though? I'll pay for it, obviously." I winced at the probable cost, but whatever it was, it would be worth it to not have to see Evan.

"Certainly." Her voice was kind, competent. "I'll have your things transferred."

She began keying things in on her touchpad. "The car is waiting downstairs. I'll walk you out the back. Is there any message you'd like me to leave?"

It would be easier for Evan if I just disappeared, I knew. "There's no message. But I'm not a secret. I'll leave by the front."

She nodded. "I've sent you my information, if there's anything else you need. And you were here as the gallery's guest. Everything has been taken care of."

I heard the door open behind me as I walked away, heard him call my name. I didn't turn around.

Everything had already been taken care of.

I wasn't sleeping, but I still jolted when my phone rang. I didn't recognize the number. I answered anyway, sure it was some small hours of the morning disaster.

"Imogen. She was nothing. I'm so sorry."

"Evan. It's four o'clock in the morning. I've been back for almost three hours. If you were sorry, you would have called sooner." Or not fucked her.

Silence on the other end of the phone. Then: "But—"

"No," I said, and disconnected.

When the phone rang again, I turned off the ringer and shut it in a drawer, so I couldn't see the display light up.

21

The car, a sleek, smoke-colored thing, slid to a stop in front of the hotel. I met the driver at the trunk, handed him my bag, and climbed into the backseat on my own.

"I hope you had a good time last night," Gavin said.

I stared. Burst out laughing. "Look, I know you guys don't really understand human emotions or whatever, but are you fucking kidding me?"

"Forgive me, Imogen, I was preoccupied at the event, and obviously missed something. What happened?"

"Well, Evan was preoccupied, too. With another woman. I was the one who found them. So no. I did not have a particularly good time."

Silence, but for the quiet hum of the car.

"We do, you know."

I looked away, out of the window. "Do what?"

"Understand human emotions. Feel them, even. Things would be easier if that weren't so."

"What would be easier, Gavin? It's been an exceedingly long twenty-four hours, and I really can't do cryptic right now."

"Very well then—I'll endeavor to be clear. I am in love with your sister, and I believe that if she goes to Faerie as the tithe, the effects of being there will kill her."

I turned away from the window and looked at him full-on. For the first time since I'd met him, he seemed mortal. Not like he was wearing his human glamour, but fully mortal—fine lines feathered his eyes, and dark circles ringed them. He looked colorless, exhausted.

"So forbid her. Tell her she can't do it. You're the king, right? Or lie—tell her you were wrong about the time. Seven years is too long in dance. She knows that." My words tumbled over each other in a rush.

"I wish I could."

"What, because you can't lie? Fine. I'll lie to her. You just keep her from going over there to die."

"I *can*not—as in, am prohibited by the magic that governs it, Imogen—interfere with the tithe. I cannot say something to your sister to directly influence her choice, nor can I prohibit her from going, if she is chosen."

"You aren't even allowed to tell her that you think she might die?"

"Magic manifests differently in all of us. Mine uses words as a channel. Sometimes saying a thing makes it true." He pinched the bridge of his nose, and a muscle fluttered along his jaw.

"Then don't choose her." Knowing as I said the words that it wasn't that simple. "Or, fine. Let her go. Just give her the same deal that Evan got. Parole her so you can dance together here. That would make more sense anyway."

"Evan is allowed to leave Faerie for temporary periods because it is to our benefit that he spend time elsewhere. That would not be the case with Marin."

"But—"

"Marin sickened when she rode into Faerie because of the strength of its effect on her, not because of an overindulgence in grief. And do not think that we, that *I* cannot tell the difference. Even though

I didn't know precisely what caused it, do you think I didn't know how you felt, that you were betrayed, raging, the second that you got into this car? I can taste it. The intensity of Marin's emotions would be like wine to us, and we would drink her dry."

The air in the car crackled across my skin. I pressed myself against the door.

"We are already spread too thin because of the leniency Evan has forced on us. Faerie is weakened, and I am weak because of it. I have no options." He breathed out, and I took in the fact that my cheating ex might be the reason that my sister died.

"I have no options," he said again, "other than you."

"Me." So tired my bones ached, I stared at him. "You are the fucking King of Faerie, Gavin. Even if you are weakened, what exactly do you think that I can do that you can't?"

"You can talk your sister out of this."

"I really don't think I can. Not unless I tell her you think she might die, and honestly, Gavin, maybe not even then. You didn't grow up in our house. You didn't live with our mother. You can't know what escaping that—knowing that finally, we could be sure that we could keep her away from us, out of our lives—means."

He continued as if I hadn't spoken. "As you said, you can lie to Marin. And if that is not enough, you might work to ensure that she isn't chosen."

"Not to spoil your big secret plan, but I am already throwing my hat in the ring for this—I'm writing the best book I can, because I want your deal. The success, and the safety it means, I want that. So maybe lay off all of this bullshit, and things will work out."

"Your being chosen in her place would work, but the odds of that are unpredictable. What I meant was that you could make certain that she does not believe that she will be chosen. Your sister is many things, but confident in her talent is not one of them." Like it was nothing, what he was saying.

"You want me to mentally sabotage Marin. To make her think she isn't good enough, that she doesn't deserve to win this thing. You want me to lie to her, and to do it well enough that saying the thing makes it true." My words tasted like poison in my mouth, bitter acid.

"Don't look at me like that, Imogen. Do I need to remind you that the alternative could be her death?"

"I loved her before you did," I said. "So no. You don't."

"And you cannot tell her."

"What, that her lover and her sister conspired to take her choice and her dream away from her? That we talked ourselves into believing that betraying her trust and breaking her heart was the right thing? Believe me, I'd already figured that out."

"Imogen, I—"

"Look, Gavin, unless it's something really important, can we not? As you already know, I had a shitty night, and this morning has been even worse. And I'm really tired, and I'm going to take a nap, so if you could please just shut up, that would really help." I curled into the corner, closed my eyes.

I didn't open them again until we were back at Melete.

Once upon a time.

Once upon a time, there were two sisters—one dark as the night, and one bright as the sun. People who knew them said it was as if one heart lived in two skins, that was how close the two girls were.

Still, as close as they were, they were not the same. The older sister was quiet and cautious, mistrustful of everyone, like a cat who has been kicked. The younger was bold and exuberant, as if the world were a safety net made to catch her.

A safety net can break if you fling yourself at it too hard.

In the course of her adventures the younger sister was changed. Her desire for everything became a desire solely for one thing, and she was never certain she truly held it. Her desire consumed her, wasted her away until she was no longer bright, but instead, a shadow. A pale form, ghosting through her life.

The older sister saw this, and saw the want that ate away at her sister like a cancer. Such a thing was unbearable to her, that her sister might want, and have only the emptiness of a desire unfulfilled, and so she left, and she went on a quest, and she vowed to find the thing that would be the balm to her sister's wound.

The older sister walked, east of the sun and west of the moon, in shoes of iron. She brought back the egg of the phoenix, the flame of the firebird, and a deathless heart trapped in an emerald. If there were a sign or wonder under the sun or hidden in its shadow, she gathered it and brought it to her sister.

And still, the younger sister faded.

One of the wonders the older sister had returned with from her travels was a wizard, sworn to her service for a year and a day. He examined the younger sister, using all the tools of his dire art.

"The only cure for her is time," he said.

"She is dying," the older sister said. "Even I can see that. How can you say time will cure her?"

She looked around at the rooms full of glittering treasure, the staggering wonders she had collected and brought back, each more rare than the next. It seemed they were useless, nothing. "Time is the one thing she does not have."

"She is not dying. Her condition will correct itself. But you must hold her close and hold her here until it does. You must be the thing that gives her time."

The older sister knew that the wizard could not mislead her, due to the vows he had made. And so she went out in search of time. She gathered grains of sand and drops of water, and the small ticks of gears. She stole leaves at the turn of the seasons, and the space between now and then.

She could see her sister improving, but still too slowly. There was not yet enough time.

And so she stole her own—greying her hair and wrinkling her skin, and weakening her bones.

"I see you finally understand," the wizard said.

"Yes," said the older sister. A clock chimed. She watched her younger sister sleep, true rest this time, whole and peaceful at last.

And then she, too, closed her eyes and slept.

22

I dropped my overnight bag on the floor of my room and dropped myself on my bed, staring up at the stars on the ceiling.

"How was the show? Was the gallery amazing?" Marin asked.

I closed my eyes and started keeping secrets from my sister. "Well, I walked in on Evan having sex with someone else, and I needed to ask the gallery's publicist to arrange for a new hotel room for me at the last minute, but otherwise, things went well."

"Seriously? That asshole."

I nodded. "She was really nice about it. The publicist, I mean."

Marin sat down next to me. "Are you okay?"

"Mostly. I'm more embarrassed than hurt."

"What a fucker."

"No argument from me on that one. He was really enjoying the whole big success thing, everyone making a fuss about him and his art. And they should. He might be a jackass, but he's a very talented one.

"He just forgot how to be a decent human being, as the night went on." And then my voice broke and I followed it, hot tears spilling down my cheeks.

Marin gathered me into her arms, and held me while I wept.

"I'm just so mortified," I said. "It was like I was nothing. And then he called, and tried to tell me that's what she was, like that didn't make it even worse."

"I'm so sorry, sweetie."

"Thanks." I sat up, blew my nose, scrubbed the remaining tears from my face.

"Are you going to be okay?" she asked.

I nodded. "It sucks, and I plan on wallowing, but my heart is insulted, not broken."

"Not in love, then?" she asked.

"No." I thought of Gavin, his desperation, and knew what I had felt was nothing like that. "Are you?"

"I think part of me has been since the first time we danced together," she said. "He makes me feel like I'm safe, and like I could be brave enough to do anything."

I squeezed her hand. "I'm so happy for you." And I was, I was. Even as my own heart pinched and folded in on itself, knowing that she loved him made what I had agreed to, hurting her to save her, not easier, but almost bearable.

"Have you talked at all about what happens if you go to Faerie as the tithe?" I asked. I wanted to know what exactly it was I would be hiding from her.

She nodded. "He hasn't said so directly, but I know he's worried. He keeps telling me I'm good enough to have a 'stunning career'— his words—without it, that I should think carefully about my options, that I should talk to Evan about what it's been like—which I'm certainly not going to do now."

"But if Gavin's worried—" I started.

"I know there are risks, but Gavin doesn't know our mother. I keep a calendar, you know," she said.

I rubbed my eyes. "Of what?"

"Days since the last time I've heard from her. Or seen her. She's pretty regular about making contact, like she doesn't want to let me get too comfortable. So this way I know when to brace myself for the random message delivered through the front office, or the bouquet of headless roses left in my dressing room."

My hand curled into a claw. I'd never kept a calendar. It was always a clock. Counting down in my head until the next time.

"There is always a next time," I said, half-aloud.

Marin nodded. "I might have a good career, maybe even a stunning one, without becoming the tithe. But I won't have a safe life. I need to do things this way to make sure we're safe. To make sure she can never touch us again."

It sounded like Gavin had been exactly right in predicting Marin's reactions. Proof of love, I guessed. The needle in my heart took another stitch.

"You don't think there's another way, something else that might work? Gavin can't curse her?" I asked.

"Apparently not, because I'm sure he would have offered. But nothing else I've done to try to get away from her has ever worked. Not completely. I know that's how it's been for you, too. She always manages to creep back in. It would be worth going not to hear her voice for seven years, never mind the rest of it. I can't make him see that, but I know you understand."

I did, was the thing. That understanding was part of the vise that Gavin had put me in. I didn't want Marin's time in Faerie to hurt her—I would do anything, everything I could to keep her safe—but I knew what she meant. There was a freedom attached to going that was worth what being there would cost.

The two years I had been away at boarding school, my mother wrote me every day. People noticed, commented on how much she must love me, how close we must be. Really, what it meant was that every day, there was the reminder that I was pathetic, I would never amount to anything. I stopped reading them, but it didn't help, because they still showed up, each new letter a reminder that even though I had left, I hadn't gotten away. She could still get to me, she was the one in control. It got to the point where the simple act of opening my mailbox had made me sick to my stomach.

"I do understand," I said.

"People ask, 'How will you know when you've made it?' When I answer, I talk about roles I'd like to dance, that I want to create a part one day, that sort of thing. But really? It will be when I finally feel like she's not waiting around the corner to pounce.

"When I don't go to bed at night wondering if the next day is the day she's going to show up to try to take everything I've worked for away from me. That was what she always said: 'I gave you this, I can take it back.' And I knew she could."

She shuddered. "Ugh. Sorry to be so bleak. I was trying to cheer you up."

"Yeah, that worked well." But I forced a smile onto my face.

"I need to go practice, but before I do, do you want me to bring you anything? Chocolate? Wine? Evan's cheating balls?"

I snickered. "I'm good, thanks. Dinner later?"

"Perfect," she said.

She hugged me before she left, and I felt how strong she was, how sinewy with muscle, full of grace. Gavin could be wrong about what she was strong enough to survive.

He could be wrong, and it wouldn't matter. Because I had promised I would hurt my sister to try to protect her. Because even if I hadn't made that promise, I might hurt her anyway, because we wanted the same thing. Maybe neither of us would be chosen. But only one of us could be.

I told Beth I had decided, I was sure. My fingers wrapped around the hourglass dangling from my neck as I spoke.

"What happens next? Do I need to file paperwork or something?" Throw my name into an eternally burning goblet? Write it on wax and give it to a blind oracle? Even though I had lived with the knowledge of what the tithe was, what Melete was, for months now, it seemed almost ridiculous to have this conversation sitting on the worn grey sofa in Beth's house, the lilac blanket she had knitted tossed over the back, the scent of coffee mingling with the smoke of lapsang souchong, like the Fae had become an ordinary thing.

"Nothing like that. There will be a gathering, the night of the spring equinox. You'll be evaluated. Showing up and presenting your work is all you need do."

"It seems sort of anticlimactic," I said. It should be harder, or magical. Something that made clear it wasn't just another story submission.

"It won't be. What does Marin think of your choice?"

"We haven't talked about it." I knew we'd have to, but I wanted to put it off as long as possible. The possibility of the conversation had become so fraught. "I mean, I'm sure she knows, because I'm still wearing the necklace, but we haven't actually gone into the specifics of the thing."

Beth set down her empty cup and picked up her knitting. "Well. Remember that you can change your mind at any time up to the equinox. Also remember that you aren't betraying Marin by choosing to believe in yourself, and in your art, and that doing so doesn't mean you don't believe in hers."

I nodded, throat tight. "Logically, I know that. But part of me feels like it's a betrayal, to want this. To compete against her."

"I haven't ever been in the situation you're in. I'm an only child,"

Beth said. "I never lived with my daughter's father. He's a perfectly lovely man whom I like a great deal, and we would have made each other miserable if we had ever resided under the same roof.

"I love my daughter, but we're not peers. She has no desire to be a writer, and I have no desire to be an orthopedic surgeon. I don't know what it would be like to be in competition with her for anything, and I never will. So it's easy for me to tell you that from the perspective of an artist, Imogen, if you want this chance, you should grab it with both hands and hang on to it.

"But from the perspective of a human"—she leaned back in her chair, set her knitting in its bag—"things are different. People who don't know any better will tell you that you can have it all. That the people who love you will support you in your choices, and if they don't, they never loved you anyway. That's not exactly true.

"I believe that you should put yourself and your art first. In the end, the art is what lasts. But making that choice means sacrifices. Before you decide anything, you don't just need to know what you want, you need to know what you're willing to give up to get it."

I came home to discover that Ariel had occupied the front room. Furniture was shoved to the side, stacked up on each other in haphazard and precarious fashion. The floor was covered with index cards, arranged around x's of tape.

"What is this?" I asked.

"I'm blocking out my new project," she said.

"The one that's not Joan of Arc?"

She nodded. "I'm trying to figure out how much of a fairy tale I can tell about this place, before it turns into something that can steal my voice. Plus I've got a main character who can only speak the truth once we get to Act Two, which makes things both easier and not."

"Pronouns," I said.

"What?" She sat back on her heels.

"Thomas and I had an entire conversation about the tithe and Faerie when we were at the gallery for Evan's show. Using pronouns. I think I only got tripped up once."

"So it's how you say things, not what you say."

"I think so," I said. "So long as you might plausibly be talking about something else, I don't think it triggers the curse or whatever it is that shuts us up."

"That helps." She grabbed a stack of index cards, made notes. "I mean, I can always rewrite in rehearsals if it turns out people literally can't say their lines, but this is good to know."

"It looks like it's going well." I could see more of the pieces now, bits of songs, dance steps, stage blocking, dialogue. Some cards layered on top of each other. It looked close to complete.

"It is." She reached over and knocked the table leg, causing it to tilt, and nearly fall off the ottoman it was perched on. "Superstition. But almost all the songs are set. Mostly, I'm working on the book and the staging.

"I was worried it wouldn't, you know? Like, the magic 'don't talk about Fae club' would kick in, and I'd be up onstage making fish faces while the music played. But it's working.

"So if I wanted to look for more fairy tales, where would I find them?"

"Like Beauty and the Beast sorts of fairy tales?" I asked.

"Exactly. Not our kind of problem, just general information."

I sat down on the floor with her, next to an index card that asked, *Does he love her?* It depended, I thought, on who the "he" was. "I can give you some books. Are you looking to add them to your story?"

"Not so much that. But I keep thinking—I wrote this because I was so angry about not being able to talk, and it's working. I mean, no one on Broadway will think it's true, but that almost doesn't matter to me, because I'll still have told the story." She shoved a hand through her hair, puffed out a breath. "Then with what you just said, about the pronouns. It just makes me wonder—how many more of what we think of as just fairy tales might be true? Not true true, but a way of talking about things without exactly saying them? Maybe people wrote them down because they had to say *something*."

"It wouldn't surprise me if a lot were," I said. "I think it would be weirder if no one had ever tried to talk about it before, than if a bunch of people had, and we just didn't realize it."

"That's what I think," Ariel said. "Because come on. I could send this show to one of the producers who danced with the Fae on New Year's, and they wouldn't see this as a true story. But if you came and watched it, you'd know right away. So I want to read the fairy tales, and see if I can guess at what else I've been missing."

I'd heard the knock on the door and hadn't thought anything about it until Marin texted. *Come down. Now. Mom emergency.*

Marin was sitting on the porch, folded up small, arms around her knees. There was a brown cardboard box next to her. "It's for us. From Mommy Dearest. I didn't even want to take it inside."

"Do you think there's a head in it?" I asked. It was, in a coincidence almost as disturbing as its origin, exactly the right size for that particular horror movie trope.

"You know that could actually be a more pleasant alternative to whatever it is she did send," Marin said. She looked almost sick, green at the edges.

"We could just throw it away."

"I'm all for that," Marin said, pushing the box farther away from her. "Why would she do this?"

"Because whatever is in there is something that will upset us, and it's been too long since the last time she shoved herself into our lives. Because even though she's not here, it will make her happy to imagine us doing exactly what we are right now, and she assumes that we will open it, and so she'll get whatever hideous reaction she's hoping for." I could hear my voice going higher and faster, like a hysterical child, and I forced myself to breathe, to relax. To remember that I wasn't a child, and she wasn't here. That I had the choice, and she couldn't force me to do anything.

Marin stood, picked up the box, and started pulling at the flaps.

"What are you doing? I thought we were going to throw it away," I said.

Marin peeled the tape away. "We will. But I'm not going to be able to relax until I know what's in there, and I don't want to be digging through the garbage at three a.m. so I can sleep."

"Fine." I stood behind her, watching as she lifted out packing materials, revealing what was underneath.

It was a picture of us. Me, with brutally short dark hair hugging my head like a shadow, next to Marin in a tutu. A dance recital. Then I remembered which one. "God, I hated that night," I breathed out, just as Marin said, "That was one of the worst performances of my life."

And so of course, of course, that was why she had sent it. A frame full of misery, that to anyone else would look like a lovely memory, but was chosen to make us feel small and sad, unworthy of where we were.

"I was just starting to get breasts and hips," Marin said. "Which, weird for any girl who does, because your body is suddenly this alien thing, but it threw off my center of gravity. So all the spins and turns and balances that had been like nothing for me went all wonky. It seemed like it happened overnight, too, and of course I was worried it was because she was right, and I was getting too fat to dance.

"Eventually, I figured out how to cope, and my dancing went back to normal, but I fell onstage that night. Over-rotated, and wiped out. Right in front of everyone. With this enormous thud that sounded exactly like 'fat ballerina' in my head." She brushed at her eyes, mashing the tears from them.

I put my arm around her. Marin's bra strap was visible in the picture, having worked itself free from the hiding spot beneath the thicker strap of her costume. Her eyes were red-rimmed.

"That was the year my teacher had recommended me for a young writers' conference," I said. "I had written an essay for the application, and I had just found out that I had gotten in. The day after the acceptance letter came, Mommy Dearest wrote to my teacher saying I'd plagiarized the essay. That she had written my essay, as a model, of course, but that I had simply copied hers and turned it in. That even though it would be hard for me, I needed to be made to face the consequences of my actions.

"I couldn't go to the conference after that, obviously. And I had to give an apology in front of the whole class, for cheating and taking the spot that should have been one of theirs. That was what I did that day."

The worst part had been the look in my teacher's eyes. Mrs. Keith. She had believed in me, encouraged me. Our mother had gone in to see her, so embarrassed at what she'd claimed I'd done, so full of talk about the pressures I put on myself to succeed in the wake of Marin's talent, and called me a liar. Took my writing from me, and took away Mrs. Keith's belief and support, too.

"Our happy family," Marin said. She tossed the picture back in the box. "Do you think there's any photo, from growing up, that doesn't have some hideous memory attached to it? There has to be, right?"

I didn't think so.

Marin stuffed everything back in the box, folded the flaps closed. We threw it in the trash. Marin shuddered. "She's always going to be there, isn't she?"

"I'm just glad she can't be here," I said. "It's the one safe place." Though not as safe as we had thought, not with packages that could show up to knock us off our feet one more time. No place had ever been as safe as we thought.

Marin adjusted her necklace, settling the hourglass back at the hollow of her throat. "We can make ourselves safer."

23

Marin had been away for the past couple of days at an audition, so I was surprised to see her in the studio as I ran past. Instead of continuing home, I opened the door and went in. Stepping inside, I was struck again by the beauty of the space. One wall was all windows, the opposite all mirrors, and the room seemed to open up forever, all golden light and silver gilt and Marin spinning in the center of it.

"How did it go?" I asked.

She finished a sequence of turns across the floor, checking the angle of her leg in the mirror. "Awful." She sounded choked, on the edge of tears.

"What happened?"

"I'm a disloyal fame whore, apparently. For leaving my old company and coming here to dance with Gavin. Which, as they explained, also makes me the other kind of whore. After the fellowship is over, I can expect a year or two of roles from companies who don't mind that sort of thing, if it means Gavin on their stage, but once he gets tired of me, I'm finished.

"Then they offered me a role in the corps." No, not tears in her voice. Fury.

It was a huge insult. Marin had been a principal dancer in her last company, someone who danced major roles. The Snow Queen, not a snowflake. The least she should have been offered was a position as soloist, and even then, only at a better company.

"What a horrible bunch of people," I said.

"It felt like the only reason they gave me the audition was to humiliate me. They were so gleeful as they explained why I wasn't a good fit." The series of turns again, and then again across the floor, each time with adjustments I couldn't quite see, each time smoother and more powerful.

"Fuck them. You're better than that. You're better than they are."

"But what if I'm not?" She stopped the spin. "It's completely possible that I will never get a job dancing with a major company. That everyone thinks I'm just Gavin's latest whatever. I never should have come here."

"You have other auditions," I said. "Anyone who sees you dance knows you're good." It felt like saying nothing, like offering a Band-Aid to someone with a chest wound.

"Except that's clearly not the only thing that matters. Because I danced great yesterday. I was on. And still. The fucking corps." She sat down, took her pointe shoes off. "I'm starting to feel like the only chance I have for anything when I get out of here is to be chosen for the tithe."

And there it was, the needle in my heart. "That's not true."

"Easy for you to say. You're a writer. You're supposed to do stuff like this, fall off the map and hide away. You'd still be a young writer if you make a 'Forty Under Forty' list. If I'm still dancing at forty, it would be a miracle."

"I wish I could help," I said.

"You can. Take off your charm."

"Marin, there are forty fellows here. Sure, some of them don't have charms right now, but theoretically, any one of them has a chance to be the tithe. My deciding not to wouldn't do anything." The worm in my brain that told me to use this, to play on her weakness, her emotions, to break her. I had, after all, promised. And besides, it would be for her own good.

"It shows you support me. That you have my back. That you understand why this is so important to me."

"I do, Marin, but . . ." Her own good. My hand shook.

"But what?"

"Isn't it better if we both try? That way there are two chances for us to be able to get away from our mother?" The words sounded weak, an excuse, even to me. But I couldn't. Even to save her, I couldn't hurt her, not like that.

"But it's not just about that anymore. I need to know there will be something for me when I get out of here."

"I'm there for you, Marin. You have me." Liar, liar, liar. And not even a good enough liar to keep her safe.

She sagged. "I know that. I do. I'm just so scared, Imogen. I knew there was the possibility I might not be able to find a new ballet company, but I never imagined something like that, you know?"

I did know. She was good. Great. She belonged at a major company. To dance like that, and then be called nothing but a whore, must have been awful. "You're a spectacular dancer, and they're idiots, Marin. You'll get the next job."

But things got worse. Two nights later, I walked into the kitchen to find her easing her way into a chair, a pack of frozen peas pressed to her hip. "Hand me the other one, too, would you?"

"Marin, what happened?" I passed her the bag from the counter.

She pressed it to her shoulder, winced. "Gavin dropped me. Well, he fell, and so I fell with him."

"Are you okay?" Falls weren't great for any dancer, but falling while being partnered, the extra height from the ground, made it even more dangerous. She'd been injured that way before.

"I will be—nothing's broken or sprained. But I'm worried about him." She lowered her voice. "I mean, that sort of thing, it just doesn't happen to him. Because of who—what—he is. And when he apologized, he said he was tired. Tired. I'm worried."

"Maybe it was just a bad day?" But he had said Faerie was weaker because of Evan not always being there, the tithe not being the source of whatever it was that it had been in the past. Maybe Faerie being weaker made him weaker, too.

"The worst part is, once I realized he was okay, all I could think about was what would happen to me, if he couldn't dance. What if no one wants me without him?" Tears smeared Marin's face.

I reached out, took her hand. "He'll be fine. Everyone gets tired. And you're brilliant. Of course they'll want you."

Except her next audition was canceled. The company didn't give a reason, so she assumed the worst—not that they no longer needed a dancer, but that they didn't want her.

"You have to promise me that you won't compete against me for the tithe," she said, flushed and furious.

"What if it were me, Marin? What if I were sending out a book, and all I was getting were rejection letters? Tell me honestly that you would step aside, and I will."

She turned away. "It's different. You have time."

"When we applied here, we promised to go. No matter what. Even if the other one of us didn't get in. I don't understand why this is different."

"Because I might be nothing without the tithe. Nothing. I literally cannot even get an audition right now. And you don't even seem to care. You just want to go, and leave me alone again."

Again? "What are you talking about, Marin?"

"Just like when you went to school. A great opportunity that only you could go to that left me behind. To be nothing. Alone with her." She spat the words.

"I had to go, Marin. You know what she did to me! I wasn't leaving you, I was saving myself. You're the one who never answered my email, my letters, anything. You could have told me what it was like, living with her. You didn't." It had been like writing to a black hole. "I would have come back for vacations if I had thought you wanted me there. If I'd thought you needed me at all. But you never answered me, and I thought you were glad I was gone."

"What letters, Imogen? What email? I didn't get anything from you. Before you left, you said you were sorry, you promised you'd help me get out, and then you disappeared into your new life. I get that she hurt you, and I know it was bad, but I was stuck there. Every day, waiting for her to snap again, waiting for that to be the day that I did something wrong, something that would make her turn on me. Something that would make her hurt me the way that she hurt you, something to take away my dancing.

"You got away, and I had to live with that, and I had to do it alone, because you left me there alone and never looked back."

"Marin, I wrote. I wrote you that whole first year. I didn't stop until I was sure you didn't want to hear from me." The horrible truth roared into my head. "She must have found them. The letters, the emails. Everything. She must have hid them, kept them from you."

"That's easy for you to say now, isn't it?"

My stomach clenched and turned. "You think I would lie about that?"

"I don't know, Imogen. You're my sister, and I don't know. All I know is that you left then, and you want to leave again. Off on your own to be amazing, and me left behind. I know that it doesn't matter to you that I want this, that I need to be the tithe so that I can have a career, a future when I get out of here, so that I can have a chance to make up for the time I've wasted here trying to make things better between us, that I wasted trying to figure out what I did that made you hate me so much that you left."

"Marin, I don't hate you. I never have. Moving out had nothing to do with you."

"I guess it didn't," she said. "Considering how little I seem to matter to you now."

Her words were a kick in the stomach, stealing my air. "You do matter."

"Then take the charm off. Show me that I matter more to you than this does. Show me that you trust me enough, that you believe in me enough to think that I can do this, that I can be the one who gets us away from her for good."

My hand went to the charm around my neck, holding on to it like it was a shield against shock, Gavin's dire certainty echoing in my ears. "Marin, I can't. I have to do this."

She shook her head. "Mom always said that you were jealous of me. That you wanted to be the sister who was the star. I guess she didn't lie about everything."

You think you get free when you grow up, when you get out of the house. Mostly, you do. Eventually, you stop only ever letting yourself half-sleep, because you're bracing for footsteps and angry hands. You stop looking for hiding places to keep safe your most precious things, to make it harder for someone to take them from you on a whim. You choose your clothing based on style, rather than on how well it hides bruises. You grow your hair out, and almost forget the metallic snick of scissors.

The muscles relax in your shoulders. You remember how to take a deep breath, how to unclench your hand, how to share a secret. Until.

There is always an until.

When it happens, everything goes back to the way it was, and you embrace your two best friends, loneliness and fear.

I closed the door behind my sister. Then I picked up my pen and went back to work. There was nothing else I could do.

And so I hid. I hid from Marin—and everyone else in the house—locking myself away in my tower, a Rapunzel who refused to let down her hair. I worked harder than I'd ever worked before, writing all hours of the day and night, leaving meals unfinished and half-drunk cups of coffee to go cold and sludgy on my desk while I wrestled with words and phrases.

I didn't leave my room.

There are fairy tales where silence matters. Where a particular truth must not be told to a particular person, where shirts of stinging nettles must be woven without even the smallest whimper of pain or else a curse will not be broken. The silence binds back like thorns, wrapping and stopping the mouth of the person who could speak the truth and save herself, who must instead stand, tied to the stake, waiting for the voice of the fire.

I didn't speak of the bargain I had made with Gavin, except to the silence of the page.

But a curse wouldn't be a curse if it were easy to bear, and my tower wasn't ringed around with thorns, or set apart like a stylite in the desert. It was in a house full of people, a house with my sister in it. Every time I saw her I wanted to speak, but I swallowed my words, and I choked on my silence.

There was nothing I could say that would help.

24

The shattering of glass brought all of us running, from the library and down from our rooms and into a storm of wings and feathers.

The birds flocked and swooped, moving in tandem like a murmuration of starlings, down the hall to where Marin stood, circling back and up the staircase again toward me. A sea of them, in radiant colors. They flew past us again, the circuit tightening, a feathered whirlwind.

With no obvious signal, they changed course, flew back into the night, disappearing through the window their entrance had shattered.

"What was that?" Ariel, standing in the hallway near Marin, asked.

"It's getting close to the equinox. The Fae are checking out their potential houseguests," Helena said from below me on the landing. All of us were frozen, still.

"Those were Fae?" Ariel asked.

"Or their emissaries. Not all of them look human."

"So if they're coming here—and next time, I wish they'd knock, because it's cold and that glass is going to be a bitch to clean up—does that mean it's Marin for sure?"

"Or Imogen. She's got a necklace, too," Helena said.

"You could still change your mind, Imogen," Marin said.

I walked the rest of the way down the stairs, began picking up the larger pieces of shattered glass. "I can't, Marin."

"You could," she said. "You just won't."

"Oh my God," Ariel said, her awe breaking through the beginnings of another fight.

"They were Fae," Helena said. "Look at the feathers."

They had fallen in the wake of flight, breadcrumbs to mark a path. Smoke rose from them now—violet, midnight, grey—a thick haze that smelled equally of roses and of rot. When the smoke cleared, the feathers were gone.

"Is this going to keep happening?" Ariel asked.

"Probably," Helena said. "It did before."

"Why did they come here, though?" Marin asked. "It's not like I dance in the house."

Helena stared at her. "Because talent is only a piece of the tithe. It's also about who Faerie wants. I thought you of all people would have figured that out."

The next morning, I stumbled out of bed to hear Ariel come into the house singing, belting the glory note so long that I wondered if it was true that the right note could shatter glass, and if we were about to find out.

"Are you drunk?" Helena asked.

"Just happy. You should be, too, because look what I got!" Ariel dangled a chain from her hand. An hourglass charm spun at the bottom of it.

The equinox was only a week away. "The new project is done?" I asked.

"It is."

"What new project?" Helena asked.

"I got grumpy at Angelica for telling me I was doing art wrong, and at the Fae for taking my voice at Thanksgiving, so I wrote this whole thing about this guy, Thomas the Rhymer, who was this amazing poet, but then he hooked up with the Fairy Queen and she stole his voice, and when he finally gets it back, he can't be a poet anymore because he can only tell the truth, and no one goes to a poet for that. It's a musical." Ariel was all delight.

Helena looked at me, and I shrugged. I had no more idea of what was going on than she did.

"Angelica says the Fae like stories about themselves, and I guess they liked mine."

"Good for you," Helena said. "Really. But why is that supposed to make me happy?"

"Because this is for you." Ariel offered the chain to Helena. "That's all you need, right? You put this on and go kick ass, and then tell Janet to fuck off."

"You'd just give it up?" Helena's hand twitched, almost reaching out, then falling back to her side.

"Going to Faerie for seven years, that whole thing's not for me. I've known that pretty much since the beginning. I need to hear people screaming along with my songs. But if you want the chance, you should take it. Here."

Helena swallowed hard, nodded. She took the charm from Ariel's hand, and fastened it around her neck. It fell to the floor. She tried again, and again the necklace wouldn't clasp.

"Let me try," Ariel said. The necklace fell again.

"Stop," Helena said. "Thank you for trying. But it knows, or they know. Whatever. It's not for me." She stepped over the charm and walked back up to her room. The door closed behind her.

"It was kind, what you tried to do," I said.

"I thought I was helping," Ariel said. "I thought if she just had a chance, maybe it would be okay." She picked up the charm and shoved it into her pocket.

"Are you sure you don't want to try yourself?" I knew Ariel was good; she could be one more obstacle in front of Marin.

"Very, very sure. Even if it weren't seven years off of a stage, I do not want to go hang out with things like those birds that broke in here. It's just too much. I will happily stay here, and make my art on my own."

We weren't the only ones afflicted by the curiosity of the Fae. As the clock ticked closer to the equinox, they were taking themselves out of hiding all over Melete to observe and consider.

"I've been standing here for an hour, and I still can't figure out where the motor is, how it's being controlled." A tall man stood on the bank, staring at the moat around the house that Marin hadn't yet staged her invasion of. "It" in this case was the smallish sea monster, acid-yellow and serpentine, swimming lazy circuits around the house.

"The motor?" I asked.

"It has to be. Some kind of engine that's propelling it. It's solid, so it can't be projected or CGI." The man's voice was distracted, his face distant, as if part of him were somewhere else, marking theories on a whiteboard or adjusting gears.

The sea monster spiraled into a coil at my feet, casting a cat-like eye on me. Then it sank beneath the surface of the water.

"Amazing, the things people are working on here. I'm going to see if the artist lives there—I'd love to collaborate with them." Shaking his head in awe, the man walked toward the house.

"That is what usually happens," Beth said, when I told her about it later. "There's always an explanation: 'Someone made that' or 'artists are eccentric' are built-in covers for nearly anything that happens at Melete. There are some years where not all of the residents know about the Fae, or the tithe."

That seemed almost impossible to believe, that there could still be people here who didn't know what kind of a place this was. Except. I hadn't known, until Halloween, when there was no choice for me but to know. I had explained away all of the strangenesses that had happened: I was tired. I needed to eat something. It was stress, or shadows in the woods. If I hadn't been chosen, or hadn't lived in a house with other people who were, it was completely possible that I could have spent my entire time here willfully ignorant of the other world that Melete was part of.

"So they think they're seeing next-gen animatronics."

"Or performers rehearsing for a play, or whatever else they can wedge into the category of artistic expression. For some people, the lie is so much easier to believe than the truth, that they'll talk themselves out of seeing what is right in front of them."

"And the secret never gets out," I said.

"And the secret never gets out. Not even the most creative of the common rumors about Melete comes close to the truth. That's helped, of course, by the prohibition on direct speech about the Fae and the tithe, but it's astonishing how little is spoken about when you consider everything that goes on."

"The Fae dancing at parties and appearing as sea monsters in a residence's moat," I said, and shrugged. "I wouldn't believe me."

"Neither would I." She poured jasmine tea into a cup with jasmine flowers painted around the rim. "You haven't changed your mind about the tithe."

"No," I said. "I'm still sure." The equinox was in three days. Campus was beginning to green and blossom, winter melting away to puddles, the trickles of the thaw a hundred small rivers, all running down to join the Mourning.

"And you can compete with—leave, if necessary—your sister?" she asked.

"I want to be chosen," I said.

Beth met my gaze, held it. "All right. Then we should talk about what will happen at the selection."

"It's not just a deadline?" I asked.

"No. You'll present your work. You'll read a piece of it. The Fae will be there. It's more a performance than a portfolio review."

It made sense. I could email a file, or hand someone a manuscript, but that wasn't an option for everyone. Marin, for example, would need to dance.

"What will happen?"

"It will be—" Beth paused, looked away. Opened her mouth to speak, closed it. "It will be intense. Forgive the word, but nothing else seems honest.

"For me, it was the most difficult thing to get through." Her eyes were very far away.

She was usually so straightforward. The fact that she wasn't now scared me a bit.

"More so than the seven years?"

"Going to Faerie as the tithe was unpleasant. Knowing what I know now, I would still do it, because what has come after has been worth what it cost me, but I won't pretend the experience itself was an enjoyable one. Still, while I was there, I had before me the knowledge that it wasn't forever, and the knowledge of what I would gain at the end. I could hold on to those things, and use them to push away everything else.

"The selection—I was afraid. Ridiculous, perhaps, but what I remember most is fear—fear that settled so deeply in me that I still can't articulate it. I wish I could, Imogen. I feel like I'm failing you, and that's not what I want.

"I'll be there that night, if it helps for you to know that. Mentors, even past tithes, don't participate in the selection, but I'll be there. And your work is good. Remember that.

"Follow the instructions you're given," she said. "Be as strong as you can, and remember what you want."

I knew what it was I wanted. It wouldn't be difficult to remember it, no matter what the circumstances. But it was a want that was divided in two. To save Marin. To be better than her. Maybe the fairy tales were right to warn about the dark-haired older sister.

"I don't know what else to do," Helena said. We were on the front steps, wrapped in fleece jackets and blankets against the lingering chill, but the air was fresh and smelled like spring.

"For as long as I can remember, being this thing, this person who wrote poems on the way to being a serious and important artist, it was my job. That same length of time, I got told that if I did my job right, the asshole who contributed half my DNA would stop thinking with his dick and come back to my mom. I'd be a success; she'd be happy. That was how the story was supposed to go. That was my fairy tale ending.

"Finding out that my mom had lied to me, that none of that was ever going to happen, I just, I don't know. I feel like I don't know the point of me now." She had pulled her hands back into her sleeves, tucking into herself.

"Do you still want to be a poet?"

"Maybe? I think so? I think I liked it. I liked the times when I felt like I was actually working toward being good at it. But I've never really thought about being anything else. So maybe I'd rather be a chef, or an electrical engineer. I just, I don't know. I don't know how to know."

"You could leave," I said. "Go anywhere else. Figure out what you want, who you are."

"But this is home. I've never lived any place that isn't Melete, except when I lived in Faerie. I was homeschooled, and then I studied poetry with Janet, because what up-and-coming young poet wouldn't give one of their limbs to work with Janet Thomas?

"I don't know if I want to go. I don't know what there is, besides here. At least here, I can keep her away."

"Janet?" I asked.

Helena nodded. She looked like she hadn't been sleeping. There were bruised crescents beneath her eyes. Even the shock of her fuchsia hair looked muted. "This year's the first time I've ever lived in a house that she doesn't have keys to."

"Have you talked to Thomas?"

"I have this half-written email saved in my drafts folder. I keep opening it up and changing three words, and then closing it again. I want to talk to him. I think. But maybe not."

"He seemed okay when I met him."

"Yes, but he might have been trying to get into your pants."

I laughed. "Point."

Robins hopped across the green-brown grass, pulling worms from the dirt. A Frisbee flew from the house next door, skittering to a stop at our feet. I winged it back, shouting an apology when it hooked left and landed in the moat.

"What would you do if you couldn't write?" Helena asked.

I sat back down on the step next to her. "For a while in college, I thought I wanted to study classics. I had this amazing mythology professor, and she read us the opening of *The Iliad* in ancient Greek, and I could feel my hair stand on end. I wanted to do that. I took enough classes to get the minor."

"What happened?"

"Latin verbs. And the fucking ablative."

"And you can write," she said.

"But if I had wanted it bad enough, I would have made myself learn the fucking ablative. Helena, you're not even twenty-one, and you've published two collections. Of poetry. Which is not an easy thing to sell. You got in here. The issue isn't whether you can write, it's whether you want to. Don't let Janet fuck with your head."

She stood up, handed me the blanket. "When you put it like that, it almost sounds possible. I'll think about it. I'll think about all of it. Even emailing Thomas.

"Oh, and good luck tomorrow."

The equinox. "Thanks. Do they make you go to this, too?"

She nodded. "I went before. When I was almost fourteen. Evan's year. It was amazing. There weren't that many choices, maybe twelve or thirteen, but they were all so good. So much talent. You could have filled stages, galleries. I wanted to weep from it, just being there.

"After, I imagined what I would do. Practiced the poems in my head. These perfect things that even the Fae would fall in love with."

Her mouth twisted. "I was a complete fucking idiot, obviously. You're right. I should leave. Because if I don't, this is what my life will be like—being reminded of my failure every seven years."

There was a letter from Evan in my mailbox. No decorations this time, no sketches on the envelope. Only my name.

I balanced it on my hand, as if the weight of it might give me a clue to its contents, contemplated throwing it away unread. Cursing my curiosity, I opened it.

Imogen—

This is not to tell you that I am sorry. Though I am, should you ever want to accept my apology.

It's to wish you luck, tomorrow. I will be there, and I will be thinking of you.

Evan

I read it again and put it away. I wasn't angry anymore, not really. Just tired, and achingly bored of the cliché of it all, the feeling that my humiliation had been part of a badly-written script. It wasn't something I had the space to deal with. Not today.

Whether I might accept his apology or not, that wasn't what mattered now. Tomorrow, the selection, that was what was important.

But first, there was one last fling before judgment day. The Night Market glittered like the last night at Versailles, light and sparkle and flash everywhere. The Fae weren't even pretending to hide anymore, but walking openly in the Commons, clothed in the extraordinary.

They glittered, too, eyes like burning darkness, clothing bound with fireflies, footsteps that rang like bells, and hair that wept blood red honey from its ends.

The booths were almost as impossible as the Fae were, and this time, when I was offered gifts, I didn't blush and demur. I knew what the stakes were, now. Knowing what I was prepared to sacrifice, I had no problem accepting all that they gave.

A silver dress, beaded like a fantasy from a speakeasy, and an opera cloak of black velvet, lined in green silk. A ring of tarnished silver, curled around itself like a climbing rose. The thorns gripped my finger as I tried it on.

"It likes you," the woman said. She wore a rose collar around her neck, and in the firelight, I couldn't tell if the red drops were blood or rubies. "Wear it for luck."

"I've seen you before," I said. "The rose garden."

"I am often there. But my roses are even more beautiful in Faerie. Do you not think you should come to see them? That you deserve to walk in those gardens?"

She moved like a serpent, grace and danger coiled, and I fought to keep from backing up, away from her regard. "I would love to come and see them."

"So many roses. Like you've never seen. You'll perfume them; they will grow in your bones like a trellis, and their petals will turn the color of your happiness, or your heartbreak."

Good. Great.

She stepped so close our shadows merged, and trailed her finger across my lips. Her touch the swift burn of bee stings. She shuddered. "Delicious. Oh, I do hope it's you."

Her ring still clinging to my finger, I rushed from the booth and back into the crowd of people and Fae. I wanted, desperately, to see someone I knew. But while I recognized faces in the crowd, even saw silver glints around people's necks—all our hourglasses—there was no one I could go to who would understand.

Silence, so well kept that I wore it like a cloak, the glitter of the Market around me like the inside of a shattered mirror.

One sharp sob barked from my throat, and I slapped a hand over my mouth in an effort to stop another from following.

Overwhelmed by the night, by the Fae, I clung to my gifted finery and walked home, alone in the cold and silent darkness.

25

The first day of spring dawned grey, misty and close, water dripping from newly budded leaf and tree. The ground squelched underfoot, and the air smelled wet.

There was a card on my desk that hadn't been there the night before, sitting on top of pages I had printed out, the ones I would read tonight. *You will be called for at sunset.* Words written in ink the iridescence of butterfly wings, such a pleasant invitation.

Follow the instructions I was given, Beth had said. I would be called for. I would go. I would will that my art would be enough.

The sun lanced through the clouds, illuminating the forest. Spring was regreening the trees. No longer the winter skeletons that had no secrets except those beneath their bones, the new leaves brought shadowed spaces, places to hide. Secrets grew up from the loam, and the roots, and the fallen leaves of the past.

In an easier life, I would have gone downstairs and talked to Marin. Told her that I loved her, that I thought she was an incredible dancer, that I believed in her. But I couldn't say that I wanted her to be the one chosen tonight. And as much as I hadn't been able to bring myself to undermine her before, I also couldn't bring myself to support her now. Speak something and make it so—what if my words were what gave her the strength to be the best, and then she was chosen, and then she died? Because I couldn't separate the one from the other in my head anymore. I wanted her safe. So I stayed where I was. I kept my silence.

I dressed too early and sat, straight-backed, on the edge of my bed in my fake-professional black dress that I never wore because it felt like zipping myself into someone else's skin, and heels that rubbed the sides of my toes. My feet would bleed like a dancer's if I had to walk too far in them.

On my finger, the rose ring from the night before. The Fae woman had said it was for luck, after all, and I needed some.

Around my neck, of course, an hourglass.

The knock on the door came just as the edge of the sun dipped below the horizon. Helena was standing in her doorway as I walked downstairs. "Are you coming?" I asked.

"Past tithes enter Faerie separately. I have to cross over with Janet."

"I'm sorry," I said.

"At least it will be the last time."

"You've made up your mind to leave? I'm glad. Go be yourself." I hugged her. For a breath she stood, stiff, then her arms crept around my shoulders, and she hugged me back.

A voice came from downstairs, one I didn't recognize, one that sounded like the tolling of a clock. "It is time. You must come now, or not at all."

Helena stepped back, nodded, and I went.

Ariel was at the bottom of the steps. "I still think you're crazy, and I'm not wishing you luck." She pulled me into a hug, tight and fierce.

Marin was already at the door, standing next to a Fae woman whose dress was nearly as dark as her eyes, her hair the green and weeping branches of a willow. Neither of them said anything. The Fae woman turned on her heel, assuming we would follow.

"Marin—" I said.

But she only turned and walked away.

And so, in silence, I followed my sister down the stairs, and into the darkening forest.

We walked through the campus, past the mentors' houses and the artists' studios. Past the thorned shadows of the rose garden. Through the Commons, and along the shore of the Mourning River. To an old bridge, its worn stones faintly green with moss.

The bridge was whole tonight, as it had been the first time we crossed it, on Halloween. The stars changed overhead as we crossed, and I stumbled sideways, my heel skidding on the stone. My skin went hot, then cold. I felt watched, as if even the trees could see through my skin. I wanted to run forward, to turn back, both at once.

My shaking rattled the pages clutched in my hand, recalling me to myself, reminding me of what I was here for. I pulled in a breath, let it shudder out, and kept walking.

No Fae lined our path through the forest tonight. There was no need. We were coming to them, in slow progress, and my feet were already bloody in my shoes, the toll for the crossing paid. I matched my breath to my footsteps, trying not to quake in fear, trying to dampen the nerves sizzling beneath my skin.

Trying not to hear the fear that had been in Beth's voice. Not to hear the silence when she hadn't spoken of what would happen tonight. The only sounds now were that of the ground, crunching beneath our feet, and the whispers of our breath. The stars of Faerie were bright against Marin's hair, and I remembered another night, following my sister through the woods when we were children. She had brought me out safe, then, and I wished, oh, I wished that she would return safely tonight.

All of us who hoped to be chosen were there, gathered. Fifteen.

Both too many and not enough. In clothing to dance in, holding violins, or like Michelle, whose face looked drawn, with painted canvases tucked under her arms. I waved to her, and she turned away. I wondered if she had read the fairy tales she was looking for, if she had found any help in them if she did.

The Fae woman who'd brought Marin and me led the others away, one at a time. From where we were, those of us who remained couldn't see or hear anyone else. Maybe it was supposed to make the waiting easier. It didn't.

"Fuck this. I'm done." The snap of a chain, and a charm tossed to the ground. A tall man with a voice like warmed honey, his face all strong bones and rich dark skin that a camera would have worshipped. "This isn't worth it."

No one stopped him when he walked away. One less person to compete against.

"Here." The Fae woman stopped. "You." She summoned me with a wave of her hand, and I followed her through what looked like a thicker grove of trees.

It was, and it wasn't. I could see the trees, smell the dark green of them, hear branches rub against each other. But it was also a stage, spotlit and set in some vast amphitheater. The one layered over the other in palimpsest, each simultaneously real and not.

My stomach slid sideways. The pages I clutched rattled in my shaking hand as I stepped into the light. I could see them, the Fae in all their terrifying glory. The humans stood out like flaws in a gem. Janet, arrogant and unblinking. Beth, who nodded, and Evan, who dropped his gaze from mine. Helena, whose eyes were shadowed. I took a deep breath, and began.

Once upon a time.

"Once upon a time, there was a mother, and she had two daughters.

One of the girls was as dark as the night, and the other girl was as bright as the day. But their mother promised them that she loved them both, each the same, and would never give one more than she gave the other."

The world shifted, and I wasn't standing, reading for an audience, but sitting in the backseat of my mother's car, upholstery pricking against the backs of my legs. Second grade, I thought. Not a memory, or if it was, one so complete that every piece of it was tangible and real. My heart beat in that moment, not this one.

"You'll never be anything, Imogen. It's time for you to face that. You're the weird little girl who sits in the back because no one else wants to sit by her. I've tried to help you be normal, but you won't even make an effort. It's no wonder no one likes you." My mother's voice, on the way home from school, and even as the past ended, and I stood again in my present life, the floral scent of her perfume burned in my nostrils.

I held the pages in my hand tighter, reminded myself that the past was over, done, and kept reading.

"A promise such as that is all well and good, and who is to say if one girl's shoes were small and tight, and the other girl's were comfortable and new? They both, after all, had shoes. Equally impossible to measure whether a mother's hand contained a pinch or a kindness, when it touches both girls' cheeks.

"But one girl grew dimmer and the other grew brighter."

The shift, again. The world dropping away below my feet. I was twelve this time.

The feel of the scissors, cold against my head, the snick of the blades as they cut through my hair. It fell to the ground in hanks. "I told you not to talk to boys. Do you want people to think you're a slut?" When my mother finished, my hair was cut so close to my head that there was less than an inch of it left.

My scalp ached, and I wanted to reach up, to check that the hair I had always kept long after it had grown back out, that was twisted and pinned into a knot at the back of my neck, was still there. That it hadn't been shorn again, wasn't heaped at my feet. It had been the one thing I had thought was beautiful about myself, and she had taken it from me, and smiled when she did. My hand fisted at my side, trembled, but I kept it there, kept reading.

"The bright sister watched as her darker sister diminished, and it grieved her. A sister, she thought, was a half of a whole, a reflection in a glass, the echo of a heartbeat. One was not possible without the other. She did not understand what she saw from her mother, but she knew it was not love."

The word cracked as I spoke it. I swallowed hard, called my voice back into my throat, and kept reading.

"So the bright sister took herself from home, and set out to find a way to help the dark sister. She had heard there was a witch in the woods. A witch, she thought, could help."

Sickness burned in my gut, bile rushed up into my mouth, and my hands shook with rage. The next year. Three days before Christmas.

All of the contents of my drawers spilled out on the floor—pens and pushpins and bookmarks mingled with sweaters and leggings and underwear. Books were unshelved, the sheets ripped from the bed.

My notebooks, all of the stories I had ever written, were gone. Burned to ash. Marin's cry as she tried to save them.

My own screams.

My hand. Oh, God, my hand, burning and burning.

"*You have to learn to do as I say. I've told you and told you, and obviously that hasn't made an impression. I'm only doing this for your own good.*"

"You're not," I whispered, and there was a rustle from my audience. I could still feel the agony as the flames ate my skin, could smell the smoke, settling in my nose and throat, choking me. I looked up, out, but I couldn't see their faces. I bit the inside of my mouth until I tasted blood, pushed my feet harder against the elegant cages of my shoes, leaned into the pain there because that pain was real, found my place on the page, and continued to read.

"'Of course I can help you,' the witch told the bright sister. 'You and your sister both. But it will cost you.'

"'I'll pay anything,' the bright sister said, because she loved her dark sister, and because she did not understand the ways of bargaining with witches—how you tell them no two times, and only the third say yes.

"'I need a servant. The last girl got rescued by a dragon. Can you work?' the witch asked.

"'Yes,' said the bright sister.

"And so she did. Cleaning the witch's cottage and cooking the witch's meals and doing the witch's sewing, for a seam sewn by a witch will never hold."

Pain. Pain for each relived moment.

The bruises on my skin. A pinch for fidgeting. A slap for talking back. Stripes from a ruler on the back of my legs when I hadn't gotten straight A's on my report card. The calm promises that no one would believe me if I told. After all, I was a liar—that was what people who made up stories were. I was a liar. I was nothing. I was nothing. I was nothing.

Her voice was a litany in my head, a counterpoint to every word I spoke, as I continued to read.

"The bright sister worked until she was barely a shadow of herself, until she was smudged with dirt and dark as a corner. But witches keep their promises, and after a year and a day, the witch gave the bright sister two finely worked chains of silver. 'They will bind you together,' she said."

Something new. Something I hadn't lived.

Marin dancing. Our mother's voice. "Imogen is just jealous. She knows she's not as pretty, not as talented as you are, and so she doesn't want you to succeed. She doesn't want you to be happy."

Marin turning and turning, her eyes spotting the wall opposite to where our mother stood.

"It's why she left. She doesn't love you, and she's not coming back."

Marin missing her spot, and falling.

My heart broke as she fell. But wasn't that what I wanted, after all? For her to fall again, to not escape, to be good, but not quite good enough?

"When the bright sister returned home, she found that the dark sister was gone. Dead and buried, with only a hazel tree to mark her grave. The bright sister put one chain on the hazel tree, and the other one on herself, and then she lay down upon her sister's grave. She did not rise from there again.

"Soon, a rose grew from the grave as well, with flowers a color unseen anywhere else, petals of purest silver. It wrapped itself around the hazel tree as it grew, so close the two could not be separated.

"And the mother came from the house every day, and in her grief at what she had done, she watered both the rosebush and the hazel tree equally with her tears."

The end. I let my hand, still screaming with pain, fall to my side, the papers rattling. There was no applause, no visible reaction from the Fae, from anyone. It was like performing to a room full of statues, marble and cold. I was led through trees to a seat with other residents of Melete. Still that uncanny double vision, the forest and a stage, strobing one to the next.

I wanted not to be there. To be gone, to be home, to be away somewhere no one would see me shaking, where my mouth didn't taste of ashes, where I could put myself back together again. My feet throbbed with every beat of my pulse, and the left-hand sides of my pages were smeared with red, the blood from a paper cut.

From here, I could watch as the remaining artists presented their work. I was feverish with nerves, sick and relieved simultaneously. So much talent. A crashing storm of something on the piano that sounded like being caught up in a hurricane. Another writer, a poet who spoke a sestina. This, at least, I knew I was better than—the technique was impressive, but there was no heart beneath it.

I understood then, too, why there had been no reaction following my reading. I couldn't move to clap or cheer. Couldn't weep or gasp from beauty. Everything was pulled from my body, the emotions, the reactions sucked out from under my skin, taken from me at the height of their intensity. By the time the performance was over, I had already given my praise.

This is what it would be, to be in Faerie. This was the first taste of all of those seven years. Nothing I would feel would be mine.

And then Marin danced. The Myrtha variation from *Giselle*, the leaps, the power, the heartbreak. The queen of the fey women who haunted the forest, who stole young men and danced them to their deaths, in revenge for how they had been treated.

She was seduction and she was power, and she danced better than she ever had.

I don't know what played in her head as she danced. What memories she relived, or if she had been given another sort of spell to break. Her face was wet with tears as she finished, but every movement that she made, from the arch of her feet to the angle of her fingers, was perfect. Was true.

Silence when she finished, as there had been silence for all of us. I could not stand, could not clap, could not weep.

Then a chiming, as silver hourglasses fell from lapels, from chains. All of them.

Except for Marin's.

26

Sick to my stomach and unable to sleep, I paced on feet swollen and blistered. I'd failed.

Failed Gavin, failed Marin, failed myself. Everything I'd poured into the work hadn't been enough. Unable to hold myself together, undermined by my past.

The past, or whatever it had been. There had been no explanation, not from any of them, at the end. No reaction from the Fae, no words from the mentors. No thank you and good luck, you weren't what we were looking for this time, but we hope to see new work from you in the future.

Just a forest full of aching, echoing silence, and us alone to stumble our way out of it.

And now, Marin would go away to Faerie, and she might never come back. The best, the best I could hope for was that she might return in seven years, that she might still be herself then. But no promises, no guarantees.

I had ruined our relationship, made her think that I didn't love or support her, that all the poisoned words our mother dripped in her ear were true, and I had failed anyway.

I stumbled to the bathroom and vomited, retching again and again until all that came up was acid. Stood, trembling, and washed my face and hands, tried to clean the taste of my failure from my mouth, and then hobbled slowly downstairs to brew a cup of tea.

Three flights of stairs on feet that were sure they shouldn't be walking.

The light was still on in the kitchen. I hoped it was Marin. I missed my sister. Maybe now that what I promised Gavin didn't matter, I could somehow convince her to forgive me.

"Helena?" I couldn't parse what I was seeing at first. A limp form, bright-haired, on the floor, the shattered mug, the spilled liquid. The stench of rot and roses. Then I understood.

"Helena." I felt in her neck for a pulse. Still there. She was cold, clammy, and there was vomit crusting her mouth. The reek of decayed flowers was overwhelming.

"Help!" I screamed as loud as I could, cursing my phone, plugged into a charger on the third floor. "Help!"

Ariel ran into the kitchen. "What's wrong? Oh, God."

"Call campus security. We need to get her to a hospital."

Helena's breathing gasped and rattled. I didn't know what to do, so I held her hand and spoke to her. "Helena. Hang on. Just please hang on. We're getting you help."

"Imogen, is everything—oh, no." Marin, Gavin behind her.

"She drank something. I don't know what. Ariel's calling for help."

"The hospital can't help her," Gavin said, kneeling on the floor next to Helena. "The plants she used—they're from Faerie."

Ariel set her phone down. "Can you do something?"

"I don't know."

"Try," Marin said. "Please."

"One of you hold her."

I gathered Helena's head into my lap, held her shoulders. She was so cold. Gavin sniffed at the shattered mug, tasted the liquid spilled on the floor. His glamour fell away from him, his eyes shading to black, the crown of antlers rising up from his head. He looked utterly inhuman. The air in the room crackled, electric.

Gavin spoke a word, all sharp edges and daggers. It scorched the air like lightning, and Helena convulsed. I pushed on her shoulders, holding her steady, willing her to be safe. Her heels thudded against the floor.

He spoke again, and the air turned sour, the stench of rot overpowering the scent of roses. Helena choked, gasped. Liquid began to dribble from her mouth.

"Help me hold her up," I said, worried she would drown in whatever it was Gavin's magic was bringing out of her. Ariel and I maneuvered her to a sitting position. Marin stood, watching Gavin, her face like stone.

One more word, that flared like phosphorus behind my eyes. Helena vomited, thick ropes of green that coiled like snakes. Her eyes opened, then closed again. She moaned.

"The poison is out of her system," Gavin said. He hunched over, looking like he might vomit himself. "Someone should stay with her, though. She'll feel horrible when she wakes."

"But she'll wake up? She'll be okay?" Ariel asked.

"I've done everything I can to make it so she will." Tired, I thought. He looked tired. Just like the rest of us, and the thought chilled me.

Gavin carried Helena upstairs, and Ariel and I got her cleaned up and into bed. She was so pale, her chest barely moving the blankets as she breathed. Her eyes hadn't opened again.

Marin came in later. "Has she woken up yet?"

I shook my head. "She was there tonight. In Faerie. That's how she got the whatever it was she took."

"She was there?" Marin asked.

"She had to be." I spoke in a near whisper, as if the words might break if they were said too loudly. "Like Halloween, everyone who had ever dwelt in Faerie and was at Melete had to be there. It must have been awful for her, watching the thing she thought she'd be doing her whole life. She was there, and Janet was too—who knows what horrors Janet might have spewed at her.

"Didn't you see them? In the audience?"

"No," Marin said, and turned away, looking toward the window. I wondered again at what magic it was that she had danced through, but I wouldn't ask her to relive it.

The pink of the rising sun illuminated the blinds, and she winced. "Gavin said if Helena hadn't been found, the poison would have killed her at sunrise."

"That seems oddly specific." But it had a horrible kind of logic. All the ritual and belief necessary for Fae magic. Sunrises and sunsets and every seven years.

"Has someone told Janet?" I asked.

"Ariel was going over there."

"I don't know what to say to you."

She turned and opened the blinds, letting in the risen sun. "Not now. Let's just not, right now."

I blinked, eyes tearing at the sudden brightness, and turned away, toward Helena, still unwoken, still a faded ghost, and nodded.

Janet refused to come see Helena.

Ariel's rage was incandescent. "She said that she had given Helena every chance to be extraordinary, and instead, Helena had chosen to be mediocre and a coward, and this was only one more example of that."

"That's disgusting," I said.

"I'm going back there later. I swear to God, I will drag that woman over here if I have to. She just stood there, looking like I was something she had wiped off her shoe, telling me that Helena was no longer her concern."

Helena still hadn't woken up. She was, if anything, paler than she had been, the shock of her hair almost obscene against the translucence of her skin.

Gavin, still looking exhausted, had checked on her, and said that she was beyond his ability to help. Later that day, the same Fae woman who had brought Marin and me to the selection came. She had, she said, some skill with healing, and she was here at Gavin's instruction to use it. Helena's room smelled like the inside of a storm when she finished.

"Will she be okay?" I asked.

"I have done what I could to make her so," she said. "But what she took, we call it Heart's Ease. If death is what will ease her heart, then that is the fate she has chosen for herself, and nothing that any of us can do will serve to undo that choice."

I wished, very much, that the Fae could lie. I could have used the comfort.

"Can you get word to Thomas?" I asked Gavin.

"I have," he said.

"Is someone with Helena now?" I asked.

"Ariel is," he said. "And Marin's here."

"Good." I shoved my feet into wellies and grabbed my coat. "I'll be back."

I knocked on Janet's door hard enough to bruise my knuckles. When she opened it, the house smelled like she had been baking.

"She took Heart's Ease. Do you know what that means?" I asked. I could taste fury in my mouth, like heat.

"That her life or death is her choice," Janet said. She sounded like she was making observations on some mildly inconvenient weather. Her hair was perfect, her clothing precisely ironed.

"Did it occur to you that if you took, oh, half an hour out of your day to visit her, she might choose to live?"

"She made her choice when she drank. I have nothing to say to her." She began to close the door.

I shoved my foot in it.

"She could die." I spoke the words slowly, as if that would be the thing that would make Janet hear and understand.

"Then she will. She is a coward, and a mediocre poet who never once used any of the advantages I gave her. And so, I have nothing to say, and no interest in keeping her in a world she has chosen to leave. Now remove yourself from my house." She didn't even look before closing the door.

I pulled my hand back, fist clenched. I couldn't even lie to myself, couldn't walk off in a rage of *I don't understand how a mother could do that.* The things that a mother could do were permanently scarred onto my body. I understood them very well.

It was worse, somehow, when it was your mother. When the person who was supposed to be the one who loved you the most made it clear that she didn't love you at all, that you were nothing to her, that a random person on the street would have showed you more compassion, more kindness. It made the lack of love all the more obvious.

I stopped, wrapped my arms around my stomach, and let the sobs fall from my throat. Cried for Helena, for Marin, for myself, until I was raw, hollowed out.

Then I scrubbed my hands across my face, and slogged back home. At least there, I could pretend like I was doing something that would make a difference.

I met Thomas on my way up to the house. "Hey, this year's girl, I've come to meet my kid." He smiled, but he looked pale, his clothing rumpled, dark crescents beneath his eyes.

"She's upstairs." I took him to Helena's room. He sat with her for hours.

That night, Helena died.

Janet never came.

27

I wore the same dress that I had worn just five nights before. Not even a week. Not even long enough for the blisters on my feet to have healed before I stuffed them back into the same shoes that had put them there.

The click of heels from all our shoes echoed down the stairs, across the wood floors of the house, on the groaning front porch. They sounded wrong, those steps from only three sets of feet, as if the house itself had forgotten someone.

Helena's body had been cremated. There would be no waxen figure in a polished coffin, no open grave like a scar on the earth, waiting for its contents. But we would stand, and speak her name, and remember. That was what you did when someone died. It wasn't enough, couldn't possibly be, but we could observe the fucking formalities.

Melete was green and budding. Young leaves hazing the branches of the trees, grass curling up from the dirt, birds singing the songs that welcomed the season. Too bright, too loud.

This was why it rained on funerals in the movies. Because anything other than muted grey, than the sky itself weeping, seemed callous and false. An abomination, that someone can be dead, and the trees be full of singing birds.

We had her memorial in the rose garden. It wasn't in bloom yet, the plants little more than thorned canes, but it was the one place at Melete that any of us could remember hearing her say that she liked.

"Which is awful," Ariel had said. "She lived here her entire life, and the best we can do is a muddy bunch of thorns to say good-bye to her in."

We were a small party of mourners. Ariel, Marin, me. Thomas, looking as if he hadn't slept since Helena died. Gavin.

Janet knew where we were. None of us expected her to show up. "She can't be bothered to show up for an alive daughter. I don't know why she'd come for a dead one," Marin had said.

"I could go tell her Thomas is here. She'd run to meet him," Ariel said.

But we decided we wouldn't tell her that. Janet had made everything in Helena's life about Thomas. We wouldn't let her make this about him too.

So the five of us stood awkwardly in the mud and the thorns. Then Gavin took hold of one of the plants, and when he took his hands away, the entire garden was in bloom. Pinks and reds and yellows and whites, the air heavy with fragrance and with velvet petals. It was beautiful.

"You think that makes it better?" Ariel rounded on him, and Gavin took a step back. "She's not even here to see them. You couldn't bend one of your own rules, help her out, show just a smidge of compassion, and you think flowers will fix it?"

"No," Gavin said quietly. "I don't. I don't think flowers will fix anything. And if there had been a rule it was within my power to break, I would have." The roses bloomed brighter and wilder as he spoke. "There are things I can't fix, no matter how much I want to. I hate knowing that I failed to heal her, couldn't bring her back, couldn't even make a chain to fasten around her neck." His glamour slipped sideways, the too-dark eyes, the curling horns flashing in and out before our eyes. Marin took a step toward him.

Gavin paused, gathered himself, all of his masks falling back into place. And again, I thought he looked tired. Mortal. "There are any number of things I would fix, rules I would break, if I could. I cannot."

He looked at Marin as he spoke the last, and Ariel looked away. She picked a rose, the same vivid fuchsia as Helena's hair had been. "She helped me move my steamer trunk."

Then Marin. "She wore a Santa hat and sang, when we made cookies."

Gavin. "She was loyal."

Then me. "She burned like a flame." I tossed my rose on the ground with the other three, our small, inadequate tributes.

Then Thomas. Who said nothing, only threw his rose to the ground and walked away.

Roses. The rose garden, the riot of them Evan had brought at Thanksgiving. I didn't walk back to the house with the others, but stepped out of my shoes, and into the mud. Through the Commons and to the studios. To Evan's. I hadn't spoken to him in weeks, and that was right, that was perfect.

I ran, almost. Wanting to be there before I cared, before I let myself think. I stepped inside, dropped my shoes, and unzipped my dress, shedding it onto the floor like an old skin.

"Imogen, what are you doing?" His hair was mussed, and there were holes in his T-shirt. I wanted to hook my fingers into them and tear. To tear, and to keep tearing, to leave marks on his skin as proof that I had been there.

"Helena is dead, and I can't feel anything. You said I made you feel real." I unhooked my bra, slid my panties down my legs. "Make me feel something."

"Imogen."

My hand on his crotch, the hardness beneath the strained denim, and my voice a haze of fury. "I can tell you want me. And I can't"—I choked on tears, swollen in my throat—"I can't breathe, Evan. I can't fucking bear this. Just make it stop."

His arms around me, a careful space between us. His hands stroking my hair. "I've got you, Imogen. You can breathe. It's okay."

He spoke a stream of nonsense words, like you'd say to a child, to soothe them as they sobbed. And I did. Until my eyes were swollen and gritty, my mouth dry. I cried for Helena, who was gone. For Marin, who would be. For all of us, lost.

When I finished, I was shaking from cold and embarrassment. I couldn't even look at Evan as I stepped away from him. "Let me just . . . I'll go." My hands shook as I stepped back into my underwear.

"I owe you an apology."

I paused, half into my dress.

"For the gallery. For what I did. I want to say it to your face. I am sorry. I was an ass."

"And a dick."

"Yes. I'm sorry."

The zipper stuck halfway up my dress. Better to walk home looking like I'd just been tumbled than to have his hands so close, to ask for his help. I'd mortified myself enough for one day.

"You don't have to forgive me. I probably wouldn't. But I am truly sorry, Imogen. I don't know if that changes anything between us, but I want you to know I mean it."

"I should go," I said.

"All right."

Halfway home, I realized I'd forgotten my shoes. They were hateful things. I didn't go back for them.

Thomas stayed, after the memorial, to help pack up Helena's room. "I don't even know what I should save," he said, staring into her closet. "Everything, I guess. Or maybe donate the clothes? Do you two want anything?"

"If you're not sure, let's pack up everything for now. Then, when you're ready, you can go through it. That way you don't regret anything," Marin said.

"You mean besides the fact that I had a daughter I never spoke to?" Thomas said. "Because as regrets go, that's a good one."

"Look," I said, setting aside a notebook half-full of poems. "You fucked up. You did what you could at the time, and you thought you'd have forever to fix it, or if it didn't get fixed then at least you could tell yourself it was her decision not to see you."

"Imogen!" Marin said.

I kept going. "You fucked up, but when Gavin called, you got your ass on a plane and got here. And no, that doesn't make you a hero, or even a good dad, but you did it. And it was the right thing.

"So no, you never had a conversation with her, and yes, that sucks, and yes, it's something you never get to fix, but she wasn't alone at the end because you were there. You never spoke to her, but you were the one who bothered to show up, and it's not enough, but it's also not nothing. Because at least two of us tried to drag Janet over here, and she couldn't even be bothered to walk across campus."

"I'm sorry," Marin said. "My sister—"

"Is right," Thomas said, setting his hair on end with his hand. "She's right."

He huffed out a breath. "Let's donate the clothes. Pack the rest of her things. Unless either of you want something. I'm going to go outside to get some air."

"What is wrong with you?" Marin said after he left.

"I'm tired," I said. "I don't just mean lack of sleep, though I mean that, too. But I am tired of walking on eggshells. Of not saying things. Do you know where I went after Helena's memorial?" I sat down in a heap of semi-sorted clothing.

Marin shook her head.

"To Evan. Evan. Because I didn't think I could count on you for comfort, and I needed it from someone.

"I feel like I've lost you already," I said. "When I'd do anything to keep you here."

"You can't, Imogen."

"Actually, she could," Thomas said, windblown, the scent of cigarettes clinging to him. "There's a way."

"What are you talking about?" Marin asked.

"The tithe can be broken. By love strong enough to wrest the intended sacrifice back from the collected desire of Faerie. Or at least that's the poetic way of putting it. Basically"—he looked at me—"you have to want Marin more than they do."

"What do I have to do?" I asked.

"Imogen, no." Marin's voice was sharp. "I'm going. I want to."

"What would I have to do?" I asked again, ignoring Marin. Because why would Gavin have told her now, now when her presence there was guaranteed, that he worried Faerie might kill her? Speak a thing and make it happen.

But if I still had a chance to undo my failure, to protect my sister, I would take it.

"I don't know the exact details, being as it's not something I ever contemplated, but when the tithe goes, it isn't like popping over to the neighbor's to borrow a cup of sugar. This is the Fae we're talking about, so there's a ritual. If you can interrupt the ritual—pull your sister down from the horse she'll be riding, hold on to her as some variety of batshit weird stuff that I imagine will be unpleasant for you both happens—do all that while Faerie flings its might against you—and it will, it won't be happy about you taking what it wants—then she stays. The tithe is broken.

"Of course, if you fail—and you will fail, Imogen, almost everyone who has ever tried has—you go to Faerie with her. And while she will only have to serve the seven years, you won't get to come back. Ever."

"That's why Janet hates you," I said. "She wanted you to save her."

"Got it in one. And there was no way in hell. I had just gotten back—even if I had loved her, there was no way I would have risked it. Faerie is not a nice place if you're human, and seven years there is a prison sentence, not a vacation. I wouldn't have been strong enough, and I didn't love her."

"Imogen, you can't," Marin said. "It's too risky."

"Not any riskier than what you've signed up for, not really."

"You're assuming I want to be saved. You don't get to make that decision for me."

"Marin, I—"

"No. This is not a subject that's up for discussion. I want this. I want to go. I am going. The only thing you have to think about is whether you support me or not. I'd rather you do, but even if you don't, Imogen, I am going."

I tried, then. I tried to force air through my lungs, force words from my mouth. To tell her what Gavin had said. That this wasn't about keeping her from what she wanted, this was about keeping her alive.

I tried, and nothing came out. Magic wrapped my throat like vines, choking off everything but silence.

"I'm going," Marin said, and I couldn't tell her no.

"I was going to speak to Marin about it after the selection," Gavin said. "The rules that govern the tithe require the opportunity to be given. But then . . . Helena."

The sun streaked down through fast-moving clouds, and the wind stole pieces of my hair from the ponytail I had pulled it back in before running. I had escaped my thoughts for five miles, only to come home and find the reminder of them on my front porch. That was fine. We needed to talk.

"Were you going to speak to her? Really? Because when I tried, I couldn't. Gavin, you took my voice." My hands fisted at my sides.

"I did. Before. I needed to be sure you wouldn't speak with her about it. I would do it again."

"Undo it. Now. You had no right."

"Of course. But once you know the truth of it, you won't require magic to keep your silence. You'll choose it on your own."

His left hand a fist that opened, and he said a word I didn't know. The sensation of a necklace snapping, of something sliding down and away from my throat. I swallowed hard. "Explain."

"Yes, Thomas is correct that the tithe can be broken, and I am required to tell Marin that she may ask someone to risk themselves for her. But not of the reasons I think she should avail herself of it."

"Right. Because that would fall under influencing. Some other easy wiggle word for why you can't do anything that's actually useful."

"Imogen, I'm—"

"Sorry. Yes. I know. Easy for you to say when you're not the one Marin hates. So, fine. Tell me how this works. Thomas said the odds weren't good."

"Faerie has existed for longer than Melete, and the tithe had always been a part of Faerie. Perhaps once every hundred years, someone has tried to break it—to save the father of their child, or to make a grand romantic gesture.

"I can only think of two times in all of our history that it has worked."

"Well," I said, "at least it's not impossible."

"Imogen, I would have told Marin about this because I had to. Because the tithe is what it is, and I can't change it. But I won't ask you to do this, and I would have asked her not to mention it to you. The risk is too much, and Marin would never forgive me if you were lost. As much as I'm able, I will keep her whole, and send her back to you when it is over."

As much as he was able. Which would be not at all. Roses grown in a graveyard, and too late. A fall in a dance studio, and a partner wearing the bruises. "Funny, but I don't think you love her any less now than you did a few months ago when you begged for my help, so forgive me for not thinking of that as being particularly useful."

"Can you help me at all—tell me anything? Why it's so dangerous to try, or who broke it before?"

His face twisted; he swallowed hard. "I can't. Not directly. But know that Faerie suffers, without a tithe, and so anything connected to it suffers as well. The old stories are sometimes true, and not all changelings are stolen."

Good. Great. That was all very helpful and crystal clear.

"Has anything changed?" I asked. "Do you still think that she might not make it through seven years?"

He opened his mouth, closed it again.

"Never mind," I said. "I can tell you're trying to figure out a way to talk around it so you're not actually lying to me. I have to try, you know. She's my sister. I have to tell her."

"There's one other thing," Gavin said. "There has to be balance. If you save her, you'd get what the tithe promises. The success. All of it. It would go to you, not her."

I sucked in a breath. "That's why you broke the spell. Because you knew she'd never believe me when I told her why I'm rescuing her if she knows that."

His face was kind. "I'm sorry. But you needed to know."

"You need to leave. I can't look at you right now."

If I was going to break the tithe, save Marin, I needed to see if it was actually possible, if I had better odds than just sheer luck. I needed guidelines, a to-do list, or whatever the situational equivalent was.

"Well," Beth said, "I don't know what went on in Faerie, of course, but forty-nine years ago, Melete almost lost its funding. There were other things that went on then, too—someone was disqualified for a major award. I think a Grammy, but I'm not positive. A resident died under suspicious circumstances. And it seems to me that things were quite precarious for two or three years after."

"Rebuilding years," I said.

"If I were trying to find years when the tithe failed, that's where I'd begin."

"That makes sense," I said. "It was the one hint of bad press I found when I was first looking into applying here."

"I'm surprised you found that much. The Fae are good about their PR. Speak no evil is fairly literal in their case."

Didn't I know it. "Those are cute." I gestured at her lap.

Today's knitting was rainbow-colored yarn, and very small. "I'm making socks for my granddaughter. You would think smaller would be easier, but these are a pain in the ass."

She jabbed at one of them with her knitting needle, but it was clear that, pain in the ass or not, Beth was delighted by knitting tiny socks for tiny feet.

"Why would losing the tithe mean that Melete loses funding, though? I understand why Faerie would have problems, but why would that carry over to here?"

"Because Faerie is woven into all of Melete. The Fae don't just benefit by having the equivalent of an artist-in-residence, they benefit by having all of you here. By surrounding themselves in the energy, the emotion, generated by the intensity of this experience.

"And the benefit is mutual. The good fortune that accrues to the tithe also disperses over Melete, and those associated with it. Or did you think all of this happened by generous alumni donations?"

I felt embarrassed, naïve. "I hadn't thought about it at all, really."

"Financially, of course, most of it does. But that generosity is moved by Faerie's influence. Faerie takes care of its own first, so if it suffers, so does Melete. Without a tithe, Faerie will suffer."

She set down her knitting, tiny socks half-formed in her lap. "Be careful, Imogen. They won't like it if you try to keep Marin from them."

I didn't particularly care what they would like. "Did you ask someone to help you?"

"No, and I think most of us don't. We agree to go because we want the benefits, even knowing the risks. I know you're worried for Marin, but it's more than likely she'll be fine once she gets back."

"She fell. At Halloween. From the effects of being there. So I'm worried." Spell or not, I couldn't put Marin and death in the same sentence. It was too big to say.

"Ah. I hadn't known. That first trip can be difficult, all the novelty. But it can also serve as an inoculation—she'll know what to expect after that.

"As it is, of course I understand your worry. She's your sister. But I don't think you need to worry excessively."

"Thanks," I said, and got up.

"Oh, and Imogen. The piece you read was quite good. Whatever else, I want you to know you've been worthy of your time here. You might keep that in mind, as you make your decisions about what you're willing to risk."

It mattered, hearing her say that. Had it been anyone other than Marin at risk, had the risk to Marin been anything less than Gavin's fear that she would die, it would have mattered enough to change my mind. But Marin had always saved me, and I had failed her once already. Leaving her to the tithe wasn't a choice.

Back home, later that afternoon, I opened the door to find Janet standing on the front porch, her hair bound up, her suit precise. "I've come for her things."

"I'm sorry?" I said, not believing what I heard.

"Helena's things. I want them. Her notebooks, her computer. The rest of it doesn't matter, but if there's any of her work that's worth salvaging, it ought to be published. I've already spoken to my editor. If I write the introduction, they expect the volume to do quite well."

I bit the inside of my mouth to keep from spitting my first response at her. Literally counted to ten in anger before I could trust myself to speak. "They're not here. Thomas—who, incidentally, did come and visit Helena before she died—took them with him."

She blinked, whitened. "He was here?"

"Yes. He came to see Helena. Maybe if you had bothered to, you could have seen him, and he could have explained, for the thousandth time, that he doesn't love you, that he never did."

She went as hard and cold as stone. "He should have loved me. If Tania had kept to the bargain, he would have. When you get back, you get everything you ever wanted. All I ever wanted was him. Every word I wrote, everything I did, I did for him."

"That's not love, Janet. That's obsession." I realized then that what Thomas thought was wrong. Janet hadn't been angry at him for not trying to break the tithe. She had wanted to go, wanted all the promises that came with it. She was angry because he didn't do what she did—spend seven years waiting on the other side.

"I spent seven years in hell for him, and what did I get out of it?" she said.

"Helena."

"And she should have been what brought him back to me. I tried everything with that girl, brought her up here, so that she would be closer to Faerie, so that she would be surrounded by art, by artists, by people who understood sacrifice." She was so calm, so logical, as if she were explaining the rules for the composition of a sonnet. "It should have turned her into an artist, too."

"Did you ever bother to ask her if that was what she wanted?"

"It should have been. You know what they are. You've seen them. Your own sister will go and live with her lover, away in Faerie. You write fairy tales—the Fae are the happy ending everyone wants." Then there was grief on her face. Not for the loss of Helena, but for the loss of Faerie. Seeing it there made me sick.

"That's not how the stories end, Janet. The thing that comes before 'happily ever after'? It's 'they lived.' Helena didn't. She's not here anymore, and neither are her things. Now please. Go. Before I call campus security, and have you removed from my house."

"They should have let me stay. If they wouldn't give me Thomas, they should have let me stay in Faerie. They tell you you've bargained for everything you've ever wanted, but nothing I had was.

"Tell your sister to remember that."

28

We kept the door to Helena's room closed, after. She had kept it like that herself, and we had gotten used to it. Seeing it open was a scar on the wall, an emptiness that looked wrong and out of place. But it was cracked now, a slant of light showing through into the hallway.

I opened the door the rest of the way. Ariel was sitting on the bare mattress, her back hard against the wall. "I never read any of her poems. I keep thinking about that. That was what she was here for, that was what mattered to her, and I never read them."

"I kept a notebook of hers," I said. "From when we packed up her stuff. I haven't been able to bring myself to open it, because I think she'd be pissed that I was reading her drafts." I imagined her face, the twist of her mouth, and my eyes prickled as I smiled.

"I'm so angry," Ariel said. "Not at her, but around her. Mostly at Janet. I have never wanted to punch anyone in the face as much as I want to punch her.

"And just . . . everything. Everything that told her that she was only as good as her art, and that her art wasn't good enough."

She closed her eyes, dropped her head back against the wall. "And then I feel like an enormous hypocrite, because we weren't friends, and I never read her poetry."

"Let's read one," I said. "You have a lighter, right?"

"Yes, because I occasionally need to ruin my own voice with smoking. Why?"

"Meet me downstairs. We'll go to the Wishing Bridge."

It was a tradition: Write down your fondest wish, the secret one that you tell no one else, the one you can hardly admit to yourself, even as you write it down. Then light it on fire, and toss it over the bridge. If it burns away completely, before the water extinguishes it or carries it away, then your wish will come true.

All the traditions that get built up around wishing, around the ways we tell ourselves that yes, this one time, we did everything right. This time, it has to come true.

This time, we'll get what we want.

Ariel and I stood at the bridge's rail, and I opened Helena's notebook. "Here's one. It fits all on one page."

I tore the poem from the notebook, and gave the page to Ariel. She read it out, her glorious, rich voice speaking Helena's words to the trees, to the Mourning River beneath us, to the air. The page trembled in her hand, but her voice was strong.

Here was the sunlight, bright in the sky, glinting diamonds off the water. The green heart of spring rising from the ground, flowers fragrant in the air. The day was beautiful, and it was broken, because all that was there was a page of words, and not the person who had written them.

Hearing the poem, I cried for Helena again. For the waste. Because, in a way, she had been right. It wasn't a great poem. It was competent, it was technically skilled. But it wasn't great.

Yet.

It might have been, though. Because in the words, there was an ear that heard language like music. There was a voice that wanted to be something it wasn't yet, but that it might have been, if she'd ever once gotten enough support to believe in herself, and in her art.

Helena wasn't a great poet when she died, but she could have been one, if she had lived.

When Ariel finished reading, she looked at me. I nodded.

She clicked her lighter on, and touched the flame to the corner of the page. The fire licked around Helena's words, flaring brighter and stronger. Ariel held the page until it burned almost to her fingers, then tossed it in the air. The page was gone, burned to ash and air before it touched the water.

"There," she said. "Now maybe she gets her fucking wish."

Because that, too, is a wish we tell ourselves when people are lost. That they go on. That their name is spoken, and so part of them remains. That the truth of who they were lingers, that what matters will never die.

That they are more than ash on the wind, more than a wish carried on water.

I wish. I wish. I wish.

I had let my guard down. Too busy thinking of everything else, of Helena, of a thousand improbable plots to save Marin. I wasn't paying attention, and so, it was my fault, really. If I had been thinking clearly, I would have hit delete when I saw our mother's name come up in my inbox, but I was only halfway paying attention, and so I opened it.

There was a friend who could get me a job teaching high school English, which was a real career, unlike fiddling about making things up. Never mind that I didn't have the degree or qualifications necessary to teach in high school. That part was relatively benign, as messages from my mother went.

She still wasn't sure why I'd run off to Melete, which, incidentally, had certainly only accepted me so that Marin would attend.

Everything she'd ever heard had said real writers could write any-where, but since I needed the crutch, she hoped I was finally writ-ing a novel while I was there. That lady on that morning talk show had written a novel, and it had only taken her three months and it had sold over a hundred thousand copies and now they were making it into a movie, and so it couldn't be that difficult to write a book. Was I sure I was working hard enough?

I shook my head. It sucked to read, but mostly it was a version of the kind of thing I'd heard before, and not just from my mother, but from any number of well-meaning friends trying to help me hit the bestseller lists. Because of course novel writing was that easy, which explained why so many people had similar experiences. Then I made the mistake of continuing to read.

No matter what I was writing, I had better not make up any lies about her to put in it. One of the women in her neighborhood had said there was a very cruel mother in a short story of mine, and had asked if we were still on speaking terms, and she wouldn't stand for people to be walking around thinking things like that about her. She had never done anything to me that I hadn't deserved, that wasn't my fault, and the times she was strict with me, it was for my own good. If I tried to play the victim card just so I could get on televi-sion, if I wrote lies about her to try and fool the people who couldn't see me for what I was, she'd get a lawyer, and she'd sue.

She knew plenty of examples of people who had decided to trade on lies instead of talent, but she wouldn't let me do that. She'd make sure I couldn't. It might hurt me, but it was for my own good.

Hand shaking, stomach full of acid, I hit delete.

Everything had been for my own good. No matter what she had done. All the meals she had refused to let me eat had been missed for my own good. I needed discipline. The books thrown in the trash, because I had to learn to live in the real world. Every memory relived the night of the selection—the sound of her voice, the feel of the scissors, the beating so visceral I had expected to be covered in bruises the next day, the shrieking, burning pain of my hand in the fire—all of that had always been done for my own good.

I felt horrible—flushed, and then chilled, like my legs couldn't hold me if I stood, like I needed to run until my muscles burned. It was my fault. I should have known better. I knew what she was like. She wanted the reaction, even if she wasn't there to witness it. She had already sent something ugly to Marin.

I scrubbed at my eyes and stood, light-headed from stress. Marin. Once might not have been enough. Our mother might have emailed both of us. I needed to check on my sister.

I stumbled and nearly fell on the top step, then clutched at the railing, made myself watch my feet as I walked down the twelve steps to the second floor.

Marin's door was open. "Marin, did you—oh. Gavin. I'm sorry. I was just . . . I'll."

"Imogen, what happened?" Gavin rushed across the room and took my shoulders gently in his hands, keeping me upright. "Here, sit down. Marin's in the shower. She'll be right out. Or do you need me to get her?"

He helped me over to Marin's bed, sat next to me, then stood again. "Let me go get her for you."

"Gavin, I'm fine. Really. I'm so sorry for acting like that. I just. I'll go back to my room." Stupid. Stupid and embarrassing, letting him see me like this.

"Please, she'd want to know."

She might not. We had hardly spoken over the last few weeks.

Maybe she thought I was a liar who had abandoned her. Maybe she'd think I deserved this.

Gavin knocked on the bathroom door before opening it, and a few seconds later, Marin stepped out, wrapped in her robe, a towel around her hair.

She sat down, put her arm around me. "Mommy Dearest?"

I nodded. "I'm sorry. I'll go. I just wanted to make sure you were okay. I'll go." I tried to get up, but my legs betrayed me, sending me falling back to the bed.

"I've got you. You don't need to go." Marin wrapped me in her arms. "I've got you."

The door closed softly behind Gavin. I leaned my head onto my sister's shoulder, and I wept.

I cried until I felt as if I had been turned inside out. For the fact that my mother could still hurt me like this, years after I'd moved out. For my sister, because even though I could feel her heart beat, I had built a wall between us, and it was a wall I would most likely build higher before this was done. "I'm sorry I fucked things up so badly, Marin."

"You really wrote me. When you left." Her voice sounded high, hesitant. A girl's voice, a child's. "I saw it. That night. I saw then, and knew it was true. You didn't think you were leaving me alone."

"I did write. So many letters, Marin. I thought you didn't write back because you were mad at me." I didn't tell her what I saw, her believing the lie that I hadn't loved her.

"Do you think she enjoyed it? Putting us against each other like that? I mean, she must have, because why else would she go to the trouble, but I just can't imagine. It's like my brain all goes to spiders when I think about all the lies she told, trying to make it so we'd hate each other."

"I've never hated you, Marin."

- 2 6 6 -

"I've never hated you, either."

"I know," I said. "You sent me stars."

"I was so scared when I did that. I thought you'd return them unopened or something. But I saw them, and I remembered the Star Princess stories, and I just missed you so much."

"The first thing I did when I got them was put them up. I take them everywhere. Looking at them is how I know I'm home."

I dragged in a breath. "I wrote you the Star Princess stories."

Her hand tightened around mine.

"I was going to give them to you. For Christmas, that first year."

"Do you"—she sniffled—"do you still have them?"

"They're in storage. But I still have them." Tears leaked hot from my eyes.

"Maybe I could read them sometime?"

"Yeah," I said. "That'd be good."

"I'm sorry I let things get so fucked up between us," Marin said.

"We're okay?" I asked, knowing it wasn't that easy, that this wasn't the kind of thing that magic words made better, knowing that they had to be said all the same. There had to be a start.

"We're okay."

The run felt like purging poison from my system. My head was clear, and I had figured out a new scene, a way to make something that had been too flat more emotionally complex. I was going to ask Marin to read my draft before I sent it to Beth, but I thought it was close to being ready.

I ran up the stairs and into the house, got halfway down the hall, and then stopped. Walked backward, slowly.

"Oh, good, Imogen, you're here." Marin's voice, but she wasn't the only one in the front room.

"It will make it much easier if I explain to you both at once." Janet. Smiling. My skin broke out in gooseflesh.

"I know a good deal about the tithe, having watched Thomas go through it, and then of course being chosen myself. And I know that the Fae can be so scrupulous about their honesty that details get left out. There is so much that's important in the details. I want to be sure you know what to expect." Her smile was a witch with a poisoned apple in her hand, a forgotten fairy extending a spindle.

"I think we both know what to expect," I said.

"I'm quite certain you do, Imogen. It was Marin I was concerned about. Concerned that she might have had second thoughts, and asked you to try to rescue her, not knowing what she'd be giving up if you succeeded.

"You do know, right, dear?"

Marin looked at me, looked at Janet. She shook her head. My unsaid words rose up in my throat to choke me.

"Ah. Perhaps I thought you were closer than you are. The kind of sisters who shared the important things. Well, I hope there are some things that you share, because if Imogen breaks the tithe, you get nothing that you were promised, Marin. None of what you've agreed to risk yourself for. She gets all of it."

"Nothing?" Marin asked, her voice shaking. "I'll be nothing?"

I closed my eyes.

"But I know how close you are. I'm sure Imogen will take care of you." The comfort of serpents, poison and green.

"Did you know?" Marin's voice, sharp as knives. "Imogen, did you?"

"Oh dear. And I was only trying to help. You two clearly have a lot to talk about. I'll see myself out." Janet smiled at me on her way out the door.

"Marin, I'm sorry. I—"

She held up her hand, stepped back. "Don't. Until you decide that you want to support me, that you're happy for me finally being the best, being better than you, until you can watch me cross that bridge into Faerie and cheer for me while I do, you stay the fuck away from me, Imogen."

She followed Janet out of the front door, closing it between us.

I went upstairs. Took off my shoes. Didn't even shower, just crawled into my bed. Pulled the blanket over me until everything was dark, until I couldn't see the stars on my ceiling, until I was completely cocooned.

29

"Get up. Away from the desk. Let's go." Ariel stood in the doorway, holding my jacket out to me.

"Where are we going?"

"Out. To the Market. To There, if we have to. I don't care, as long as it's somewhere that doesn't make me feel like I am the neutral country in a war zone. Come on. Now."

All of the progress that Marin and I had made was destroyed. She was convinced I was jealous of her, that I wouldn't be happy until I had stolen all of her chances for success. Impossible to tell her "I am trying to save your life" when my reward for doing so would be exactly the thing she was most afraid of.

Plus, I still wasn't sure I could save her. The Fae's magic, or PR savvy, or whatever it was that kept the responses to Melete so uniformly positive in the press, had also all but obscured whatever happened when the tithe was broken forty-nine years ago. I could find traces of the fallout, but nothing of the actual events.

"Okay, you're right. I could use the air. And the company." And the mad glitter of the Market. I pulled on my boots, shrugged into my jacket.

The sky was late-evening lavender-blue, and almost warm enough to make the jacket unnecessary. The greening trees were dotted with birds.

"I can't see them anymore without wondering if they're real birds, or if they're Fae," Ariel said.

"There's no reason for them to be watching now, though," I said. "They know who they're getting." Everything smelled like spring. The dark richness of the earth, the green sweetness of the grass.

"Unless you steal her away from them." Ariel looked at me sideways. "Is that still the plan?"

"If I can figure something out by May first," I said. The birds lifted from their trees, flocking ahead of us. "Even if I can't."

"Do you ever think, 'Fuck it, it's only seven years, her boyfriend can handle this, I'm out'?"

"All the time."

Ariel stopped walking. "Really?"

"She's so angry at me. And I pretty much have no idea how to pull this off. Which makes me wonder if I'm throwing away our relationship, my future, for nothing.

"But I have to try, Ariel. She's all I have."

Her arm around my shoulders. "I know."

The Market opened before us, in all its color and chaos. But this time, I no longer held the key to the treasure trove of wonders. The Market, the people in it, they didn't want me there.

We walked though the booths, the sky still light enough that the fairy lights hung in the trees were dim against it. Time and again, I was ignored. Shoved aside, my foot stepped on by someone trying very hard to pretend I didn't exist. The Fae knew. Somehow, they knew that I would try to keep Marin from them, from the tithe, and even if they couldn't stand directly against me, they were under no obligation to make my life pleasant.

No gifts, no offered food or drink. Just lines of turned backs and deaf ears. Of accidental elbows and feet catching my heels. It got worse the longer we were there.

"This is kind of weird, right?" Ariel asked, after I got jolted hard enough to spill iced chocolate down the front of my shirt.

"It is. I think I'm going back home."

"Do you mind if I stay? One of my friends is singing later, and I want to hear her."

"Of course. Not like I can't find my way home. And it will probably be better for you once I'm gone."

Holding the hem of my shirt away from my body, I walked back through the people, the booths. The attention was a buzz in the back of my head, their eyes static electricity on my skin.

The same eyes, the same booths, the same people, even as I walked around and through. Even as I could see my way out. Could see it, but couldn't walk to it. I couldn't tell if the path was shifting under my feet, or if my feet couldn't find their way. Either way, I was trapped.

Trapped in a sea of faces increasingly feral, increasingly Fae.

I sat on my heels, head in my hands.

"Imogen?"

Evan's voice. Fabulous.

"What's the matter?"

"They're fucking with me, and I can't leave." I stood up, watched his eyes take in my ruined shirt, the rest of me, frazzled and worn.

"You're going to break the tithe."

I nodded.

"They can't interfere with me. I can get you safely home." He held out his hand.

So familiar. The warmth of it, the calluses and scars. It might almost have been a comfort, but for all that had passed between us. Still, I held on and we walked through the lights of the Market, now bright against the unrelieved darkness of the sky.

"Better?" he said, and it was, my brain no longer buzzing, my skin no longer feeling like it was crawling with ants.

"Thanks," I said, pulling my hand out of his.

"You should check your library, when you get inside."

"For what?"

"Fairy tales."

"Seriously?" I stopped walking. "I'm not new here, Evan."

"These will be more autobiographical in nature than the Grimms'."

"Why are you helping me?"

"Because when I'm in Faerie now, I don't see Tania anymore. I don't feel grief over her. I see you. I feel the grief over what I did, the guilt, the regret. Because I want to make it up to you, or at least to show you I can be a better man than I was."

For the first time since he had started apologizing, I believed him. "All right," I said. "I'll look."

I went into the library even before changing out of my disgusting shirt. I didn't even need to look for fairy tales—they were all piled up in a stack, where Ariel had left them in her hunt for some way that someone might have written about the Fae, the tithe, without making clear what they were saying.

I sorted through them, skimmed titles, and everything was familiar. Most of these I could have retold without looking. Knowing fairy tales hadn't helped me before, and it probably wouldn't now. But maybe it was Ariel who was right, not Evan—someone might have tried talking about what happened the last time the tithe was broken.

Not caring about the lateness of the hour, I made coffee, and went upstairs to work.

"You were right," I told Ariel over breakfast the next morning.

"I usually am," she said. "About what?"

"That people would try to talk about what happened here. The roommate of the woman who broke the tithe last time—she was pregnant, apparently, and not keen on her baby's father being stolen away—she wrote a book."

"And we had it in the library?"

"No, but I downloaded the ebook. *Seven Years Broken*, by Ellen Sherman. It's full of symbolic language and metaphor, so I know I'm still missing things, but there's enough there that with her connection to Melete, I know that's what she's talking about."

"Does it tell you how to break the tithe?"

"The only thing I can figure out for sure is that I have to keep Marin from crossing the bridge that day. Which I'd pretty much gathered already from Thomas and Beth, but it's nice to have the confirmation. But after—she talks about a land that sickens and almost dies. Magic fades from the world, and the shadow world that's left behind makes lesser art. There's a plague. Disaster after disaster, until someone offers themselves up as sacrifice to restore the balance."

"Well, hell, Imogen, I'd spill chocolate on your shirt, too."

"Two years after Ellen Sherman's roommate rescued her boyfriend, the boyfriend's mentor went missing. From here. He was never found."

She shivered. "Do you think he went voluntarily, or . . . ?"

"I have no idea."

"Does any of this change your mind? I mean, that is a lot of bad shit that could possibly happen."

"No," I said. "It's Marin."

It's one of my oldest memories, still utterly clear. The night I got lost, and Marin rescued me. It should have been the other way around,

I know. I was the older sister—I was seven, Marin was five—so I should have been the one who was responsible, the one who did the rescuing.

But I wandered off from the family reunion, desperate to get away from the rowdiness of the drunk uncles, the shrieks of the cousins I saw too rarely to be friends with. I was never a child who could find my balance upon being thrown into a group. Too many new people made me feel small and awkward, as if I had been dressed up in all my flaws and strangenesses.

I didn't want to play baseball, or whatever other team sport the kids, too young to drink and gossip, were being made to play. I wanted to read. So I took my book and walked into the park until it was quiet, until I could no longer hear the raised voices of people I didn't want to be with, and then I sat under a tree and I read.

I read for hours, blissfully undisturbed, until the sun set and it got dark enough that I couldn't make out the words on the page, even with the book pressed so close to my face that I could smell the slight bitterness of the ink.

Even when it was dark, it didn't occur to me that I was lost. I don't know if I could have found my way back to the area of the park I had wandered away from, but I hadn't tried, so there was none of the panic of disorientation. It was a warm summer evening, and while I was slightly hungry, I was also used to missing meals if I lost myself in a book. There were rules, and there were consequences for breaking them.

But the dark was moonlit and comfortable, and I wasn't thinking of rules. I was thinking about the book I had been reading, replaying scenes in my head until they felt solid and real, until I could see myself in them as they unfolded. So I stayed where I was, back pressed against the bark of the tree, watching the neon blinks of fireflies, until I heard Marin's voice. "Imogen! You have to come back right now. Mom says you're lost, and she's so mad at you."

Her voice snapped me back to reality, and the obvious passage of time. My skin went cold and my stomach hot and acid as I realized how mad my mom probably was. So, so mad. The combination made me so dizzy I nearly fell, standing up from the tree. "Do you know the way back?"

"It's not far. Come on. Once you're not lost, it'll be okay." Marin smiled, the dimple in her right cheek flashing, and held out her hand.

I was still young enough to think that was the way it worked. That if I could undo whatever it was I had done wrong, that would be enough. Things would be put back, magically restored. I had been lost, and if I came back, everything would be fine. No harm done. "Okay," I said, and followed my sister out of the woods.

That wasn't, of course, the way things worked.

When I said that Marin rescued me, I didn't mean from the darkness in the woods.

My mom grabbed me and shook me so hard that there were bruises on my arms when I changed for bed that night. Five on each, the shape of gripping fingers. My book went flying into the forest, lost.

She yelled as she rattled me back and forth, about how I was being a drama queen, the way I always was, and hiding so I could be the center of attention, and I was a selfish brat to be that way. My behavior had ruined her day, and she wouldn't stand for that. If I couldn't behave, I needed to be punished. It was for my own good.

She slapped me, her hand cracking across my face. My tooth cut through my bottom lip, and blood filled my mouth, bitter as salt. I swallowed hard, trying not to choke. I had already learned not to cry, unless I wanted to be given something to really cry about.

But when she raised her hand to slap me again, Marin screamed, "It was my fault!"

Mom's hand held still.

"I wanted to play hide-and-seek, and I was supposed to find Imogen. She was still hiding. I'm sorry. It was my fault."

It was enough. Marin, with her blonde hair and blue eyes, was the pretty one, the one everyone looked at, the one everyone made a fuss over, and the attention they gave her transferred seamlessly to my mother—all praise hers, for having such a lovely child. She would have never raised a hand to Marin and risked marking that beauty.

Instead of getting slapped again, I got shoved into the car along with the lawn chairs and the leftover potato salad, now rancid-smelling grease. It was my fault, of course, that I'd been yelled at and hit—I should have said something earlier, and I shouldn't have let Marin play a game like that in the dark—but I was used to things being my fault.

Marin held my hand all through the dark and silent drive home. Tight, so I'd know she was there.

That was the first time she saved me. The one constant through the first sixteen years of my life, the years I lived at home, while my mother made my life a misery, was Marin. She saved me every time. Always.

And so even if she hated me for it, I would save her.

30

The next evening, I chased the setting sun as I ran toward the bridge that led into Faerie. That was where they would cross, and I would need to pull Marin from her horse before then, or she would be gone.

"It will likely be more than that," Beth had said. "You know how they are."

I did, now.

The sun dipped lower, and the shadows stretched toward me from the trees, reaching out, grasping.

Cold hands under my skin, tearing at me from the inside, catching and pulling. I ran faster, away from the bridge, away from the river, away from Faerie. Even as I ran, it got worse. The coldness, the terror. Feeling myself being pulled apart from the inside as I ran, those strangers' hands inside me making my footsteps falter, my heart skip.

Out of the shadows and into the dying light of the sun. Free of the hooks inside my skin, the hands in places that should have been impossible.

I didn't stop until I was home, the wind of my passage drying the tears to salt on my skin. The water in the shower ran from steaming to lukewarm before I stopped shaking, before I felt almost warm, almost safe.

The tithe would not take kindly to being opposed. That was fine. I didn't need kindness. I needed my sister.

———◆———

I shifted my weight against the cushions of Beth's couch, my fingers plucking at the threads of the throw heaped on the end of it. So tired I couldn't focus, and anxiety licked at my nerves like electricity through wires.

"Are you all right?" Beth asked, her raised brows indicating that she already knew the answer.

"Just a lot on my mind." It was mid-April. I had seventeen days.

"Is there anything else you wanted to talk about?" Beth asked.

"There is, actually. I'm going to give you a copy of the file for my book, sometime before the night of the tithe. If I don't . . . if things don't go well for me, would you take a look at it?"

Expressions chased themselves across her face. Then she smiled and said, "No request for a blurb, or that I pass it to my agent?"

I smiled back. "It's good enough. You'll do those things anyway."

It got worse, the interference from the Fae. The feeling of being watched, haunted, chased. The sound of footsteps echoing mine, even when I wasn't walking. The hillside that developed lumps and holes to turn an ankle or send me falling as I ran on it. A hissing of snakes sent, slithering, across my path.

Pebbles buried inside the sheets of my bed, and milk that curdled in my coffee. A thousand tiny cruelties. We wanted different things, the Fae and I, and I would be opposed.

I couldn't write. Not because of anything so simple as writer's block. Files disappeared from my computer, only to show up days later with new names and rearranged contents. Notebooks went missing from drawers and showed up in the oven, or on the shelves in the library, or outside on the porch, the wind riffling their pages.

My pens ran out of ink, the battery in my laptop wouldn't charge. I couldn't write.

It was easy enough to brush things off at first, to tell myself that none of this would be happening if the Fae or whatever it was that governed the tithe didn't see me as a threat. But the little things accreted—the nights of interrupted sleep, the aches and bruises from yet another fall while running, this one that tore the skin from my palms and made trying to write a white-hot agony. It became exhausting. There were two more weeks until May first, the night of the tithe, and I didn't know how I would get through them.

Marin was still furious. Not speaking to me, walking out of a room if I walked into it. If Gavin had a house on Melete's campus, I'm sure she would have moved into it, but he didn't, and he was spending more and more time in Faerie besides. She was probably angry with me for that, too.

I ran through the studios, around a corner, and straight into Evan. I cartwheeled to a fall, wiping out completely. Staggering back to my feet, I brushed the worst of the grit from my legs and burning hands, half-expecting him to be another thing sent to torture me.

"Imogen, are you okay?"

"I'm fine," I said, rolling my ankles to test them, blood sticky on my hands.

"You look terrible. Like someone's been beating you up, like you haven't been sleeping. Come on, I have a first-aid kit in my studio. That's not much, but it's a start." He slid an arm around my waist, taking my weight, and after a couple of staggering half steps, I let him.

He opened the door. "You should know that they can't get in here. The Fae. It was part of what Gavin did, in getting me temporarily out. This studio was my place to recover. There's an extra key."

He rummaged through a drawer, and set the key on top of a series of sketches of new work. "If you want it, it's yours. Come here anytime."

"I won't be interrupting anything?"

He knew what I meant, but met my eyes as he answered. "If it makes it easier for you to come here and take care of yourself, I'll stay out of your way. I'll even leave when you get here. But think of this place as yours."

I nodded.

"Also, there are things you can do to protect yourself from them. They can't cross a threshold if there's rowan over it. None grows here, but you might be able to order some. Wear your shirt inside out, and it will force them to drop their glamour to see you. If you pass through running water, it will wash away any enchantment that has been cast on you."

"How do you know all of that?"

"Gavin. Some of the Fae didn't think I should be out, even if my being in Faerie was hurting them. They'd try to take me back to Faerie, or to torment me while I was here. So he gave me ways to protect myself."

Which was probably part of why he couldn't protect Marin. I shoved the thought from my head. It might be true, but I couldn't think about it.

"You'll need the protections, Imogen. Things are going to get harder for you." He took the bandages from my shaking hands and fixed them over my palms for me.

"You should know that she'll fight you, too."

"She's already pissed." I flexed my hands, testing the bandages.

"No, I mean actively fight you. That day." He leaned against the edge of his worktable.

"I wouldn't have asked anyone to try to break the tithe for me, so I don't know how the fact that you are changes things. But I remember, in the days leading up, being less than sure about my decision.

"Spring was beautiful here that year. Everything bloomed early, and the weather was perfect and green. I was doing work I was proud of, starting to change my style, and really feeling like it was mine, you know?"

I did. "Like finding your voice."

"Exactly. I missed Tania, but was beginning to think that agreeing to run away to Faerie for seven years to grieve her hadn't been my best idea. Besides"—he smiled—"I knew I was good enough to be a success on my own, and more and more, I wanted to see how good I could be without their help.

"But when I woke up that morning, I wanted to go to Faerie like I had never wanted anything in my life, and the feeling only increased as the day went on. By the time the ritual started, I was nearly blinded by it.

"What I'm saying is she might be pissed now, but it will be worse then. And even if she does change her mind and ask you for help, don't rely on her. The tithe doesn't want to be broken."

"She won't ask," I said. "She hates the idea. Hates me for trying this. But Gavin." I pulled in a breath, then shuddered out the words. "Gavin thinks she'll die if she goes."

The relief at finally telling someone was like a fever breaking— hot and cold and shaking all at once. "He's afraid she'll die, and he's told me to stop her from going because he can't, and I'm terrified that I can't either, and that she'll be gone, I'll lose her, and she'll go and die, and the last thing I will have done will be to fail her."

His hand, soft, on my shoulder. "I wondered why you were trying so hard. Imogen, I'm sorry."

"Thanks," I said. "So am I." Stupid small words. Overused ones. Tiny things, hardly any letters. We expect them to do so much, and when it comes down to it, they're nearly empty, all their color leached away, all the meanings that should have been there hollow and inadequate in the face of the weight they're meant to carry. We know, and we say them anyway. "So am I."

"Also, this doesn't really have anything to do with that, but since you're here, I have something for you." Uncertainty in his voice now, in his bearing. He opened the drawer again, took out a necklace. A chain, the leaf of an elf maple hanging from it. "I made it. Before. But it's for you. So if you want it, it's yours."

Our pasts always haunt us. But sometimes the ghosts are friendly, and the memories they bring with them sweet as well as bitter. "It's beautiful," I said. "I would love to have it." I held out my hand, and he dropped the necklace into it.

"And I meant what I said, Imogen. Use the key. Come here. Take care of yourself. If I can help you, I will."

"Thank you," I said. Small, tiny words.

I turned my shirt inside out before I left Evan's studio, and for the first time in almost three weeks, didn't feel watched as I walked home. My shoulders uncoiled, just a bit.

A box of rowan branches—thin green leaves and clusters of orange-red berries—arrived that afternoon. I hung them over my windows, and over my door, and fell, exhausted, into a dreamless sleep.

31

For two days after, I thought I had gotten lucky. That Evan's advice had been the silver bullet.

But then I slept with the windows open, and woke, shivering, in a bed that had been the target of an extremely localized rainstorm, the orange berries of the rowan floating in the puddles on the floor.

I had forgotten that I had a sister who wanted to go to Faerie as badly as I wanted to keep her from it. She had taken down the rest of the rowan, leaving the house unprotected. My dreams were full of her dying in Faerie, with me there to watch, and I couldn't wake myself from the visions until dawn broke.

The sky's cold grey light was comfort after that. Shivering from the nightmare, I shrugged into my robe—worn brocade in a pattern of roses, the threads going out at wrist and hem—and went downstairs. Coffee brewed, and brewed again after the milk I'd poured in had proved to be curdled, I sat at the table and pillowed my head in my hands.

"How are things?" Ariel said, as she poured herself coffee. "Or should I not have asked?"

"We're still at the same levels of armed truce," I said. "Though be careful with the cream—they're spoiling it again."

"And that's why I've been taking mine black. Do you have a second to talk?"

"Sure."

She leaned against the counter. "I got an offer from a producer. Cynthia Dickinson. She wants to stage my Thomas the Rhymer musical, but as immersive theatre."

"That's where the audience interacts, right? Like that *Macbeth* that was on multiple floors of a hotel?"

"Exactly. She's got some great ideas, too, like that people can get True Thomas to tell them their futures, and then you go to different parts of the performance based on what they are. Some really cool ways to work the staging. She built mini-sets as part of her proposal. Hang on—I've got pictures on my phone."

They were photos of what looked like an elaborately staged dollhouse, full of detail.

"These are gorgeous, Ariel."

"Right? I got chills looking at them. She really gets what I want to do with the project."

"And it would give you the audience interaction you've been wanting," I said.

She nodded.

"That sounds great. Congratulations! We should celebrate."

"Thanks, but that's the thing—I'm not sure if I want to do it." She slid the phone back into her pocket.

"Why not?"

"Because I don't know if I want to think about this place anymore, once we're done with it. I mean, I wrote this as a fuck you to the Fae, but now Helena's gone and Marin's going, and that feels more like getting screwed over."

"She's not going," I said. "Marin."

Her voice softened. "Sorry. You're right. Of course she's not. But it's not just you guys. It's everything associated with the place.

With the Fae. I don't know if I want to keep dealing with the bull-shit, or turn my back and walk away clean.

"Because, honestly, Imogen, I might be the only one who walks out of this house in June. I know you have a plan, but look at the odds."

"I can't look at the odds," I said. "I understand what you're saying, but if I start doing that, none of this works, because I curl up under my desk and never come out.

"But, Ariel, no matter what happens, none of us get away clean. This year, this place, it's always going to be in our art. Even if we decide to walk away from art completely, and take up law or sell real estate, this will always be in our past."

"Like a graveyard of fucking ghosts," she said.

"That's what it feels like, sometimes," I agreed. An entire life as a haunted house.

"You know, I remember the first time I heard you sing," I said.

"At the Night Market," she said, and smiled. "That was a good show."

"It was, but that's not when I meant. It was our very first day here. You were singing Puccini on the porch, and I thought it was one of the most perfect moments I'd ever experienced."

Ariel shook her head. "God, we were naïve. I still thought this whole place was perfect, then."

I laughed. "I thought the same thing. That it was like magic."

"We were idiots," Ariel said.

"But we weren't wrong."

"No, I guess we weren't. Here's to our past selves, and all the ghosts that we are," she said. "May we haunt the Fae forever."

It was the last night of April. Tomorrow would be May, and tomor-row would be the tithe. I opened all the windows in my room and let the night in. I drew a long breath, gathering the wet, green scent of spring, jasmine rising through the air like holy smoke.

My email notification pinged. Beth.

She had read the file I had given her, and had been impressed enough to send it to her agent, who would like very much to speak with me at my earliest possible convenience.

My heart butterflied in my chest, and I felt a grin stretch itself across my face. I read it again, to make sure the words were still the same.

They were.

Beth apologized for doing this without my permission, but she had wanted me to know that I had options. That there were things I would be leaving behind.

I read it one more time, then closed the email without replying. Part of me wished I hadn't read it. Hadn't known that particular piece of what I might be losing, this first part of everything I ever wanted.

I turned off my computer and picked up my pen. I had an idea for a new book, one about what happened after "ever after," and I wanted to get the first pieces of it on paper. It was important that I do that now, that I treat the night as no different than any other. To not think it was possible that tomorrow night I would be far away from this room, and this desk, and a life of writing.

To not think that I might be even further from Marin, downstairs in her room, than I was now. I had to try, one last time, to talk to her.

Downstairs, a knock at the door. I stepped out to see who it was, so late.

"Hello, Marin. I know you said you'd come by when you were ready, but I wanted to help you with your things." Janet's voice.

"Marin?" I called down from the landing.

"Your sister is going to stay with me tonight. I thought it might be nice if she had someone, someone like a mother, who could be there for her, and help her prepare for tomorrow."

"Marin, wait!" I started down the stairs, and they shifted beneath my feet, tripping me up. I fell.

Picking myself up off of the floor, I saw Marin sling a bag over her shoulder. "Thanks, Janet. I'm ready to go."

"I'm sure you are, dear."

And then they were gone.

This is the thing about fairy tales: You have to live through them, before you get to happily ever after. That ever after has to be earned, and not everyone makes it that far. There are stories where you must wear out your iron shoes to right a wrong, where children are baked into pies, where jealousy cuts off hands and cuts out hearts.

We forget, because the stories end with those ritual words—happily ever after—all the darkness, all the pain, all the effort that comes before. People say they want a fairy tale life, but what they really want is the part that happens off the page, after the oven has been escaped, after the clock strikes midnight. They want the part that doesn't come with glass slippers still stained with a stepsister's blood, or a lover blinded by an angry mother's thorns.

If you live through a fairy tale, you don't make it through unscathed or unchanged. Hands of silver may be beautiful, but they don't replace the hands of flesh and bone that were severed. The hazel tree may speak with your mother's voice, but her bones are still buried beneath its roots. The dead are not always returned, and roses do not always bloom from graves.

Not every princess climbs out of her coffin.

Happily ever after is the dropping of a curtain, a signal for applause. It is not a guarantee, and it always has a price.

I tried to sleep. I needed the rest, needed whatever strength and advantages I could give myself. Exhaustion wasn't one of those things.

But when I closed my eyes, I saw Marin galloping away on a bone-white horse, saw myself opening a door, three or four years from now, to see Gavin, stone-hearted, telling me she was dead. I heard my mother's voice, telling Marin that I had always been jealous, that I didn't want her to succeed.

I turned my shirt inside out and stuffed a sprig of rowan in my pocket.

I walked all over the campus. Through the artists' studios. There were lights in some even now, in the smallest hours of the morning. Someone played the cello, sobbing and deep.

Through the mentors' houses. Only a few lights on there. Beth and Janet were the only ones here who had served as tithes, I thought. I wondered if they were awake, waiting for this year's ritual, or if they slept, secure and comfortable now that their service was done, that they couldn't go back. Or if Janet sat with Marin, and wished that tomorrow's white horse would be for her instead, that there was a door left to open her way to Faerie again.

I kept going, past the rose garden, still in riotous bloom. Across the Commons, so still and quiet, like the whole of Melete had silenced its clocks, was holding its breath. Then to the banks of the Mourning River, held there by bridge after bridge, arching from one side to the next.

And one bridge that didn't, one bridge that stopped in midair. I walked up and across, until the stones ended, until I stood on the precipice.

I looked over, into the still-dark forest where Faerie was. I stood, until I could look unflinchingly at it, until my heart did not gallop like a horse, until my breath did not rush like the water beneath me.

"I will not let you have her," I said.

All around me, laughter. It was the only thing I heard as I walked home.

32

A ticking clock, counting down. Time, always and ever the enemy. Time, that turns a dancer's grace into mere mortality. Time, that stretched the bridge between sisters until it snapped. Time, the drumbeat mark of a prison sentence.

One more day. Seven years. Forever.

The tithe was tonight.

The rising sun scattered color across the sky, painting the low clouds in sherbet shades. Birds sang. Everything was green and new. Everything I saw told me to stay. To surround myself in the beauty. I could have everything I wanted on my own. A writing career. Days full of sunrises and glory.

The air smelled of roses, and the walls were covered in a kaleidoscope of butterflies, glowing reds and oranges, and that bright, impossible blue. Their wings folding and unfolding in time with some great heartbeat. Open, close. Open, close.

And then they flew, hundreds of multicolored stars, searching for brighter skies. I reached—

"Imogen!" Ariel's voice, and hands that shoved me back, hard. I crashed to the ground.

"You were about to take a header down the stairs. What the hell?"

"I saw—" I shook my head. "Nothing true."

"Was it them? Of course it was them." She answered her own question, looking around as if she expected the Fae to slither out of corners and shadows. I wouldn't have been surprised if they did. "They're fuckers. I get the feeling that Gavin is literally the only one who plays by their rules, much good it does him.

"So when do we go kick their asses?"

"You're coming with me?"

She grinned, fierce and bright. "You can't even walk down stairs on your own, so yes, I'm coming with you."

I hugged her tight, as if she were my sister. "Thank you."

There wasn't a dress code for the evening, or if there was one, no one had bothered to put it on my invite. I wasn't even supposed to be there, unless it was to wail and wave as Marin rode over the bridge and away from me.

But this was the Fae, and appearances were their own kind of magic. They had wanted me, once, and so I dressed to remind them of that. In a silver dress, beaded like armour. In a black velvet cape, lined in silk as green as a forest. In a rose ring that clung to my finger as if it had been made for me.

In a necklace, the leaf of a tree, made by one they had embraced.

I stood on my bed and plucked a star from the ceiling. One that Marin had given me. I tucked it in my bra, a talisman. A reminder.

Then, because glass slippers would have been a bitch to run in, I laced on a pair of boots, and went down to Ariel's room.

She looked me up and down. "Yeah, okay. That actually makes sense. Ready?"

No. "Yes."

The Fae were waiting.

Stepping out of the house was flinging myself into a wall of naked want. So much emotion pulling at me. A gaping maw of desire so terrible I went to my knees before it. The Fae, welcoming the tithe.

"Right. Okay. That's how it's going to be then." Ariel pulled me to my feet, and I clung to her like a drunk.

Walking was stumbling, slow and graceless. It wasn't simply want that saturated the air. Time seeded itself in my eyes like grit. The hair on my neck rose as I heard the echoes of hoofbeats close behind, urging me to run, to find a place of safety. Not here, not here.

The ground, the universe itself disappearing beneath my feet, ice beneath my skin, as I danced with a partner whose eyes were as black and as far as forever.

Ariel's hand slid from mine. I fell backward. Easier to stay here. Marin wanted to go. I should respect her choice and let her.

A hand cracked across my face. I blinked. Swore.

Ariel, in front of me, hand raised. "Imogen. Pay fucking attention. Do not let go of me again. You turned into a zombie for a second there, and we are running out of time. It's almost sunset. We have to go."

"Thanks." I held on, didn't let go again. Stumbling and half-stunned, Ariel dragging me, we made it to the banks of the Mourning. To the assembled crowd. Faces I recognized mixed in with those that weren't human.

"I still want to punch her," Ariel said, looking at Janet. She stood close to a group of Fae, who paid no more attention to her than if she had been a tree.

"Me too," I said. Easier to stand on my own feet, to focus, now that we were here. A respite only temporary, I was sure.

Other fellows there, too, ones who had been at the selection, some wearing their hourglasses. Hoping, maybe, for one last chance, still thinking this was the easy way to success. Their chains were fastened again. I hadn't worn mine since.

The light fell, the sky darkened. My heart beat like the ticking of a clock. My head was full of voices, telling me to leave, telling me I would fail. That I would die. That Marin would. That her last thought would be that I hated her, that I wanted what was hers.

"How will you know when it's time?" Ariel asked.

The wind picked up, whipping the river to white.

"Storms come in fast here," I said. I let go of Ariel's hand and held on to the chain around my neck, the elf maple leaf, pressing the points into my skin to keep my mind and eyes clear.

I wanted the storm to come.

The ground beneath my feet shook with the thunder of hooves. The wind blew harder, sending my hair stinging into my face, pulling leaves from the trees and scattering them. I was buffeted, pushed. Unwelcome.

My mother's voice rang in my ears, telling me to go. To take my jealousy and get out of Marin's way. That I didn't deserve anything good.

But it was nothing that I hadn't heard before. The same insistence that I was worthless, that I was nothing, that I would fail.

All the things that I had proven wrong. I had done everything she said I couldn't. She hadn't even been able to burn my stories out of me. I was nothing that she said I was, and she couldn't touch me.

My mother didn't matter. Marin did.

The first horse was black as a raven's wing, and Gavin sat upon it, his face stern and unreadable. Not the face of a lover waiting for his beloved, but the face of a king who had made a bargain for his country. He held the reins of a second black horse, and Evan rode that one, the tithe at the end of his sentence.

Evan wore the tithe's circlet, silver thorns binding his head. Everything silent but for the rush of the river, and as they reached the foot of the halfway bridge, the horses halted.

Evan dismounted, lifted the crown from his head, and handed it to Gavin. His service done, his burden passed, Evan walked away. Away from the horse, from the bridge, from the assembled hosts of the Fae—and came to stand at my back.

Gasps and hissing as he did. The fangs and the claws of the Fae were out, and the worse things, the things we couldn't see, were here, too. Greed reached out with clasping fingers. Hunger. Such hunger I felt like I might starve from it. Despair to weaken legs, to stop a heart. Counterfeit memories that sent flames licking over my hand. I closed my fingers around the burning, held it tight.

Gavin set the tithe's crown on his own head.

The horses came faster then. Not quite the gallop of a hunt, but fast enough to race the wind, in shades of brown from the dried blood of a bay to rich chocolate to near sand pale. The Fae rode these horses, in clothing made from cobwebs and silver, from the leaves of autumn's trees woven with velvet, in roses and brocades. Watching them pass was an ache. Surely I should be there, should throw myself after these riders, or perhaps below their feet.

I stepped forward.

A hand on my shoulder yanked me back hard. "If you go now, they will take you into Faerie with them. Wait for Marin. The white horse."

I turned to glare at whoever had kept me from the riders. Evan. Blood at his temples from the crown worn by the tithe.

Marin.

I fought my racing heart and stood, weeping, as they rode past and left me behind.

Then. And then.

A white horse—white as death, white as truth, white as hope—galloped past. On its back, the tithe.

Marin.

In a dress as white as her horse, seven braids woven into her hair, fairy lights binding her hands before her.

I ran. The ground itself rose up to trip me, sending me tumbling forward in a headlong heap. I clawed at the grass, digging with hands and feet to stop the slide. Fetched up hard against the stones at the base of the bridge.

Clambered to my feet, the reins burned through my hands. Trying again for purchase, I grabbed at the hem of my sister's dress, clutched at her ankle. She kicked at me and urged her horse to run faster. I held tighter, felt my fingernails tear from my hands, and pain like burning iron as the horse crashed down on my foot.

I took hold of my sister, and I pulled her from her horse, and I held on as if she were my life.

"Let me go!" She struggled and flailed, her elbow cracking into my cheekbone, her knee slamming the breath from my lungs.

And then it was not Marin beneath me, but a swan, beating violently with its wings. I nearly let go in shock, looking around for my sister.

"Imogen, hold on!" Ariel's voice, clear above the chaos. The swan's beak stabbed at my eyes, its feet scraped my stomach raw.

Then gone.

A snake, small and fast and hissing, that nearly slithered into the darkness before I grasped it again. It whipped itself around, sinking fangs deep into my wrist. My blood burned.

The poison bubbled through my veins, and my legs went out from under me. Bile rose up in my gorge, and I turned, vomiting pale green foam onto the ground, the snake that was my sister still writhing in my hand.

A bear, carrion-scented and roaring, its breath hot on my face as it snapped at my eyes. In its eyes, not my sister, but my death. Then a lion, its claws sharp through the thin fabric of my dress. Tight as the lion's claws pierced me, I held tighter, and then smelled my skin burn as the lion turned to red-hot iron in my hands.

The crackling stench of burning skin, the hiss and drop of metal beads melting and falling from my dress. The voices of the Fae in shrieks and cheers.

Somehow, impossibly, Ariel singing. The very first thing I had heard from her, her rock-star voice mourning through *"O, mio babbino caro,"* singing of a lost love that drowns itself in the river.

The river.

Running water breaks their magic.

I rolled across the ground, clutching the iron to my chest as I did. Farther still, down the bank and into the rushing water of the Mourning, falling as deep as I could below its surface, deep enough to drown. The water hissed and steamed around us. My lungs burned, and pain like a knife pierced my head. White sparks burst behind my eyes.

As we drowned, me and the white-hot flame of my sister, I felt her hand on mine, shelter in the darkness. Tight, so tight, and if I just held on, if I held on long enough, we would be safe.

We drowned in a sky full of stars. One slipped away from me, and I watched it float, up and away, into the bubbles of our fading breath.

And then the weight in my arms was no longer the weight of iron, but the weight of my sister, of Marin.

Hold on, hold on, hold on.

Weighted down by dress and cloak, by Marin, limp in my arms, I kicked back toward the surface, heaved her onto the bank of the river, and struggled out after her. Dropped my head to her chest, where I waited for her heart to beat.

Nothing.

She was naked. The transformations that had wracked her destroying her clothing. Cold, I thought. She was cold. I had to get her warm. I struggled out of my sodden cloak and wrapped her in it, the green silk pressed to her skin.

Someone was sobbing. It might have been me.

"God damn it, Marin," I said, "wake up."

Nothing, and nothing.

I pressed my hands against her chest, my breath into her body. She didn't move, and she didn't breathe.

Too long. It was too long, I knew. The voice in my head wasn't my mother's. Not this time. It was Janet's. *It's not everything you ever wanted. Not really.* I hung on to Marin, laid my head on her unmoving chest, and sobbed, begging her to not be gone, to come back.

"I'm so sorry, Marin. Please. I love you."

The lonely echo of hooves, and the shattering of a crown.

A riderless white horse galloped across the bridge, and into Faerie. Half of the bridge disappeared behind it.

Marin's eyes opened, and all the clocks struck midnight.

33

This is how happily ever after begins.

These are the things that happen.

After.

Pain. Skin burned and torn, a foot smashed under a horse's hoof, fingernails ripped from their beds. Marin's hand ripped out of mine.

Other hands then. Gavin's, and the pain diminishing. "I'm sorry. There will be a scar."

I didn't ask where. I already knew there would be. One that was visible was just a more obvious reminder. Besides, I had others.

The worst of the pain receded. I sat up. The bank of the Mourning River. Dress in tatters. My boots much the worse for their drowning. I probably was, too.

Marin and Gavin, and he looked fully human now. Exhausted and diminished, and there was no crown of any sort on his head. She was shouting, wrapped in my sodden cloak and her own anger. Bits and pieces floated down to me. "You kept her from telling me!"

Gavin, implacably calm. "And if she had told you, and failed. If you had gone, believing that you would not survive. If believing that had made it happen. What then?"

"At least I would have gone knowing my sister loved me. Believed in me."

"I love you!" His voice not calm then.

"It wasn't your choice to make." The crack of her hand against his face. His eyes closed, his head bowed as she walked away from him.

Her arms around me, and even though the weight, the pressure of them was an agony, I didn't ask her to let go. "Come on," she said. "It's over. Let's go home."

I shook my head, looking at Gavin's ravaged face, the blood on Evan's temples, on Ariel's scratched arms. "It won't be that simple."

It wasn't.

"You should go," Gavin said. "Leave Melete. All of you, as soon as you can. Probably Beth, too. I'll tell her. I'll buy you what time I can, but we, the Fae, aren't generally gracious losers."

"They can't harm you directly—"

"But we all know how well that's worked out for Imogen the past month or so," Ariel said. "You really are shit at this, Gavin. We'll go."

"I'll help if I can," Gavin said, watching nothing but Marin.

"We've taken care of things just fine on our own so far," Ariel said.

We stumbled home in the darkness, as if that helped, as if the Fae wouldn't be able to see what we did. But they would be weaker with no tithe, and maybe that would help. We stuffed what we could carry into tote bags and wheeled suitcases.

"Do you need any help?" Marin asked, voice hesitant.

"Can you get the stars down for me? I want to bring them, but it hurts to lift my arms that high."

She climbed onto my bed and started undoing constellations. "I dreamed about the stars, when we were under the river."

"I brought one with me. I wanted something that would remind me of you." It was gone. Floating somewhere in the Mourning River, a wish carried beneath a bridge.

"Imogen. I'm so sorry."

I held up a hand. "I know. But we can't, not now. We need to go."

"Right." She nodded. "But thanks."

The three of us shoved together in the back of a cab that we'd had to walk to Melete's front entrance to meet. We drove away as dawn broke over the horizon, Evan and Beth in a second car behind us.

"Just like a fucking fairy tale," Ariel said.

After.

As the cab sped away in the dark, Marin's phone and mine lit up. Same number. I answered. Listened. Hung up.

"There's been an accident."

"Gavin!" Marin gasped, horror in her voice.

"No. Our mother."

"Is she—"

"She's still alive, but partially paralyzed. They're not sure if it's permanent, and there's other damage. Serious damage. She's asking for us. They say to come now."

"Marin. We don't have to go."

I wasn't sure I could. I was so tired. So goddamned tired from the night, from the month, from the most recent forever. And I had nothing I wanted to say to that woman.

"I need to," Marin said. "This one last time. I need to go, and then I never need to see her again."

"Okay," I said.

"Imogen." Her voice so small, and I knew what she would ask. "I need you to come with me. Please."

I closed my eyes, leaned back into the seat. "Of course I'll come with you."

"Would it help if I came too?" Ariel asked. "I can change my plane ticket."

"Thanks," I said. "But no. This is the last time. We need to do this on our own."

"Okay. I'll tell Evan and Beth when we get there."

In the dark, as the cab took us toward the airport, Marin held my hand.

The hospital smelled like antiseptic and fear. Marin and I were bleary-eyed and travel-faded. She had closed her eyes on the plane, but I didn't think she had slept. I hadn't. Adrenaline and nerves raced beneath my skin.

"It was at midnight," Marin said. "The accident."

"I know." Midnight. When the tithe had officially been broken. Everything I ever wanted.

"Do you think—I mean, with everything I said about keeping us safe—did they do this?"

Yes. That was exactly what I thought, though not for the reasons she did. The Fae, backhanded and precise about their gifts, knew that deep dark wish from my childhood. Not the safety Marin wanted, but the one that I did. It is possible to tell a truth, and tell it in pieces.

"She was drinking, Marin. There is no way that what you wanted caused this, okay?"

She nodded.

We turned the corner and were outside her room. I looked at Marin, and she nodded. "The last time."

"It took you two long enough to get here," our mother said as we walked into her room. I had braced for her to look terrible, the stepmother from a fairy tale, the witch who locked Hansel in a cage. The monster of my childhood memories. But even bruised and swollen and covered in tubes and machines, she looked flat.

Ordinary. Small. "I'm not sure why. Nothing is more important than family, didn't I always tell you that? I assume you told that place you won't be coming back."

Marin snorted out a laugh.

"Did I say something funny? Someone has to take care of me."

"Someone might," I said. "But not us."

"You ungrateful bitch," she said. The machines beeped louder. "I always took care of you."

"I suppose you might call it that," I said. "But that's over. It's done."

"We only came to say good-bye. That's the only thing we owe you," Marin said. "We never want to see or hear from you again."

"Ungrateful. Spoiled. Too many people making a fuss over you. You've forgotten you're nothing." Blood leaked from the side of her mouth, and bubbled up into a froth as she spoke.

"No," I said. "We know who we are. Good-bye." Marin and I turned to the door.

"If you leave, you're no longer my daughters."

Marin smiled, and kept walking. "Good," I said. "I've waited my whole life to hear you say that." I followed my sister out of the door.

After.

I poured tea into a mug that said WRITE YOUR OWN HAPPY ENDING, and handed it to Beth. She raised a brow.

I rolled my eyes. "Oh, I know. My publisher sent them, though. Could have been worse. Could have had a smiley princess on it."

"You escaped the smiley princess cover, which is good," she said. "What you have is gorgeous—Evan's work, right?"

It was. A black-and-white photo of his trees. "I thought they looked like a fairy tale the first time I saw them. I was glad the art director agreed."

"So are you two . . ." She let the words trail off.

"Friends. His art is, of course, doing very well. I'm happy for him."

Beth walked around the edges of the apartment, then settled into a worn leather chair. "You look like you're doing well yourself. And Marin's living with you?"

I sat down across on the couch, the Brooklyn skyline through the windows at my back. "She is. It's what we talked about, before. Finding a place together. And it's nice to be around someone who gets it."

Who got everything. It was the life we had talked about wanting as kids, before it had been taken from us. Before we were almost taken from each other, by our mother's lies and manipulations. That was over. Done. And we were here.

When I sold my book, Marin went with me to the shelter, and paid the adoption fee for my kitten.

"And your success hasn't been a source of friction?"

"Marin's having plenty of success on her own. She got hired as a soloist at NBT, and she loves it there. They seem to love her, too."

"If I remember correctly, that's Gavin's company."

I nodded. "He abdicated."

She set the mug down with a rattle. "Does that mean what I think it does?"

I nodded. "He'll turn mortal. It's why they don't usually live here in the human world, or not for very long periods of time, anyway. Too much time away from Faerie, and you forget what you are. And the place forgets you. He says that soon he won't be able to go back." I thought he was relieved. It was easier that way.

"And he and Marin are still together?"

"They are." It was a complicated thing to watch. He was almost too careful around her, and I wasn't sure whether that was his residual guilt at not being able to protect her from Faerie, or if it was awkwardness as he became human. But Marin was happy, and so that was enough.

"And they're dancing together. In fact—you'll love this—their premiere performance this fall? Oberon and Titania in *A Midsummer Night's Dream*."

Beth laughed until tears streamed from her eyes.

"I did the same thing when she told me. I'll get us tickets."

"On to less entertaining things," she said. "I was wondering if that reporter—I know she's spoken to Ariel—has she gotten in touch with you, too?"

The early consequences of breaking the tithe were beginning to manifest. There was a delay in the announcement of next year's mentors, due to three of them having sudden scheduling conflicts. A mutual fund that held a number of Melete's assets had crashed, losing over a third of the value in the space of days. A magazine profile of Melete had revealed more scandals, and was being widely quoted in an ongoing conversation about toxic influences on artists, and the pressures to succeed. That one had been written by the reporter Beth mentioned, Christine Jenkins. She was sure there was more going on behind the scenes at Melete than she had found, and since I had been one of the people who had fled campus at the beginning of May, their residencies left unfinished, surely I could talk to her.

I hadn't, yet. But I could, and Faerie knew that. When Gavin had lifted the no-speaking enchantment he'd put on me, he'd lifted it well enough that none of the normal prohibitions against speaking about Melete remained. If I wanted to, I could tell everything.

Ariel had found talking to Jenkins cathartic enough that she had finally signed the contract with the producer, was moving forward with her play. But I wasn't sure that I was ready. "I'm sure I'll write about it someday," I told Beth. "But I want to tell the story on my own, not give it to someone else."

Even without my piece of it, there would be more, Beth said—more evidence that Melete's foundations were rotten, that the gold was only gilt. "The next seven years should be interesting."

I imagined they would be. I was looking forward to them.

"Will you go back?" I asked her.

"I don't think so. There are other ways for me to mentor new writers, and I'm looking forward to being a grandmother in my non-writing time.

"The real question is, will you? Melete does love the prestige of having successful former fellows return. I'm sure they'll ask you."

"I'm sure they won't," I said. "Or if they do, it won't be in seven years, or any multiple thereof."

"You never know. The Fae have always liked a challenge," she said, and stood up. "It was good to see you. You'll come over for dinner next week?"

I nodded. Marin came home as Beth was leaving, and the two of them smiled and hugged.

"I'm craving Thai. Are you writing, or do you have time to grab dinner?" Marin asked, unpacking her dance bag.

"Thai sounds great," I said.

"Perfect. Let me just shower and change."

"Sounds good," I said. "I'll be waiting."

Once upon a time.

This is how it should have happened.

If it had been a fairy tale, it would have ended on a kiss. A double wedding. A king and a queen—not an abdication, a broken crown.

Evil would still have been part of it. No story happens without some sort of evil, after all. No one leaves a house that's warm and safe and comfortable to brave the terror and uncertainty of the forest without a reason. If you have an easy life, you don't wake up and find yourself in a story.

All of the evil would have been punished, been undone, had it been a fairy tale.

If it had truly been a fairy tale, I wouldn't bear the scars of Marin's transformations. They are less than they should have been, but my abdomen is streaked white with healed-over burns, and the marks from the snake's fangs are an angry red on my wrist.

If it had truly been a fairy tale, Helena would have lived.

We were left with ever after. Not happily, not quite. Not all the princesses climbed out of their glass coffins. Not all the kisses given were those of true love. There are reversals that remain, even after the turn of the page.

This is what happens, when things are not quite a fairy tale.

You go into the woods to find your story. If you are brave, if you are fortunate, you walk out of them to find your life.

Once upon a time.